Layover

by

Max Martínez

Arte Público Press
Houston, Texas
1997

This volume is made possible through grants from the National Endowment for the Arts (a federal agency), Andrew W. Mellon Foundation, the Lila Wallace-Reader's Digest Fund and the City of Houston through The Cultural Arts Council of Houston, Harris County.

Recovering the past, creating the future

Arte Público Press
University of Houston
Houston, Texas 77204-2090

Cover illustration and design by Vega Design Group

Martínez, Max, 1943-
    Layover / by Max Martínez.
        p.   cm.
    ISBN 1-55885-199-2 (cloth: alk. paper).
    I. Title.
    Ps3563.A73344L39   1997
    813 .54—dc21   96-39824
                                                           CIP

The paper used in this publication meets the requirements of the American National Standard for Permanence of Paper for Printed Library Materials Z39.48-1984.∞

Layover

1

Ralph Mason stood near the edge of the bed shaking his dick at Priscilla Arrabal. She lay on the bed, baring the whitest shoulders he'd ever seen. Ralph pinched his dick with his thumb and forefinger, holding it halfway down the shaft, wagging its puff-adder head in her direction.

"I'm going to get this in you," Ralph Mason said, shaking his member up and down, "and I'm gonna tickle your tonsils with it!"

When he'd first seen her at the Ligon Wells Saloon, sitting at the bar, eating fried chicken with Georgene Henderson, it never occurred to him that she was Mexican. Later, when they sat next to the jukebox and somebody had punched in the Texas Tornadoes' "Laredo Rose," Priscilla told him she was Mexican. Ralph had never seen a Mexican so white that nobody would ever suspect that she was one. Mexicans were supposed to be dark, and short, too. But, not this one. She was as tall as he. It took all two inches of the heels on his boots to give him a little height on her. If Priscilla was Mexican, it didn't make much difference to Ralph Mason. He'd had his share of Mexican women, and more. In fact, the first woman he'd ever had was Mexican.

Good thing that plenty of people had seen him with her at the Ligon Wells Saloon. It would make bragging on her easier. He knew that the best part of fucking was bragging about it afterward. Even before he crawled into bed with Priscilla, Ralph was anxious to brag about how he'd brought her to the motel and fucked the shit out of her.

She came from San Antonio, which made her a big-city girl. Home was in a little town north of Laredo. She'd left there to go to college in Austin. Learning those two things about Priscilla had caused Ralph Mason's throat to swell. What Ralph Mason knew about city women who went to college: they didn't mind taking sex in the mouth. Ralph Mason concentrated his eyes on the scarlet lipstick that ringed Priscilla's mouth. Thinking about what she could do with that mouth sent a jolt through his pecker.

Priscilla lay on the bed. Her white shoulders rested against the rickety headboard. The white sheet beneath the bedspread was folded back and tucked beneath her arms. Her breasts were cradled in her arms, large and soft, with traces of dark blue veins. When she moved her shoulders, the milky white mounds wobbled like mercury. At the center of each breast was a brown circle dotted with tiny little hillocks surrounding the nipples. The nipples erupted as dark brown, almost black, thimbles against the whiteness of her skin. Her hands were clasped together between her breasts, holding a can of Miller Lite beer.

Ralph Mason sucked in a beer belly the size of a small watermelon. He held in his breath to appear slim, lean, and hard. He stood at a corner of the bed, across from where Priscilla rested her head. On the carpeted floor in front of Ralph was the pile of clothes he'd just removed. His brand new ostrich-skin boots were off to one side, neatly positioned side by side.

Priscilla smiled broadly, revealing her perfect teeth, even and white in the contrast of her scarlet lipstick. She furrowed her forehead and lowered her eyes, as she knew Ralph expected her to. Her gaze drifted to his midsection where he wiggled his dick at her. Satisfied that Priscilla liked what she saw, Ralph Mason smiled. His teeth were large and square, stained to the color of egg yolks from cigarette smoke and chewing tobacco. His dark blond hair fell over his forehead. He leaned forward, bringing up his right leg as if he were swinging it over a saddle. He dug his heel into the soft mattress, pinched the shaft of his half-hard pecker. He shook it once more in Priscilla's direction.

"Are you ready for some of this?" Ralph Mason asked.

Priscilla raised the can of beer to her lips, took a deep draft. She leaned forward and stretched out her hand, reaching for Ralph. There remained a yard of distance between her hand and what he wanted her to grab.

"You really know how to turn on a girl, Ralph," Priscilla said, disappointed with his antics. There was a surge of sarcasm in her voice.

The sarcasm was lost on Ralph Mason.

Ralph Mason said, "Damned right, honey! That's what all the girls love about me!"

Before he could say anything else, Priscilla heard the crash of shattered glass in the window behind him.

The sound of the breaking glass sent Priscilla scurrying backward, recoiling in fright, until her back was against the cold headboard. She squeezed the beer can until a little of the beer spilled on the bedspread. It took a second or two before she noticed Ralph Mason swaying unsteadily on his feet. She looked beyond his shoulder to the window. She could hear the rain outside, loud and persistent. The rain overflowed the gutters on the second-floor roof, falling in a noisy sheet on the concrete walkway bordering the rooms.

The light spilling out of the room from the lamps on each side of the bed caught in the bright metal of the pistol. The barrel turned until her eyes fixed on a narrow circle with a black center.

The barrel was aimed at her.

Behind the pistol, she saw in the dark shadows the face of a man wearing something black on his head. There was the glint of something metallic on the face. He was too far back for the light to fully reveal all of his face.

The smile left Ralph Mason's face. In its place came a grimace of pain. His right hand came up on his chest, pressing against his skin, lifting his left breast upward. The upper part of his body swayed forward. For a moment, it seemed to Priscilla as if he were about to take a step forward, unaware that one foot was on the bed and the other was on the floor.

Then, he let go, his strength unable to sustain his weight.

Ralph Mason fell face forward, sprawling onto the bed.

Priscilla Arrabal looked at the back of his body. She saw a thin trickle of blood coming out of a quarter-inch hole, black and gurgling, just below his left shoulder blade.

Priscilla screamed, but the sound was stifled by the fist she jammed into her mouth.

2

The bus driver's voice on the coach PA system was scratchy, as though he had a piece of barbed wire lodged in his throat. It was a hissing, crackling sound that gargled in the speakers overhead. The driver announced to the passengers that he was leaving the interstate and would be going into Lexington for a scheduled rest stop.

Lexington, the bus driver announced, was the beginning of Texas history. The town had its origins as a military garrison and grew as a remote settlement of Mexico after its independence from Spain. The beginning of Texas history, the driver droned on, occurred when the first American colonists came to the area.

"We were already here when you motherfuckers showed up," Priscilla Arrabal said to herself. Why was it so important, she further asked herself, for white people to always be at the center of the universe?

The driver slowed the lumbering road behemoth, veering into the exit ramp to Lexington. For the two hours since they'd left San Antonio, Priscilla had been absorbed in the countryside, which was green and lush beyond the tinted windows of the rolling bus. The cultivated fields of corn, sorghum, and hay were neat and square, perfectly etched into the landscape, offering an array in the shades of green. Here and there, a copse would appear and beside it she'd see a farmhouse and its outbuildings. There might be a car, or a pickup truck, or a tractor visible. All of it was just far enough away from the interstate to make them look as if painted on a canvas.

As the driver brought the bus to the yield sign, the coach pitched and rolled. The air brakes hissed below and the gears rattled and shook as the bus came to a rolling stop. Slowly, the bus picked up speed, heading due south. Priscilla saw the road sign indicating Lexington still twenty miles away.

Priscilla was immediately jarred by the difference between the two-lane road the bus now traveled and the wide expanse of the interstate they'd left. Earlier, Priscilla had been lulled by the easy flow of the landscape, rolling by in a measured tableau, giving her plenty of time to absorb its colors and textures. On the two-lane road, the woodland was closer in, the tree line tall and dark, speeding by as a blurred and indistinct memory. The lull of the interstate had placed her in a trance of sorts. The scenic lay of the land had occupied her in a twilight of thought, somewhere between consciousness and sleep. As the bus sped forward on the two-lane to Lexington, it took an effort to concentrate her thoughts on the landscape to avoid thinking about why she'd left San Antonio.

The bus strained to climb a slow gradient. The forward motion of the bus appeared for a long moment to be suspended in time. It was a separate dimension as the driver downshifted, and then there was the grinding of gears and the drag of gravity as the coach groaned onward. Near the summit of a fat hill, the first signs of the town began to appear. Homes were settled among the trees, with tractors and farm machinery nearby. A lumber yard sprang into view on the opposite side and next to it a car repair shop. The rusting carcasses of cars and trucks were scattered about.

The bus cleared the top of the hill and the driver began to brake for a stop sign at the corner of a divided road ahead. In the grassy median was a traffic light. The vehicle gradually slowed to a crawl five yards before the intersection, where the bus driver turned to the left. To the right, on the crest of a rise in the land, Priscilla saw a whitewashed building with an ancient metal soft-drink sign that said, Ligon Wells.

The driver steered the bus into the white-gravel parking lot of Tiny's Kozy Korner. It was a long narrow building with every inch of its exterior covered in metal advertisements for everything from soft drinks to chewing tobacco, cattle feed and cowboy boots. It had been many years since the bus company found worthwhile profits taking or delivering passengers in and out of Lexington proper. With the construction of a bypass connecting the highway between San Antonio and Houston, the bus station had been moved way from the central business district to Tiny's Kozy Korner. The bus traffic going east and west stopped for passengers to get out and stretch a bit and relieve themselves. They could also load up on the sodas, chips, and sandwiches.

The bus passengers stood on their feet, trying to shake the hum of the rattling bus from their flesh. They stretched and yawned, eventually leaving their seats, cluttering the narrow aisle between the cramped seats. Some of them checked their carry-on things stowed in the overhead storage compartments, as if someone might have stolen them during the first leg of their trip to Houston. Gradually, almost reluctantly, they filed out of the bus.

Priscilla was the last of the passengers to walk off the bus. She slipped on her designer sunglasses, squinting in the brightness of the early afternoon sun. The bus driver stood beside the open door of the coach.

"How long are we stopping here?" asked Priscilla.

"Thirty minutes, maybe a little more," the bus driver said, leering.

He wore dark aviator glasses. Priscilla could tell from the angle of his head, his eyes hidden behind the mirror glass, that he gazed into her cleavage. She wore a low-cut black leotard and a wraparound skirt over a black pair of tights. On her feet, she wore *huaraches,* campesino sandals. Suspended from her ear lobes were large hoop earrings.

"I guess I have time to go across the street for a beer," she said, turning her head in the direction of the Ligon Wells sign. "Is that place open?"

"Yes, ma'am," said the bus driver. "There's plenty of 'em do that. My passengers, that is. Be sure and be back before I take off, though."

"What happens if I don't?"

"I take off and leave you," he said, grinning maliciously.

"You mean, you wouldn't walk across the street to let me know it's time to go," she said, laughing, turning toward the saloon and walking away before he could answer.

"Company rules," the bus driver yelled after her.

The bypass was four lanes, two in each direction, separated by a wide grassy median. The two-lane road coming down from the interstate traversed the bypass and continued into the central business district of Lexington. The light at the crossroads changed as Priscilla Arrabal came to the road shoulder. She stopped while several cars went north, in the direction of the interstate. She waited until the light changed again before going across the road.

3

The asphalt parking lot of the Ligon Wells Saloon sloped upward to the whitewashed side of the building and swept around toward the back. Priscilla went up to the door, tried the knob, and found it locked. A crude sign, with an arrow at the bottom of it, pointed around to the back. She frowned. She turned to her left, rounded the corners of the building, came upon a larger parking lot. There were three pickup trucks in the lot, all of them with gun racks above the seats. Priscilla shook her head.

"Boys and their toys," she said to herself, shaking her head.

Priscilla opened the door and stood for a moment framed in the doorway by the bright sun. She removed her sunglasses and closed the door behind her. She took a few tentative steps forward while her eyes adjusted to the dimness.

Inside, the Ligon Wells Saloon was dark and cool. The place smelled of resin from the sawdust on the floor. It was illuminated by the square of light flowing out of the jukebox, several neon beer signs that hung on the walls and others that were propped on the shelves behind the bar. The bar was L-shaped. The short leg of it began immediately to the left as she entered. A few feet in and it made a right angle, running the length of half the building. The edge of the bar was padded with elbow rests made of a synthetic material resembling black leather. No one sat at the bar.

Priscilla made her way around the corner of the bar and took a barstool at the far end of it. She sat sideways on the barstool, placing an elbow on the black padding.

The Ligon Wells Saloon was deserted, save for two old men who sat playing dominoes at a square slate table pushed against the wall next to the entrance. One of the men kept score using white chalk on the black slate of the table. The man keeping score erased the chalk marks with the heel of his hand.

Priscilla gave herself a minute more for her eyes to become accustomed to the darkness within. Behind the bar, she saw the opened door to a walk-in cooler. Inside the cooler a pale yellow light cast a murky glow over stacks of beer cases. A woman came out, carrying two cases of beer. The woman had curly blonde hair pulled back into a bun at the back of her head. She wore a white T-shirt and tight blue jeans to squeeze in her ample hips. Priscilla guessed her age to be forty. The woman set the beer cases on the floor and leaned on the bar in front of Priscilla.

"Can I help you with something?" the woman asked, slightly out of breath.

"Miller Lite," Priscilla said, swivelling her bottom on the barstool.

"Would you like that in a draft or a bottle?" The woman ran the back of her hand over her forehead.

"Doesn't matter, draft will be fine," Priscilla said, lifting her purse from the footrest, dropping it on her. She reached inside for her wallet.

"It'll be seventy-five cents," the woman behind the bar said, placing the glass of beer on a coaster and sliding it toward Priscilla.

"Seventy-five cents? That's not very much. How do you make any money?" Priscilla had her wallet open. She extracted a five-dollar bill and placed it on the bar.

"You can pay when you get ready to leave," she said, leaving the money on the bar.

Priscilla brought the glass to her lips and drank deeply, swallowing half of the beer in the glass. She opened wide her eyes as she returned the glass to the top of the coaster.

"Gosh, I needed that," she said.

"My name is Georgene," the woman behind the bar said, extending her hand across the bar.

"Priscilla," she said, taking Georgene's hand in hers.

"You're passing through on the bus," Georgene said. "Where from?"

"Laredo. Laredo is where I grew up," Priscilla said. "I live in San Antonio. Ever since I finished school."

"On your way to Houston?"

"How'd you know?"

"It doesn't take genius, honey. Strangers walk in here at this time of day," Georgene said with a shrug, "they're on the bus to Houston. The bus to San Antonio passes by in the morning before I open up for the day."

Priscilla drank a quick sip of the beer, sloshing it in her mouth to savor the full taste of it. She finally swallowed and took another long draft, draining the contents.

"You want another?" Georgene asked, retrieving the empty glass, placing it under the beer tap.

"Yes, please," Priscilla said. "You know, it's funny about beer. I don't usually drink beer. Then I have a little sip of it, and I ask myself, 'Why don't I drink beer more often?' Is this your place?"

"Yeah, sure is."

"How long you had it?"

"Not long, a little over a year, maybe," Georgene said, pushing the beer tap forward to stem the flow of foaming liquid. She placed the glass in front of Priscilla.

Priscilla turned on the barstool to face Georgene. She took another sip of the beer.

"Women tend bar and wait tables, but you actually own this place. What made you go into the bar business? If you don't mind my asking."

"Until about twelve years ago, I worked as a waitress in a restaurant on the town square. A little restaurant that was there forever. Eight years I worked there, and then there wasn't enough work for three waitresses. I was the youngest, so they let me go. The place didn't stay open more than a year before it finally closed. In this town, there's not that many jobs. This was the only place where I could find work."

"You said this is your place."

"It is. I tended bar here for a little more than ten years. Then, the owner died. The widow sold me the place."

"Sounds like a nice lady," Priscilla said, finishing the last of the beer. "I guess I'll have another."

Priscilla sipped the beer, lapsing into a profound silence. Her face became wooden, her eyes drooped, taking in the length of the bar. She had resolved to not think about San Antonio and the life she wanted to leave behind. The thoughts came upon her when she least expected. It was all she could do to turn them away. What she wanted most, what she in fact needed, was a clear, empty mind, void of the past, closed to the uncertainty of what lay ahead.

Sensing that Priscilla wanted to be alone with her problems, Georgene shifted beer bottles in the cooler boxes beneath the bar. She added bottles from the two cases she'd brought out from the walk-in cooler. When she finished stocking the beer, she took boxes of chips, peanuts, and beef jerky and restocked the display racks behind the bar.

A few minutes later, Georgene served Priscilla a final beer in a plastic cup. Priscilla took the two singles from the change that Georgene put on the bar. Priscilla slipped the strap to her purse over her shoulder.

"I guess I'll be going," Priscilla said, waving her sunglasses in front of her. "I'll miss my bus."

"Come back and see us," said Georgene, picking up the empty glass and dropping it into the rinse water in the sink under the bar.

Across the road, the passengers were already formed in a line next to the bus, filing inside. Priscilla stopped for a few cars and trucks to go by before crossing the road. She took a sip from the beer in the plastic cup.

As Priscilla approached the bus, an explosion of sunlight, reflected from the aluminum side of the bus, pierced into her eyes. She squinted and then blinked, momentarily blinded. She stood beside the road, placing her free hand on her hip, standing still, trying to decide whether she would go back to the bus or not. The beer had made her lightheaded. She wavered on the stones of gravel, the color of powdered milk.

Ever since leaving San Antonio, she'd kept her mind off things. The pressure of what she'd left behind once again weighed in on her, insistent, clamoring for attention. She looked at her fellow passengers as they went up the steps into the bus. The solicitous bus driver lifted his arm as each passenger went up the steps, helping to steady their climb without ever so much as touching them. The sun overhead burned into her bare shoulders.

Priscilla took another sip of the beer. By the time she reached the bus driver, she'd made up her mind. She walked up to the bus driver, who smiled and dropped his gaze to her bosom.

"I want my bag," Priscilla said, holding the hand with the plastic cup at shoulder level.

"Your ticket says you're paid up to Houston, lady," the bus driver said, annoyed.

"I think I'll lay over here and do some sightseeing," said Priscilla, taking another sip of her beer.

"You can't take that beer on the bus, it's against regulations," said the bus driver.

"Well, then, all the more reason for me to stay behind," said Priscilla, smiling thinly. "I want to finish my beer."

"If you want to go on to Houston tomorrow, you'll have to buy another ticket, lady," the bus driver said, tossing his company cap back on his head. He opened the side hatch of the bus to retrieve her suitcase. He set it on the white gravel of the parking lot.

Priscilla shrugged her shoulders, picking up the suitcase. The bus driver touched the bill of his cap with his fingertip and climbed inside the bus. The bus roared up beside Priscilla as she waited to cross the road to return to the Ligon Wells Saloon.

The bus driver waited for Priscilla to walk across the road, before going on. He watched the sway of her hips in the hot sunlight.

4

Inside Ligon Wells Saloon, Georgene was surprised to see Priscilla come back in. This time, she carried a designer suitcase. Georgene drew another Miller Lite from the tap, placing it on the bar where Priscilla had sat before. Priscilla placed her suitcase on the footrest in front of the barstool and sat.

Georgene smiled her greeting. "I see you missed your bus," she said.

"I changed my mind about going on," Priscilla said. "I decided I want to stay."

"Any particular reason?" Georgene asked, drying her hands with a bar towel.

"No. No particular reason, except I don't really like to travel," Priscilla said. "I think I just need to be away from San Antonio. This is Lexington and it feels far enough away to suit me for right now."

Georgene Henderson placed her elbows on the bar, a look of concern on her face.

"What's troubling you, honey?" Georgene asked. "Husband? Boyfriend? Children? Boss? Work?"

"The simple answer," Priscilla said, taking a gurgling swallow of the beer, "is boyfriend."

Georgene placed her hands flat on the bar.

"Better take it easy on that stuff, honey," she said. "You keep drinking it like that and it'll crawl up on your backside and knock you silly. It might be light beer, but it can land heavy as hell on you."

"I'll be all right. I won't embarrass you. I promise," said Priscilla.

"Honey, I ain't the one that'll be embarrassed," Georgene said. "Why don't you tell me a little about your boyfriend?"

"I don't even want to think about him, much less talk about him," she said. "I feel like he's a son of a bitch, but he's really not."

"It might help to talk about it."

"I said that the simple answer to your question is boyfriend," Priscilla said. "But, now that I think of it, though, that's not it. Not really. You see, not long ago, I felt like everything was sort of closing in on me. What happened, what actually triggered it, I suppose, is when I found out that my boyfriend has been going out with somebody else. I knew he had a girlfriend already lined up. For a long while, you see, it's been over between us. I just didn't know how to get away from him."

"There's plenty of women, wives, who find themselves in the same predicament, honey," said Georgene. "Don't feel like you're the only one it's ever happened to."

"I don't. I don't know how I feel," said Priscilla. She tapped her forefinger on the bar. "My boyfriend, if you can believe this, moved his new girlfriend into the same house where we were living. Instead of moving out, I stayed in the house. I lived downstairs and the two of them lived upstairs."

Georgene's forehead became a row of jagged furrows.

"I know what you're thinking," Priscilla said. "I can't tell you why I stayed. For months before it happened, I had already become unhappy with my friends, my job, my entire miserable existence. Not until yesterday did I decide to leave and find a place of my own. I also gave notice where I worked. I wanted a complete change. At my job, they paid me and escorted me out of the building that same day. I woke up this morning feeling a lot better just knowing that there was nothing to keep me in San Antonio. So, I went to the bus station and got on a bus to Houston. And, here I am, not going to Houston after all."

Georgene Henderson watched Priscilla's face for a moment and decided against asking any more questions. Priscilla suddenly lifted her face, her eyes opening wide. She lifted the beer glass in salute. Georgene nodded her head.

"I'd say you've had it a little on the rough side, honey," said Georgene.

"It feels good to get it out like that, tell somebody about it," Priscilla said. "I've been trying to not think about it at all."

"Confession is good for the soul, they say," Georgene said.

"I bet you hear a lot of confessions in here."

"Enough."

Georgene poured another beer in a clean glass.

"This one's on me, honey," Georgene said, placing the beer in front of Priscilla.

"Well, I feel like meeting new people. Where's all the men in this town, anyway?"

Georgene grinned, drawing back to place her elbows on the edge of the bar. "They're working, honey," she said. "This is a working town. It's early in the day yet," she said, glancing at the clock on the wall. "Going on three o'clock now. They'll start drifting in here in an hour, a couple of hours. The ones who work in town. The others, those who work on the farms, they come in a bit later."

"Is there a place close by for me to stay the night?"

"Sure. We have two motels here on the bypass. That's mostly where people passing through stay overnight. There's an old-time hotel in town, just off the town square. That's the one that gets the tourists. It's not very big, not many rooms, and they're usually all taken. Other than that, there's a few bed and breakfast outfits. They're kind of romantic, but expensive. And, you'd need somebody to be romantic with to really get your money's worth. That's the lot. It may not be much, but you have to admit, there is a choice."

"Maybe a big, strong, handsome rancher man will come in and sweep me off my feet," said Priscilla, sarcastically. "Carry me away to a ranch house, one that looks like that mansion in *Gone with the Wind*. Maybe he'll dress me up in a ball gown that belonged to his great-grandmother."

"Not much chance of that," Georgene said, a smile crossing her face. "You won't meet that kind of man in here."

"What kind do you get?"

"Working men," Georgene said, surprised by the question. "The landowners you're talking about, they stay to themselves. They drink and visit at home. Working men is what we get here. Sometimes a few of them'll bring their women, wives, girlfriends. Sometimes their children."

"Any cowboys? Now that I'm interested in meeting new people, I'd like one of them to be a cowboy."

"Not much real cattle ranching left around here anymore," Georgene said. "There's only one big cattle spread. They say it's owned by a German company that runs it out of Denver. Everybody else who works cattle only do it once in a while."

"Just my luck to look for a cowboy when there's none of them left," Priscilla said, in a mock dejection. "I was never lucky where men are concerned."

Priscilla drank two more beers. Her head felt heavy, but she kept her body straight and steady on the barstool. She'd lapsed into another silence, which allowed Georgene to finish her work behind the bar. When she had finished, she returned to Priscilla.

"There's one more thing to do," she said, "before people begin drifting in. I need my dinner."

Georgene yelled across the bar to one of the old men play-ing dominoes.

"Hector, does that trashy truck of yours still run?"

"It'll take you anywhere you want," said Hector, keeping his eyes on the dominoes.

"How's about that truck of yours takes you over to the Golden Pullet, get me and this lady here some fried chicken. It's worth a beer when you come back."

"Why can't you walk over to Tiny's and get a barbecue sandwich?"

"Because I want fried chicken, that's why."

"Well, if he's got to drive all the way into town, how about a round for both of us?" said the other old man at the slate-top table.

"It don't take two of you to run and get me some chicken, Sam," said Georgene in mock irritation. "You gotta earn your own way around here."

"If we don't get a round for the both of us, Hector don't go," said Sam, returning his attention to the game of domi-noes.

"Okay. A round for both of you," Georgene yelled. Under her breath, she said, "Son of a bitch." Turning to Priscilla, she said, "It's two dollars and change for a three-piece order, and that gets you french fries with it."

"I guess I'd better eat something," Priscilla said, opening her purse again, taking out her wallet.

"You sure better," said Georgene.

Priscilla handed her a twenty. "Here," she said, "I'll pay for both of us."

"You don't have to."

"I want to," Priscilla said. "You've been very nice to me."

The fried chicken was greasy and cold and the french fries were soggy by the time Hector returned from the restaurant. Georgene spread the food in the space on the bar that separat-ed her from Priscilla. Priscilla asked for a Seven-Up to drink while she ate. When Georgene shook her head, Priscilla settled for a Sprite. Georgene took one bite of the french fries and gagged.

"Hector, where the hell did you go to get these?"

"The Golden Pullet. Ain't that where you told me to go?" said Hector. "When do we get our round of beers, anyway?"

Georgene brought two bottles of beer out of the ice box, flipped the caps off, and took them to the short end of the L-shaped bar.

"There they are," said Georgene, putting the beer bottles on the bar. "You'll have to come up and pick'em up yourself."

Priscilla rested her elbows on the bar. She held a fried chicken breast in front of her face. She peeled away a bit of the breading and skin, and she bit into the plump white meat. Georgene returned to take a piece of chicken from the container on the bar and joined Priscilla for their meal.

5

The door opened suddenly, sending a swath of sunlight into the dimly lit bar. A shadow moved in quickly as the door fanned opened. Just as suddenly, the door slammed shut.

In two strides, the man who entered came around the right angle of the bar. The heels of his boots made loud, thumping noises on the wooden floor. He walked over to where Georgene and Priscilla sat eating their chicken.

The man went through the open space between the bar and the wall, taking one of their french fries as he passed by. He stopped beside Georgene and lifted the lid of the beer cooler. He brought out a bottle, squeezed it several times to make sure it was cold, and then twisted the cap away.

"My beer is always cold, Ralph Mason!" Georgene said.

Ralph Mason guzzled the entire contents of the bottle in one gurgling swallow. He burped noisily as he slammed the bottom of the bottle on the bar.

"Damn! That's good!" he boomed, bending over the ice box to grab another bottle. "First goddamn beer of the day! Always the best one! Always!"

He wiped his mouth with the back of his hand before he took a long swig from the bottle.

Ralph Mason wore a straw hat, tilted far back on his head. His forehead was two-tone in color from sunburn. The top part, going up to his hairline was light and pale, while the bottom part was darker, matching the ruddy complexion of his face. His blue gingham shirt flowed over his belt buckle in a prominent beer belly. From his hips down, he was lean, with hardly any definition to his rear end. On his feet were cream-colored ostrich-skin boots.

"Who's this?" he asked, looking at Priscilla, pointing the bottom of the beer bottle toward her.

"This is Priscilla," Georgene said, her mouth full of chicken. "She's visiting. And you, Ralph Mason, you'll be going to sit at the bar over there, away from us while we finish eating."

"I'd be pleased to make your acquaintance," said Ralph Mason, "whenever you're done eating."

"Maybe you will," Priscilla said, swallowing some chicken, wiping her mouth with a paper napkin.

Ralph Mason walked around them and went to the jukebox. He placed his hands on the top corners of the jukebox and leaned forward. His head dangled loosely between his shoulders.

"He's cute," said Priscilla, picking out another piece of chicken from the cardboard tray.

"Ralph is trouble," said Georgene. "I'd be careful with that one, if I were you."

"All I said is, he's cute," Priscilla said, picking up the can of Sprite. "What kind of trouble is he?"

"Ralph has a way with the ladies," Georgene said. "Thinks he's got a right to treat women however he wants. As soon as he has his way, he doesn't want any more to do with any of them."

"He could be very interesting," Priscilla said, watching him as he wiggled his hips at the jukebox. "Don't worry, Georgene, and I'm always careful. Not that it helps, but I'm always careful. Besides, I'll be on my way tomorrow, or the next day. How much trouble can I get into?"

"With that one, you never know," said Georgene. "His daddy is pure ornery and mean. Raised Ralph and all his brothers to be the same."

The jukebox began to play George Jones' "He Stopped Loving Her Today."

Ralph Mason finished his jukebox selections and took a stool at the far end of the bar. Priscilla caught his eye. Ralph smiled, lifted his beer bottle straight up in the air in a gesture of salute, and then tilted the neck of it into his mouth.

Priscilla finished eating and drank the last of the soda. The ladies' room was next to the walk-in beer cooler. She went in to pee, rinse her face, and put on some fresh lipstick. She was interested and excited. The look Ralph Mason gave her left no doubt that he, too, was interested. Let's see what develops, she told herself.

When Priscilla came out of the bathroom, she asked Georgene for two beers, one for herself and one for Ralph Mason. This time she wanted the beer in a bottle. She picked the bottles up from the bar and walked to where Ralph Mason sat.

"You ready for one?" said Priscilla, taking the barstool next to him. She placed the beer bottle before him. "Georgene says you're trouble."

"Georgene talks too damn much!" said Ralph Mason, grinning, obviously pleased with Georgene's warning.

"Watch your damn mouth, Ralph! I can hear you over here," Georgene yelled, frowning good-naturedly.

Ralph Mason swivelled on the barstool, facing away from the bar, bringing his elbows behind his back to rest them on the bar.

"Georgene's got a deputy-sheriff boyfriend," he said. "That's what Georgene has got."

"How about you? What've you got?" Priscilla asked.

"I got more than you can handle, girl, if that's what you're looking for," he said, staring along the length of his shoulder at Priscilla and cocking an eye at her.

Priscilla settled her head into her shoulders, compressing her lips. She thought for a long moment, drinking more of her beer. Behind her, the jukebox blared Waylon Jennings' "Are You Sure Hank Done It This Way?"

After a long moment, she turned to face Ralph Mason.

"I don't like to drink alone," she said. "You can keep me company, for the time being. Don't get any more ideas than that."

"You were talking to Georgene just a minute ago. Georgene is company. I've even talked to Georgene myself. She's pretty good company, in fact, when she wants to be."

"Bartenders are nice to talk to," Priscilla said, drinking more of her beer. "After a while, talking to a bartender is like talking to yourself."

"Why pick on me?" he asked. "There'll be plenty others come in after awhile."

"Let's just say that I had a feeling when you walked in."

"What kind of feeling?"

"It's a feeling. There's no words to it. Let me wait and see what it is."

"Listen, Priscilla. That's your name, isn't it? Priscilla? I only know one thing. And, I'll tell you plain. You're hot for me. I can tell. When you're done with my company for the time being, I'm pretty sure I know what'll come after."

"You sound like women are always hot for you," said Priscilla, frowning.

"Ain't many turn me down, if that's what you mean," Ralph Mason said. "There's few that'll turn me down, once I set my mind to it."

He swivelled on the barstool to face her, placing his toes on the chrome footrest of her barstool, his legs opened wide.

"I bet I could turn you down, if I were to set my mind to it," she said.

"Yeah, you might could do that," said Ralph Mason, leaning close enough to her to smell the fragrance of her perfume. He whispered, "The real truth is, I don't believe you'll want to pass up what I got. You can think on that. For the time being."

After had it gotten dark outside and the Ligon Wells Saloon had filled with at least two dozen men and nearly a dozen women, Ralph Mason took Priscilla by the arm and led her to a table beside the jukebox. Georgene had cranked up the volume on the jukebox, making it possible to hear the music above the chatter of the crowd. Ernest Tubb sang "Waltz Across Texas."

Ralph carried their two beers to the table. Priscilla walked slowly, unsure of her bearings, determined not to weave across the small area in front of the jukebox where people danced. As she took her seat at the table, she looked at the clock above the entrance. Nine o'clock.

Ralph Mason dragged a chair from the table, placing it next to Priscilla so that his leg pressed against her as he sat. Ralph drank from his beer, dropping his hand on her thigh in a gesture of possession. Priscilla removed his hand, dropping it over his own thigh. He next dropped his arm around her shoulders, his hand hanging loosely over her right breast. Again, she removed his arm, shoving it toward him.

"I'm sitting here with you," she said, cross and exasperated by his forwardness. "Isn't that enough?"

"Enough what?"

"Enough showing off to your friends," she said, annoyed. "You don't have to paw at me to let them know you're sitting here with me."

"I don't much give a shit that they look at me or not," said Ralph Mason.

"Then, behave," said Priscilla, sternly. "Keep your hands to yourself."

"You bring out the horny in me something fierce, girl!"

"Keep fucking around and you'll end up staying horny," she said. "Or, you're going to have to find somebody else. So, just sit there. Behave yourself."

"I got what I want. I can wait for it," said Ralph, confident as he drank his beer.

"Don't be so sure," Priscilla said, beginning to think thoughts of things she'd buried long ago.

6

The noise of the crowd in the Ligon Wells Saloon, the music of the jukebox, Ralph Mason's leering face, all drifted into a blur of sights and sounds, becoming a background to Priscilla's thoughts. For one thing, the pattern was back, repeating itself. It was a pattern of one night, one man. It would be a night of sex with one man. If the next night she felt unsatisfied and wanted more, then it would be a different man. There was never an exchange of telephone numbers, addresses. Never a promise to see each other again.

Priscilla could recall how it began with the treachery of her first boyfriend, Jaime. She and Jaime had known each other since childhood, when her family would travel from the ranch to Laredo to visit relatives. His family lived close to her aunt and uncle. Jaime and his brothers and sisters were friends of her cousins. When Priscilla's family left the ranch for the comforts of the city, they moved into the same neighborhood. Jaime had become her best friend. As they grew older, the pangs of first love brought them closer together.

In the last summer of school, after they drank a few beers to bolster their resolve, Jaime had driven his car to a bluff overlooking the Rio Bravo. They'd spread a blanket on the ground, the both of them trembling in anticipation. Jaime had only enough time to put on his condom and penetrate her body before he came. She had soothed his bruised ego by assuring him that he could try again. It would be better the next time, she'd told him, but Jaime had had just the one condom in his wallet. She wouldn't take the chance of a second attempt without protection.

Priscilla had been raised to believe, mostly at home and partly by the nuns at school, that chastity was the supreme gift that a bride could bestow upon her husband. Jaime had pleaded with her until she could no longer resist. After all, there remained only their marriage vows to sanctify their union. Marriage, though, would be five years away, delayed by a final year of school and four years of college. The assurance that they would marry had been sufficient to convince her, and thus she and Jaime began to have sex regularly.

Ralph Mason brought Priscilla out of her past. He got to his feet, stooped over the table, pulled on her arm to get her to her feet. On the jukebox, Willie Nelson and Ray Charles sang "Seven Spanish Angels." Priscilla stood up and followed Ralph to the dance floor. He held her tightly, his head slightly inclined, their foreheads touching.

The gentle sway of the music took Priscilla into the past again.

As the end of school approached, Jaime had decided to attend junior college classes in Laredo. Priscilla had been accepted by the University of Texas, something which made her parents very proud. Jaime assumed that she would stay at home to be with him, even though she continued with her plans to study in Austin. Jaime became impatient, proposing that they marry right away. Two years of college should be enough. He intended to work in his father's hardware store and she was to stay at home and care for the children they would have.

On the night before she was to leave, Jaime became distraught. She listened to his entreaties and threats. She could not convince him that going away to college was what she wanted to do. It became clear to her, as they spent their last hours together, that Jaime was more concerned with his self-interest. She later reasoned that it had been her disobedience that had most disturbed Jaime. She had failed to accept the decisions he made for her own good.

Priscilla had made frequent trips home during her first two years at the University. Toward the end of her second year at school, Jaime finally confessed that while she was away at school, he had begun to date someone else. He had not intended for it to become more than a passing fling, something he owed to himself. However, the new girlfriend was pregnant. He would have to marry her. More than that, he wanted to marry her. The new girlfriend was content to let Jaime make the decisions that affected both of them.

She had been stunned by Jaime's confession. She had walked away from Jaime in a daze, numbed by the collapse of her future. What upset Priscilla the most was Jaime's two-timing her. And worse, he told her that it was a fling he owed himself. She had enjoyed sex and she felt sure that she needed it as much as he. Despite the flirtations and opportunities on campus, she had always looked forward to having sex only with Jaime. It was one of the principal reasons she returned home so often. It was a betrayal that she'd never thought possible.

The slow song on the jukebox ended, and it was followed by a faster piece. Ralph Mason straightened and slipped into a two-step, a dance she loathed, principally because it called for her to step backward, led by the man in front of her. She let go of Ralph's hand, slipped out of the arm that encircled her, and returned to the table, where she leaned back in her chair and went back to her thoughts.

For the next two years of school, until her graduation, Priscilla had refused to allow any man to become a serious interest in her life. She had decided that she was too inexperienced when it came to men, too gullible, too trusting and too quick to give all of herself. Her surrender was total and unconditional because love could not endure anything less. She decided to keep men at a distance until she could devote more time to understanding how men and women function together.

College life, at best, was transient and so were the people she met. Priscilla had thrown herself into her studies with renewed vigor, which had left her with little time for anything else. Nevertheless, she did have the urge to have sex from time to time. Her solution came from the transient nature of her life.

She would go to one of the numerous student hangouts in the vicinity of the campus, settle upon a likely prospect, drink a few beers to ease her reservations, and bring the boy home to her apartment. No one she brought home ever got a second chance. If she were to run into someone on campus with whom she'd been out, she'd be polite, but she'd refuse to even chat. She had drawn a line across her life that she would not permit a man to cross.

As soon as she finished school, she spent a month at home with her parents, and then she'd settled in San Antonio.

She continued with her one-man, one-night resolution until she met René Chapa. On the threshold of a new career, she had been introduced to him. She felt herself prepared to face a new direction in her personal life. In the three years since Jaime, Priscilla felt she had learned enough about men to make René Chapa a good prospect for a long-lasting union between them. Even though she was wiser and more experienced, in the end, René Chapa had behaved as Jaime had behaved. It had taken months before she could bring herself to admit defeat and give him up.

As she sat with Ralph Mason at the Ligon Wells Saloon, René Chapa was safely relegated to her past. Until she could put things back together, she resolved to allow only one man for one night in her life.

Once again, Priscilla was filled with doubt, determined to insulate herself in the presence of men.

"Listen, it's getting to closing time," Ralph Mason yelled into her ear over the bar noise.

"What are you talking about," Priscilla shouted back, looking at the clock above the entrance. "It's eleven o'clock. Bars close at two."

"Not in this town," said Ralph Mason, cupping his hand at the side of his mouth. "Midnight's closing here. I ordered us a six-pack to go."

"I want one more before we go," she said, swaying her shoulders back and forth in time to a song blasting from the jukebox. Patty Loveless sang "I'm That Kind of Girl."

"It's nice here," said Priscilla. "I like it."

"When I went outside to piss, I saw there's a bad storm coming up," Ralph said, inching his chair closer to hers. "It's going to get real bad weather pretty damn soon out there. There's a motel just down the road right quick. What do you say we go down there, get us a room and get about some serious business?"

"Business, you say? Did you say, business?" Priscilla said, her words slurred, weaving in her chair from side to side. "If we had business to transact, I don't think you'd have the money in your jeans to pay for it. That's what I think."

"I didn't say any such thing," he said, becoming petulant. "You're too damned good-looking to be a whore."

"We're discussing what your financial health looks like," said Priscilla, "and whether you can even pay for a motel room."

"Nothing wrong with my health, lady, financial and otherwise. I might not choose to carry a big bundle on me, like some others I know, but I have it stashed away," he said, feeling insulted.

"Tell me about all this money you have stashed away," she said.

"What do you care about any money I got stashed away?"

"I don't. I'm curious. Are you bragging or not? You have an uncle die and leave you a big bank account?"

"We don't trust banks in my family, not for a hundred years," said Ralph Mason. "We might take their money, borrow it and such, but that's all. My daddy says there's a grandfather or two in our family that robbed banks. This money I told you is something I got coming. I wouldn't put it in no bank."

"What do you do that brings in all this money that you say you have coming?"

"You be real good to me, and I might let you in on it," he said, smiling smugly. "How about it? Are you ready to go?"

"Nope," said Priscilla. "I'm still thinking about it."

7

A few minutes after midnight, Ralph and Priscilla went through the rear door of the Ligon Wells Saloon. The storm had come in as it had threatened to do, pouring rain in thick sheets that smashed against Priscilla's face. Priscilla, carrying her suitcase, bent forward heading into the driving wind. She followed Ralph Mason to his brand new pickup truck. He carried the six-pack of Miller Lite that he'd bought at last call from Georgene.

Priscilla tossed the suitcase into the cab of the truck and scampered in. Ralph jumped in on the driver's side, handing her the six-pack of beer, which she put on the bench seat between her legs.

"Fucking rain!" said Ralph Mason.

It took less than five minutes for the drive to the Settler's Motel on the bypass. Ralph steered the pickup into the brightly-lit porte-cochere. The motel lobby and office were enclosed in plate glass to one side. Ralph left the engine running and opened the door. Priscilla grabbed his arm.

"Back up a little bit, back where it's dark," she said. "I don't want anybody to see us."

"You don't know a goddamn soul in this goddamn town," said Ralph Mason. "What the hell you afraid of? Your reputation? It's fucking raining out there!"

"It's not my reputation I'm worried about, Ralph," said Priscilla.

"What's this about parking back in the dark for, then?" he asked.

She laughed. "I want to protect your reputation."

Ralph Mason became confused by the remark, a shadow darkening his face. He took a long hard look into Priscilla's face. Priscilla leaned over to touch his arm, her grin revealing her white teeth.

"Come on," she said, "why don't you move the truck?"

Ralph was hesitant, unsure of what Priscilla was up to. He laughed and shook his head, shifting the pickup to reverse gear. He let the truck roll backward, braking when it was alongside the motel rooms where no one at the registration desk could see them. Large drops of rain thundered on the roof of the truck.

Ralph Mason slipped his hand between Priscilla's legs, just in back of the cold cans of beer, patting the juncture of her legs.

"Keep this warm for me while I'm in there," he said, squeezing the inside of her thigh. "I don't want to come back out here and find that the feeling you had about me is not there anymore, and all you really want is a motel room."

"I've got money for my own motel room, thank you. And, I'm not a tease, Ralph," Priscilla said. "I know what I want."

"Good," he said, squeezing his crotch as he stepped out of the truck. "And, I'm just the man to see that you get what you want. I got it right here."

Ralph ran from the truck to the shelter of the port-cochere. Priscilla watched him run along the glass enclosure of the lobby and registration desk. She yanked one of the cans of beer out of its plastic yoke and popped the top. She sipped the beer absently for a few minutes until Ralph came running back to the truck, carrying a key in his hand.

He drove the truck in reverse across the parking spaces in front of the motel rooms. When he came up to the room, the last one in the building, he turned in a wide arc, aiming the hood directly at the door to their room.

Priscilla waited in the truck. Ralph leaped from the truck, jumping over a puddle of water. At the door to the room, he slipped the key into the lock and pushed it open. He went into the room, leaving the door open for Priscilla. She grabbed the suitcase at her feet on the floorboard, opened the door a little and waited for a break in the hard-falling rain. When she saw that there was not going to be a break, she stepped down from the truck and ran into the room.

Priscilla's shoulders were wet and she'd spilled some of the beer on her skirt as she ran. Ralph Mason already sat on the edge of the bed as she ran inside the room. He was pulling his ostrich-skin boots to remove them, which he stopped doing when Priscilla spoke to him.

"I'm going to the bathroom to get out of these wet clothes," Priscilla said. "Why don't you go back and get the beers?"

"You didn't bring in the fucking beers?"

In the bathroom, Priscilla removed all of her damp clothes except for a pair white bikini underpants. She wrapped a large bath towel around her waist. Her large white breasts swayed easily on her chest as she rinsed her face. Before coming out of the bathroom, she applied more of the scarlet lipstick. She picked up the can of beer from the sink before returning to the bedroom.

Ralph had gotten the remainder of the six-pack from the truck and had placed it on top of a dresser which stood against the wall next to the entrance.

As Priscilla came back into the bedroom, Ralph sat on the edge of the bed, once again removing his ostrich-skin boots.

He picked them up by the rims of the shanks, placing them neatly on the floor a few feet away from the bed.

Priscilla finished with the can of beer and tossed it into the waste basket beside the bed. On unsteady feet, she walked to the six-pack on top of the dresser for another. She returned to the edge of the bed, took a swig of beer, jerking on the towel to let it drop to the floor. She pulled the covers to one side and slid under, tucking them under her breasts.

Ralph Mason undid his belt, pulled on the zipper of his blue jeans and slid them down his thighs and over his knees. He sat on the bed to shake his feet out of them, leaving them on the floor where they fell. He unsnapped the round mother-of-pearl buttons on his blue gingham shirt. He removed the shirt and tossed it on top of his jeans. He got to his feet as he yanked his T-shirt over his head.

"Let's see some skin, woman," he said, turning to look at Priscilla, and grinning.

Priscilla laughed, taking a sip of her beer. She rapidly yanked the covers to one side and just as quickly covered herself again. The rain and the splash of water to rinse off her face had sobered her a little.

Ralph Mason remained on his feet so that Priscilla could get a good look at his naked body. With his boots off, Ralph wasn't as tall. Except for his protruding beer belly, there seemed to be little fat. He dug into his crotch to scratch his balls.

"You still have your drawers on, woman," said Ralph Mason.

"Why don't you get in bed with me and take them off?" she said, sipping more of the beer.

"I wanted to get down with you soon's I walked into Georgene's and saw you sitting there," Ralph Mason said. "I said to myself, there is one fine-looking woman."

Ralph Mason walked across the room to get himself a beer from the top of the dresser. He came around the bed and stood by the corner of it, taking a long swig from the can. He drank the entire contents of it.

He dropped the empty can of beer to the carpeted floor and grabbed his dick, swinging his leg around to drop his heel on the mattress. Ralph grinned, shaking his dick in Priscilla's direction. She lowered her gaze and smiled.

Then the glass in the window shattered.

8

The shattered glass in the window fell noisily on the still, spilling over onto the floor.

Ralph Mason fell forward, landing on his right cheek. His head touched Priscilla's hip. Priscilla slid away from him. A trickle of blood flowed out of the tiny black hole in his back. The blood followed the contour of his back, coursed down his side below the rib cage and onto the bed where it welled beneath his left breast.

Priscilla backed up against the headboard of the bed into a sitting position.

She looked at the window, trying to see past it, into the shadow and darkness. The barrel of the pistol was gone, and so was the outline of the face she'd seen. All she could remember was the glint of metal on the face.

Priscilla scurried off the bed as the sudden panic took hold. Her right foot became entangled in the bedclothes, throwing her off balance. The beer can she held in her hand flew in the air and dropped into the waste basket.

She stumbled for a few seconds until she could plant her feet firmly on the carpeted floor. She looked to the window again, sensing that the figure in the shadow might still be there. All she saw was a small hole in the aluminum screen, a pile of glass shards on the window casing.

She turned to look behind her, desperate for a door or hole to run through, any means of escape.

Her attention came back to the bed, where Ralph Mason grunted. He brought his hands up, placing them flat on the mattress and began to lift his torso, as if he were doing a push up. When his chest was clear of the mattress, he shook his head from side to side, trying to stem the flow of the rolling fog settling in. He grunted once more. She saw his right arm begin to shake in the palsy of death. There was a visible trembling along the ridge of his shoulders. His strength finally ebbed and he fell face forward once more.

"Oh, shit! Fuck!" said Priscilla Arrabal, making fists out of her hands, banging on her thighs.

She ran into the bathroom, shutting the door behind her. She jumped into the shower, drawing the plastic curtain to shield herself. She cowered low in the shower stall, sitting on her heels, her arms wrapped around her breasts. The shaking in her body felt like recurring jolts of electricity.

The trembling stopped suddenly, and Priscilla became numb with fear. She felt an uncontrollable rage as she realized that she had been a target in the room. The pistol had been pointed at her. There was nothing she could do about it. An onslaught of rage set in as she considered how powerless she was.

She was a witness to Ralph Mason's shooting. Whoever shot him, the face in the dark shadow framed by the window, would want to make sure Priscilla did not live long enough to tell anyone of what she'd seen.

Priscilla began to cry softly as she talked to herself, the words hurried but barely audible, a faltering whisper.

All I wanted, she told herself, was company for the night.

All right, so what if one-night stands are dangerous these days! AIDS and deadly diseases all over the place! At least, I had rubbers in my purse! Fucking rubbers! I had them!

"I don't need this shit!" she said, firmly, and louder, the sound of her voice echoing in the bathroom.

She pushed the shower curtain to one side, trying to see something in the darkened bathroom. She stood on her feet and stepped out of the shower. Her toes nudged her clothes on the floor.

She did not turn on the bathroom light. The clothes on the floor were damp, but she didn't want to take the chance of getting a dry outfit out of her suitcase. In the semi-dark of the bathroom, she grabbed her leotard from the floor, pulling it roughly over her head. She had trouble negotiating her arms into the sleeves because of her frantic movements. Once she stretched the leotard over her stomach, she couldn't connect the crotch straps.

"Fuck it," she said aloud. "I have to get out of here!"

She picked up the rest of her clothes and ran back to the bedroom. She sat quickly on the bed and slipped into her black tights. She thumped the side of her head with the heel of her palm, as a reminder to pay more attention, and she ran back into the bathroom to gather her black sandals and put them on.

The burst of sudden but sure activity settled her mind. She felt more protected by the clothes she wore. Priscilla moved quickly, with renewed sense of purpose and assurance.

The past few minutes had sobered her more than a gallon of coffee and ten hours of sleep. There was a disagreeable taste in her mouth from the beer going stale and the bile in the vomit that she'd forced back down into her stomach.

She grabbed her purse and looked around the room, trying as best she could to ignore the naked body on the bed.

What else?

For the moment, there was only one thing to do: get moving. Get as far away from the motel room as possible.

But, what if the killer was outside, waiting for her to come out?

Of course, she could not stay in the room and wait for the shooter to decide at his leisure to come back and kill her. She could go straight to the police. No, she did not want to report the shooting and deal with the police. For all she knew, the police would probably arrest her for the shooting.

The thing to do, she told herself, is get the fuck out of here. I can figure out what else to do when I'm safely away. I've got to have more time to think.

Ralph Mason had dropped the keys to his truck beside the cans of beer on the dresser. She picked them up. Her suitcase was beside the door. She grabbed it hurriedly and cracked the door to a sliver of an opening. All she could see in the weak light from the fixture over the doorway was the grille of Ralph's pickup truck.

The rain continued without letup.

She opened the door enough to get her head out to look both ways. She didn't think the shooter was close by. She did worry that the noise of the shot had attracted attention.

There were only the dim, musky yellow lights underneath the concrete walkway overhead that ran the length of the oblong building. There was no one outside. No sign that the shot had aroused anyone. There was only the sound of hard rain falling.

Nothing out of the ordinary, all things peaceful and quiet.

The suitcase dangled from her arm as Priscilla took long and determined strides to Ralph Mason's pickup. She opened the driver's door, had some trouble lifting the suitcase onto the bench seat, but finally she shoved it in and pushed it to one side.

Priscilla got behind the steering wheel, slipped the key in the ignition and cranked the engine to a roaring flutter. Before shifting into gear, she reached down the side of the bench seat, between it and the door, for the seat adjustment lever. Ralph Mason's legs were not longer than hers, but the seat was too far back for her to comfortably reach the gas pedal and the brake. She slid the bench seat forward until the hard plastic of the steering wheel nudged her breasts.

Slowly, she backed up the truck in a half circle and pointed the hood out of the parking lot.

There was no traffic on the bypass, which glistened wetly under the street lamps. She eased the truck across the east bound lane, crossed the median, turned left headed in a westerly direction. Up ahead, she saw the traffic light at the crossroads turn to green. She mashed on the gas pedal. The speedometer inched over forty as she went past the crossroads.

On top of the hill, to the right, she saw the Ligon Wells Saloon. The parking lot was empty. The low-slung building settled in greenish shadows cast by a street lamp nearby on the corner. A few minutes later, she steered the truck along a wide gradual curve and came upon a straight stretch of highway. There was only darkness in the rearview mirror.

Priscilla began to breathe more easily.

The thing to do now, she told herself, is figure out what to do. She felt calm. Nevertheless, she knew that panic was just below the surface of calm, ready to return at any second. She tightened her grip on the steering wheel to quell the shaking of her hands.

She could use a cigarette. Four long months before, an eternity for those who quit smoking, she would've had a package of cigarettes in the purse that lay on the bench seat next to her. There were certain benefits to smoking, she thought. For instance, a smoke would be relaxing to someone in deep shit, as she now found herself. In her predicament, it was no time to worry about her long-term health.

The roadside sign told her she was headed in the direction of San Antonio. Another mile up the road, she drove by another roadside sign, telling her that Seguin was twenty-eight miles away. If she remembered correctly from a previous time she'd been on the same road, she'd pick up the interstate just west of Seguin. From there it was a little over thirty minutes to the outskirts of San Antonio.

The obvious choice, she told herself, was to stay on the loop circling San Antonio and drive north, headed for Dallas. Except for changing airplanes at the airport, she'd never been to Dallas. No one would recognize her there. It was a good point in favor of Dallas. She knew no one in Dallas. This meant there would be no one who could help her. A bad point against Dallas.

Priscilla felt her blood racing, throbbing at her temples. She kept driving, blinking repeatedly in counterpoint to the windshield wipers. She tried desperately to order her thoughts into the clear thinking she'd been trained to do. There was the sporadic flurry of trembling that threatened to erupt into uncontrollable panic.

To keep control of herself, she gripped the steering wheel and fixed her eyes on a distant spot on the road. She forced her mind to empty for a few seconds. When the spasms of fear passed, she returned to the question of what to do.

The initial reactive decision to head for San Antonio, skirt the city itself and connect with the interstate to Dallas began to appear as an increasingly distant possibility. Hardly a solution at all. If she was going to devise a plan for her safety, she would have to rethink the events of the past few minutes. She would have to organize the events in their proper order. The answer to any question was in the order of things.

The training in accounting that she'd received at the university should be helpful. Everything has an order. Chaos is nothing more than indiscernible order. It's just a matter of finding that order. Everything has a grouping to which it belongs, a category to tame unruly details.

There was always a beginning in business, an opening balance where assets sustained expenses. From there it turned into the ebb and flow of revenue and expense. The telling of the tale, its underlying truth, lay in the order of the numbers.

The beginning was Ralph Mason's body sprawled on the bed in the motel room. With any luck, the body would not be found until the morning when someone went in to clean the room. That would give Priscilla from six to ten hours to find a safe haven.

The missing pickup truck was sure to be discovered soon after. She paraphrased one of her economics professors. If a redneck Texan falls in the forest, there must be a pickup truck parked nearby. No question. They'd know she had the truck.

She had struck up a fast, transient's friendship with Georgene, the owner of the bar. They would surely learn her name, where she came from, what she looked like. There had been nearly three dozen people in the Ligon Wells Saloon. She'd had too much beer and had dragged Ralph Mason into a number of dirty dances in the small area in front of the jukebox. It wasn't much to be embarrassed about, but it had sure drawn attention to herself.

It was no doubt that it would be a night to remember, more so when all those people in the bar heard about Ralph Mason's killing. There were only a handful of people in the bar when she and Ralph had gone out into the rain. Those last people in the bar would recall that there wasn't any doubt as to where she and Ralph were headed after closing time.

As soon as the police came to see about the body, it wouldn't be long before they'd know who to look for.

If she were caught with the truck, it would implicate her in the shooting. The more she thought about it, the more she realized that remaining with the truck was to take a chance she could ill afford. Without the truck, the police could only suspect that she'd taken it. They would have to work harder to make the connection between her and Ralph Mason's body. She could hang tough and claim that she'd left him alive and healthy in the motel room. She could even add that he'd had a smile on his face when she left. She could insist that she knew nothing about the pickup truck.

The thing to do, she told herself, is get rid of the truck.

Of course, she couldn't pull over to the road shoulder and leave it. She had to keep moving. Until she figured something out, she'd have to keep moving in the truck.

Her mind became too much of a jumble as her thoughts converged on the moving truck. She couldn't think anymore. She decided to let it rest for a moment.

This was no time to make hasty plans or decisions.

9

She steered the truck into a bend in the road and saw a pair of blinking yellow lights, warnings for a stop sign ahead. She slowed the truck and arrived at an intersection in the short distance. Priscilla began to shake uncontrollably as the roaring rhythm of the truck decreased in intensity. The change in the ambient sound of the truck cab threw her off balance.

For twenty minutes, she'd thought through everything possible for her to do. She'd considered every possibility. No sooner did she decide on something, when doubt set in. There came a flood of good, solid reasons for changing or discarding the things she'd decided to do. What she needed above all was time to think.

There was the taste of flat beer in her mouth and her stomach felt queasy. Her head felt light and hazy, spinning and making her dizzy at odd moments. The tremors that coursed through her body made her head ache, swirling in pain. She would have to stop the truck and rest. If she could only have an hour or two to sleep.

Priscilla had never been a quick study, and she was incapable of snap decisions. She had never been one to cram for course examinations. She was plodding and methodical. Priscilla had to absorb and turn everything she learned into an intimate knowledge that flowed from her own mind. She had to know a subject thoroughly and it had to settle into the reservoir of her experience before she could do well on an examination.

She had delayed taking the examinations for Certified Public Accountant for more than a year because she could not look through review materials and satisfy herself that she actually knew the subjects. She could not take intensive courses of study to prepare for the examinations. When she finally did take the examinations, she had little reason to worry. There was no doubt in her mind that she had passed.

What she faced at the moment was not an examination. But she did need the time to thoroughly cover every aspect of the options open to her. Once she thought it through, saw the order of things, she would know what to do. If only she could bring herself to do it.

She was determined to keep moving, despite the strong fear that pulled her in all directions at once. She was desperate for a respite, a few hours to kick back, to rest and then to think. Her instincts told her that movement was the only thing that would keep her safe. So long as she kept moving, she'd be fine. Eventually, though, she'd have to stop.

The red octagonal sign ahead came into view in the glare of the headlights. She brought the pickup truck to a complete stop at the intersection. The sky was pitch-black above the headlights. There was a fine mist that bathed the windshield. Suddenly, there was a break in the black cloud cover above and she saw the clouds drift rapidly across the horizon. The crescent moon appeared for a brief instant and then the night around her turned black again.

The intersection remained in the glare of the headlights. She was nervous, feeling an urgent pressure to move across the junction. She looked in the rearview mirror, as if there might be an angry driver behind the pickup, impatient for her to get moving. All she saw was the red haze of the tail lights.

The crossroads brought her back to the same dilemma as before. She couldn't convince herself that she had the time to get far enough away. How much time she had depended upon when they would discover the body at the motel. The pickup truck was the only hard connection to the body and to the motel room. Even if they did look for someone else as the shooter, she could be arrested for just taking the pickup. The thing to do, she told herself, is ditch the pickup truck. The quicker the better.

On the right of the intersection, there was a bank of white signs, stacked atop of each other. The arrangement resembled a restaurant menu. Arrows pointing upward indicated Seguin and San Antonio and the miles left to go. An arrow pointing to the left, going directly south, told her she was twenty-two miles away from White Leg. The interstate and the city of Latham, the arrows to the right, were ten and twelve miles away.

She thought briefly of turning to the right, heading for the interstate and continuing on to Houston as had been her original destination. She could pull into an all-night truck stop, park the truck where no one would see it and hitch a ride to Houston with a trucker. She could hope that when they found the pickup truck, the long-haul driver would be several states away and wouldn't connect her with it.

A fit of trembling overtook her upper body. She fought against it, tightly gripping the steering wheel. She breathed deeply, and as the shaking began to subside, she settled on getting rid of the truck. That was the first thing she must do.

She turned left at the intersection, going in the direction of White Leg. Three minutes later, she drove by a road sign that read, White Leg 20. There were plenty of roads that fed into the paved highway. She had never realized how many paved, gravel, and dirt roads there were in Texas. She sped onward toward White Leg.

The plan, as it formed itself in her mind, called for her to pick a gravel or dirt road, any one would do, and get off the paved highway. She would continue on the road she chose until she found the entrance to a pasture or some deserted piece of land where she could leave the pickup. It had to be far enough away from the road so no one would see the vehicle, but not so far that she couldn't walk back to the road.

Eight miles down the road she traveled, she came upon a collection of scattered buildings; old dilapidated homes and the ghostly shells of former businesses. The road sign called it a town. Larson.

She slowed the truck as she rolled into town. On both sides of the road she saw the skeletons of buildings from a time when Larson would have been a thriving little town. To her right, she saw a lone wall, bent so low that it was almost level with the ground. From its beginning nearest the road, it swept upward, warped and curving, until it stood erect and perpendicular to the ground at the opposite end.

An ancient, rusted gas pump rose out of a clump of Johnson grass. The insides of it had been ripped away, but its tubular glass hopper was still intact. Amid the weeds and grass that fronted the road were tree trunks and concrete supports for buildings long gone. As she looked at them through the windows of the truck, they appeared to be creatures of prey, lurking in the night. A blue-greenish light hovered over the town, emitted by a single street lamp, which stood in the center of town.

Priscilla stopped the truck. Ahead of her, stretching into the darkness where the headlights couldn't reach, the paved highway went on to White Leg. To the left, was a paved farm-to-market road bearing the state outline of Texas, and to the right, there was a county road graded with rust-red gravel.

She turned on the narrow, paved road, driving about half a mile until the headlights shone on a white church with a pointed steeple. The paved road went into a sharp curve to the left at a Y fork. To the right, a sand and gravel road spun

straight and narrow, going south. The church stood at the
juncture of the Y. There was a lawn of dark-green grass in
front of the church, running evenly with a line of stubby fence-
posts parallel to the gravel road.

Priscilla mashed down hard on the brakes, going slightly
past the Y before the truck stopped completely. She threw the
truck into reverse gear, going back until she turned to the
right onto the gravel road. There was a canopy of tree branches over the road. The headlights made it seem as if she
steered the pickup into a narrow tunnel.

A quarter of a mile along the road, she came to a muddy
water crossing. There must be a river or a creek close by, she
told herself. Her spirits lifted knowing she could find a good
place to ditch the truck.

The road was coarse and rocky, making the bed of the
pickup rattle. She tried to speed up to thirty miles an hour,
desperate to keep going, but the rattling and noise of the truck
made her nervous. It was entirely too much noise. She had
already seen a farmhouse or two and several mobile homes.
She wanted to reduce the chance that anyone would notice
and remember that she'd driven by.

She drove for three or four more miles. With the rattling
beneath the truck, the shaking in the truck cab and having to
keep the speed below twenty miles an hour, she became disoriented and confused, but not enough to keep her from pushing on. The stale taste of beer lingered on her palate, her
stomach still felt unsettled. She thought of coffee. What she
wouldn't give at that moment for a plate of greasy eggs and
sausage.—the kind of sausage her grandfather used to make
every November when the weather cooled and he'd slaughter
a pig. For once, to hell with dry toast. She'd give in to a nice
piece of buttered toast or an English muffin.

Up ahead, she saw a turnoff to a dirt road, with a wide
sandy apron at the entrance. In the headlights, the apron was
a soft sandy-gray color, bordered with weeds and grass. She
stopped the truck just before the entrance to get a better look.

A few yards inside the pasture, the terrain was covered in young mesquite, six to eight feet tall—high enough to shield the truck from view by anyone passing by on the gravel road. She turned into the pasture and followed the ruts that led into the light-green foliage of the mesquite.

The lane into the pasture snaked to the right and left, seeming to go on without purpose, following the growth of the mesquite. At several points, the branches of the trees whipped and snapped at the sides of the pickup.

Priscilla kept her eyes open, going slowly in first gear, wishing the truck had an automatic transmission. Further on, the mesquite ended suddenly and she stopped the truck. In the glare of the headlights was an open space, with a few saplings rising from a mound of dirt scraped out of the earth. Beyond, she saw the dark wall of an oak-tree line.

She eased the truck forward, coming up to a stock tank, with a raised earthen rim on one side. The tank was full of water, either from recent rains or fed by an underground spring. She steered the truck around to the shore of the tank, seeing that there was plenty of room to maneuver between the oak trees ahead of her. Keeping the stock tank to her right, she drove on, going a few yards into the blackened forest of oak.

When she calculated that she was far enough into the woods to be shielded from view by the trees, she stopped the truck and shut off the ignition. She leaned back on the bench seat, closing her eyes, still tasting the stale beer. Her mouth watered from the hunger she felt. She took a deep breath and tossed her head over the backrest of the bench seat.

So far, so good, she told herself.

10

Priscilla sat quietly for a few minutes, breathing deeply, exhaling in a slow measured rhythm. She struggled to keep her mind blank. For the first time in more than two hours, she felt relatively secure. There was more to be done, but for the moment she could rest. She cracked the window of the truck to let in some air.

It was hard for Priscilla to believe everything that had happened since she'd become fed up with René Chapa. Everything ran together in her mind, overlapping, seeming to have happened all at once, out of order. No, she told herself, it didn't just begin yesterday. It's been going on for months. Maybe from the day I first met René. I was too involved with work and with myself to pay attention to it.

René Chapa. He, so innocuous and bland, convinced that the only life worth living is measured by money and possessions. Respect and envy from friends and strangers alike is the only true sign of success. Hence the two-story house in a gentrified neighborhood of San Antonio. His ten-year-old Volvo; a car that impressed people but which was not economical in light of what it cost for its upkeep. There were the Saturday mornings spent at the flea markets and rummage sales, looking for bargains in furniture and other items to create and then to maintain the image of success.

Priscilla shook her head in dismay, remembering René's Nakamichi. He bragged to anyone who would listen about his Nakamichi stereo. What René never told anyone was that he'd been able to buy the Nakamichi for fifty dollars because the amplifier didn't work. He'd taken it to several technicians in the hope that it could be repaired for fifty dollars or less. The technicians all said the same thing. The machine was so old that in the event that an amplifier could be found, it still would cost more to fix than he'd pay for a medium-priced outfit from a discount store. They all told him to spend a thousand dollars and get something he could really listen to. In the end, René bought a stereo at K-Mart for less than a hundred dollars. To entertain their guests, he powered up the Nakamichi to light up the faceplate and played the inexpensive system, which was kept carefully hidden. Priscilla was mortified each time they had guests for fear they'd discover the ruse.

When they'd first met, René worked for a community-service agency as a government and corporate relations specialist. What his job entailed, he never precisely specified. It was part of his job, he told her, to attend all manner of openings, receptions, political rallies, and other gatherings. There was hardly an evening that René spent at home, unless they entertained what he termed, important people. They seldom went out alone to enjoy each other's company. If they went out, it was to some function or other which he said was important for him to attend. After many months of subsisting on hors d'oeuvres for supper and the inane conversation of such people, Priscilla had opted to stay home where she could at least feed herself a decent dinner out of the freezer.

She loved René Chapa. She loved how naive he was and how endearing he was in his attempts to fashion an image of success for himself. He did work hard, at least at first he did, dedicating himself to his job earnestly and diligently. What he lacked in education, native intelligence, and skill, he more than made for in the way his drive knew no bounds. He had a single-minded willingness to grasp any and every opportunity that came his way. Because she loved him and because she felt it was her duty to avoid subjects that could bruise his ego, she minimized her accomplishments, her job promotions, and the wide-open future she had with her own career.

The worst of it, she thought, was his inability to hold on to a job for very long. In the three years they spent together, René had switched jobs four times. René might lose a job, but he'd remain upbeat and optimistic. And, he had good reason, for within two or three weeks of losing one, he'd have another. He'd never let up attending his evening functions. When he'd land a new job, he'd say that the evenings out paid off.

So sure was she about René Chapa that she'd thought nothing of sustaining their joint financial obligations. She deposited her salary into their joint checking account, keeping only enough for her minimal needs, letting René pay the bills and manage the money. Even when she discovered that he kept an account hidden from her, Priscilla did not complain, nor did she find it a cause for concern. She simply pretended to not know. She expected that they would marry and that the money he set aside would go toward a home or a honeymoon trip. She surrendered to René Chapa her complete trust.

When she thought about it, the evidence for René's two-timing was always right there in front of her. She was too busy with her job, too much in love with René, too trusting, and finally, although she would never admit it to herself, she honestly felt sorry that René Chapa would never really amount to much. He could get by with the image he created, but when it came to actually delivering on his promise in the jobs he took, he fell woefully short.

She came to feel responsible for him and eventually René could not help but notice. Hence, the changes in jobs, the chronic shortage of spending cash, and his increasing hostility in the house they shared. Despite René's insecurities, Priscilla continued to believe he loved her, and once past this phase of their relationship, she looked forward to a long and productive life together.

The first instance that René strayed away from her bed occurred at a party celebrating his birthday.

"I think René is just so wonderful," Priscilla remembered the black-haired, dark, rotund woman saying. Her name was Rachel and she had layers of makeup on her face. Her stomach flared out in what appeared to be a perpetual pregnancy, made worse by the dress she wore, which was too tight around the midriff and buttocks.

"It must be wonderful to be Rene's roommate," Rachel had continued, gushing on about him. "Everyone just adores him! Is your part of the house upstairs or downstairs? I just envy the way you two keep this house!"

Priscilla had politely excused herself, turning away from the woman, and had gone up the stairs to hide in the bathroom. She wanted to have a good cry, but she wasn't the kind to cry. The thing to do, as she well knew, was to confront René. But, he'd been without a job for nearly two months at the time, longer than any other time. She knew he was hostile and irritable, erupting savagely at every comment she made, however slight or mundane it might be. She could not bear another shouting match with him. She decided to wait until he found another job. By the time he did find a job, she had virtually forgotten the incident. She had downplayed it and had decided that she'd made too much of it. Things became settled between them.

Then she came home early one afternoon. She was the lead accountant in a long and tedious audit of a business teetering on the verge of bankruptcy. The telltale signs of company officials sacking the cash reserves of the company were there, with little finesse at hiding the questionable transactions. The numbers leaped at her in their spreadsheet cells. All she had to do was go back to the beginning and listen to the story the numbers told. Then, she'd have hard proof.

She'd discussed the matter with her boss, who reminded her that her job was not to investigate the potential wrongdoing of a client but to render a professional evaluation of accounting procedures. He counseled her to scrupulously note all the exceptions to standard practice and she would have complied with all of her responsibilities and obligations. There would be no professional or legal repercussions. She'd remained unsure whether it was the right thing to do, but she'd finished the audit of the firm. The months of long days and nights had taken its toll. Her boss had given her a bonus of a few days off. She'd left the office early, planning on spending the remainder of the afternoon at the mall. She went home to change clothes.

She came in the door, carrying her briefcase and her umbrella. She hung the umbrella on an antique hatrack and deposited the briefcase on a cherry wood table. She was too tired to walk upstairs to change clothes. In the living room, she slumped into an armchair by the window. She kicked off her shoes and removed her pantyhose.

As she tried to summon the energy to go in the kitchen for a beer, she saw the naked rotund woman going up the stairs. It was Rachel, the woman with the perpetually pregnant belly. Rachel's fleshy buttocks bounced along merrily. Her hands were extended, holding a glass of wine in each. Priscilla was too tired to be more than curious.

She got a beer from the refrigerator in the kitchen and returned to the armchair in the living room. She sipped the beer slowly, wanting to get drunk, but not before she confronted René.

It did not take long. René was obviously watching the clock. Minutes before she would normally come home from work, the two of them came down the stairs, fully dressed. Priscilla sipped her beer, watching René over the rim of the beer can. He tried a smile as a cover to his fidgeting.

"You're home early," he said, surprised, controlling his response. "How long have you been sitting there?"

"Long enough," said Priscilla. "Who is she?"

Before René could respond, the rotund Rachel wiggled a hello to Priscilla with her fingers.

"Hi, there! Good to see you again," she said to Priscilla. She turned to René. "Come on, baby, I don't want to be late." Turning back to Priscilla, she said, "Bye, now. We won't be out too late."

Priscilla crushed the beer can in her hand.

"Have a good time," she told them, without sarcasm or malice.

Later, she realized that she had actually meant it. There was little point to anger or ill will.

After they'd left, Priscilla remained in the living room throughout the evening. She drank all the beers in the refrigerator and after they were gone, she decided that she was too drunk to drive to the store for another twelve-pack. She went to bed but the alcohol kept her awake.

René returned home at four in the morning and undressed with a great deal of noise. Priscilla lay on her side, still unable to sleep. René got into bed with her. She could smell the rotund woman's mass-market perfume and, worst of all, the sweat and body excretions of sex. René was still slightly drunk. He put his hand on her breast.

Disgusted, Priscilla swiped his arm away and went down the stairs to the living room. She lay on the couch, where her fatigue finally got the best of her, and she slept.

For two months, Priscilla slept on the couch. René would beg for forgiveness.

"It's just something men do," René had told her. "You just have to understand that."

"Bullshit!" Priscilla exclaimed. "I don't do it."

"Of course, not. You're a woman," he said. "Men are always going to have little flings. Women understand that. There's really nothing to it. I don't know why you're so upset."

"I put my trust in you, René," she said.

René went on to swear that the rotund woman meant nothing to him and, if she insisted, he would never do it again.

Only twice in the two months they were separated by the two floors of the house, early on and after drinking too many beers, was she unable to control herself enough to go up the stairs to spend the night with him. The two episodes left her tense and unsatisfied. She no longer loved him. His physical touch was repulsive to her.

It took two whole months before she could bring herself to leave the house.

11

Priscilla opened her eyes to see the pale light of morning filtering through the leaves of the trees. Through an opening in the branches, she saw a bright cobalt sky above, not a trace of clouds. The storm of the night before had passed, leaving the ground soaked and a dampness in the air that stuck to her skin.

She glanced at her watch. It was nine in the morning. She remembered thinking about René as her body became relaxed, exhaustion settling in to take over the events of the night. The tension and fear had faded gradually until her thoughts of René gave way to a black and dreamless sleep. She had not intended to sleep for so long.

She stretched on the bench seat of the pickup truck, arching her back to yawn, feeling the stiffness in her bones. There was a kink in her neck from having slept on the bench seat without movement all night. A film, dry and cottony, with the taste of stale beer, coated the inside of her mouth. Her eyelids drooped and her eyes felt sluggish and brittle in their sockets. She felt an urgent need to pee.

She opened the truck and stepped outside onto the wet ground below. She walked a few steps until she came to a clearing not far away. She pushed down her black tights, lift-ed her leotard, and rested her weight on her calves as she peed. The sweet acrid smell of alcohol in her urine wafted up between her knees.

After she finished and arranged her clothing, she went for a walk further into the woods. She came upon a dry creek with steep banks. If she could maneuver the truck through the trees and into the dry creek bed, it would be a perfect place to leave the truck.

Priscilla returned to where she had parked the truck. Past the trees, she could see the stock tank nearby. She want-ed to splash some water on her face, rinse her mouth, brush her teeth. Her hair felt oily and stiff; she had no idea when she'd be able to wash it. No sense thinking about that now, she told herself, it'll have to wait until I get rid of the truck.

She opened the door of the truck, took out her suitcase and purse, and placed them on a dry spot beside the trunk of an oak tree. She climbed into the cab, started the engine, and made her way through the trees. Thankfully, they grew sparsely enough to steer around them, and she quickly arrived at the dry creek bank she'd found.

The only sloping piece of ground leading to the creek bed was obstructed by a clump of chaparral. She stopped the truck a short distance from the chaparral, seeing right away that there was only one thing to do.

She gunned the engine, popped it into gear, and the truck lurched forward, mashing down some of the chaparral. At one point, the rear tires spun noisily, but she was able to keep the truck moving. When the truck was firmly on the dry creek bed, she turned the steering wheel to follow the curves of the creek for a short way until she found a suitable place where the bank was higher than the cab of the truck. It was a spot where the side of the creek went straight up, nearly ten feet to the level ground above.

She thought of covering the truck with brush and branch-es as an added measure of protection. There was nothing handy that she could use. If she had the time and if she had the implements, it would have been a good idea. As it was, although she'd slept a little, her mind was not entirely clear and she did not have the will to do it. She left the truck, keys in the ignition, and began to walk back to the stock tank.

At the tank, Priscilla dropped her suitcase and purse and began to walk along the edge of the water until she found a small area, like a miniature lagoon, surrounded by willows. The tank went a little deeper there and the water was bright and clear. She got on her knees, scooped water in both hands and doused her face. She tasted the water, which was sweet and cool. She was suspicious of the water, but she was thirsty. She lowered her face into the water and drank. She rinsed her mouth, rubbing a finger over her teeth to remove a little of the night film that had accumulated on them.

She felt an urgency to get moving, put as much distance as possible between her and the truck. She had to brush her teeth. The stink of the night before was on her clothes: beer and cigarette smoke. She opened her suitcase to retrieve a plastic bag containing her toilet gear.

A simple thing, she thought, brushing your teeth. Hardly ever take notice of it. The toothpaste was tart in her mouth, prickling her nerves, restoring a sense of vigor to her body. From the suitcase, she pulled a change of clothing: a pair of jeans, a white T-shirt, and a clean pair of underpants. She wadded up her dirty clothes to stuff in the suitcase.

She stood naked at the water's edge. The midmorning sun had already blistered away the dew. She turned her face up to the sky, feeling the water dry on her cheeks. Under other circumstances, she would have loved to jump in the water and swim for a bit.

She dressed quickly and then took a minute or so to brush her hair. She deciding against applying more lipstick. With the suitcase zipped up and dangling from her arm, Priscilla began to walk to the sandy gravel road.

Right now, she told herself, it's best to get moving.

In minutes, she had lugged her suitcase to the sandy gravel road. She walked swiftly, her long legs carrying her in strong strides. She worried that someone might drive by and offer to give her a ride. Tired as she might be, she didn't want the inevitable questions of a good Samaritan: What was she doing on this road? How had she gotten here? Just as certain, whoever picked her up would not soon forget her.

Luckily, it was a little-traveled road, busy only during the harvest season. She had the road to herself until she reached Larson.

Just before noon, she'd managed to walk back to the white church with the pointed steeple. From there, it was a short walk to Larson itself, where she stopped at the cross-roads to consider what to do next.

To her right, she saw cars and pickup trucks parked in front of an unpainted wooden building, weathered to a gun-metal gray. A rusted Coca-Cola sign dangling from the eaves identified the place as Dottie's Restaurant.

Larson had seemed so desolate, deserted, that she had completely missed it when she'd driven by just eight or nine hours earlier. Only the vehicles parked in front gave any indication that the place was open for business.

She picked up her suitcase. In a minute, she reached for the door and went inside the restaurant.

The screen door had a bell attached to it, which rang as she opened it and went inside. Priscilla walked to a small Formica counter. Below the counter were three swivel chrome stools with red upholstery. She placed her suitcase on the floor and sat on one of them.

The remainder of the seating area contained three tables with red-and-white checked oilcloths over them. Four men sat at one of the tables. The men wore scuffed roper boots with their trousers tucked into them. They were red-faced, bulky men, broad at the shoulders. They could be ranchers, heavy equipment operators or oil field workers, she told herself.

The three old men who sat at another of the tables had the look about them of fixtures in the place. It was obvious to Priscilla that they gathered at the restaurant every morning. She remembered seeing the same kind of men in the little town outside of Laredo, where her family had their ranch. The old men, she remembered, were Mexicans.

A lone man sat at the third table. He was a young-looking Mexican. The expression on his face told her that he must be in his late thirties, early forties. She had seen him lower his head after he'd watched her come in.

No one sat at the counter swivel stools. She lowered her shoulders and rested her elbows on the Formica counter. The waitress was in the back part of the restaurant, in the kitchen, preparing an order. She'd heard the bell and showed her face in a rectangular opening in the wall which had a stainless-steel shelf wedged into it. The waitress was a large, tall woman, over sixty, with a round face that glowed with perspiration that accented her rosy cheeks. A few strands of yellow and gray hair were pasted to her forehead.

"What can I get you, honey?" the waitress said, coming through the swinging door to tower over Priscilla. "And, call me Dot."

"Coffee, and a donut, or sweet roll, or whatever you have," said Priscilla. in a tired voice, having lost the ravenous hunger of the night before.

"Is that all you're gonna have? We have a blue plate special today. Meat loaf, gravy, mashed potatoes, mixed vegetables. It's a good deal. Fills you up, anyway. If you're hungry."

Priscilla decided she ought to eat something, even though she didn't feel very hungry.

"Could you fix eggs and bacon, and some toast with lots of butter on it?" Priscilla asked, staring up at the waitress with wide, clear eyes.

"I stopped serving breakfast hours ago, hon," Dot said.

She saw how worn Priscilla looked. She poured coffee in a cup, which she set before Priscilla. From a white box, she took a donut, dropped it on a small plate and handed it to Priscilla.

"I can make you breakfast, hon. There's no problem," said Dot. "How do you want your eggs?"

"Fried. And, could I have four strips of bacon? I'm kind of hungry."

"Coming right up, hon," said Dot.

The four working men behind her arose in unison with a scraping of chairs on the floor. Their heavy footfalls echoed in the small restaurant. The bell on the door jingled, paused while they walked out, and when the door slammed shut, the bell jingled some more.

Priscilla picked up the cup of coffee that the waitress had placed in front of her. She swivelled on the chrome stool to get a better look at the place. Above the rim of the cup, she took a look at the Mexican who sat by himself at the table beside the front window. He was watching her intently.

Priscilla smiled in his direction.

He returned a thin smile before he calmly lowered his eyes to the plate of food.

12

D ot finished with the two orders in the kitchen. She pushed open the swinging door with her elbow, coming through, carrying plates to the two old men. She slid the plates in front of each, pausing to place a large hand on her hip while she wiped her brow with her forearm.

"I don't know why you two can't have the blue plate special, like everybody else," Dot told them.

"We ordered what's on the menu, didn't we?" one of the men said, stern and gruff. "If you can't cook it, don't put it on the menu. That's what I have to say about that."

"Menu ain't been changed since ol' Morton did the cooking in this place," the other man said.

"Now, there was a cook for you! Right up to the day he up and died," the first man said.

"Ol' Morton didn't give you no lip, neither," the second one said.

"What's not on the menu is you two being contrary. You eat, and hush up," said Dot, smiling, leaving the two men to their lunch.

She went back into the kitchen and in a matter of minutes came back with a plate of eggs, bacon, home fries, and toast. She put the plate on the counter for Priscilla and turned without moving her feet to fetch the coffee pot in back of her, with which she refilled Priscilla's cup of coffee.

Dot returned to her customary place behind the counter, a straight-back chair set against the wall. She clasped her hands, dropping them into her lap.

Priscilla finished with the donut, pushing aside the small plate, substituting her breakfast plate.

Dot became conversational. "You look to me like you could use something to eat, hon," she said. "That's what I said to myself when you walked in. You finish up what's on that plate and if you're still hungry, there's my blue plate special. And, I'm not saying that just because I'm an old woman that hates to see young thin girls."

"Thank you, ma'am," said Priscilla, softly. "That's very nice of you. I wonder if you could do something for me. Do you know of anyone who could give me a lift to White Leg? It's not very far, is it?"

"Did your car break down, honey? Is that your trouble? Where is it?" Dot said. "You can't be around these parts without a car. I might could find you somebody to go out and fix it for you."

Priscilla thought quickly. She leaned forward on the counter, lowering her voice. "I don't know if I should tell you this. I guess I'll have to trust you."

She paused before saying any more. Dot became very interested, leaning forward in the straight-back chair, her face at the same level as Priscilla's, her eyes opened wide.

"My boyfriend and I had an argument. A very bad, nasty argument. It happened this morning. He was taking me to the coast, and we were on our way, and all of a sudden he threw me out of the car."

"You don't say?"

Dot left the chair and came over to lean on the counter, her forehead inches away from Priscilla's. Her lower lip drooped a little in her rapt attention.

"This is very embarrassing, telling you this," said Priscilla, skewering her face as if trying to suppress her tears. "We've been fighting all week . . . Well, I guess I can tell you the truth. Actually, we fight all the time. This trip to the coast, we planned it for a long time. It was supposed to clear the air between us, you know? He promised he wouldn't fight with me anymore. To prove it, he said we could spend a week at the coast, just the two of us. Paradise. We would be in paradise. That's what he promised."

"And, what happened?"

"Well, we were supposed to leave early this morning, before all the traffic going to work in Austin gets on the road. I couldn't get him to wake up in time. He just rolled over and kept sleeping. When he finally got up, he blamed me for sleeping late. We left and we got into the middle of all that traffic, not moving at all, hardly. He just got madder and madder. And then he started asking me about what I had packed in his suitcase. When I didn't pack his favorite shirt, he got mad. I didn't bring his boots because I thought they'd be ruined in the sand if we walked on the beach. Well, he said I should've brought his boots; he can't be without his boots. And, he got madder. It went on like that. He'd ask me something, and I'd give him an answer, and he'd get mad. I don't know why he gets so mad."

"Men are such dogs," said Dot, bobbing her head up and down, agreeing, commiserating. "I buried my own husband twenty years ago, and I ain't never felt the urge to marry another one."

"Then about a couple of miles from here, he tried to hit me. I told him I wouldn't let him hit me. I just told myself, that's enough! He's not going to hit me. Well, I can tell you, it just made him all the more madder. He was trying to hit me and was not watching the road. I was sure he was going to wreck the car. I told him to stop the car and I'd get out."

"You did right, hon," Dot said. "When men act like that, the best thing is to leave them."

"I walked all the way here," Priscilla said, lowering her face.

"No wonder you look like you could use something to eat, all worn out like that," said Dot.

"All I want is to get to White Leg. If I could only get there, maybe I could get a bus back home to Austin."

"You'll have to go to San Antonio first, hon. Ain't no bus between here and Austin."

"That'll be fine, I'm not in any hurry," Priscilla said. "Just so I get back home."

"Say, that man of yours didn't take your money, too, did he?" asked Dot

"No, ma'am, he didn't do anything like that," said Priscilla. "I can manage. I have a little money. I can pay whoever takes me."

"I was just worrying about you paying for your bus," Dot said, a worried look on her face. "We'll get you to White Leg, don't fret yourself about that. If you'd've just come by this morning, my boy, Harmon, could've taken you. He won't be back until tomorrow, though."

"I'd be very grateful if you could help me," Priscilla said.

"We'll do all we can for you, honey," Dot said. "You can bank on that. Let me just ask Paco over there."

Priscilla had her purse on the counter. She opened it and took out her wallet.

"How much do I owe you?" she asked.

"Just let it go, honey. You don't owe anything," said Dot, patting Priscilla's hand, shaking her head from side to side. "After what you've been through this morning? Lord, it's the least anybody can do."

"Paco!" Dot yelled over the counter and across the room. "You wouldn't be going into White Leg this morning, by any chance?"

"I hadn't planned on it, Dot," said Paco Rangel, staring at the side of Priscilla's face from the angle where she sat at the counter. "What's up? You need for me to get something in town for you?"

"You mean you haven't been eavesdropping, Paco?" Dot said, laughing. "I bet you heard every word!"

"I might've been curious what you two were talking about," Paco said with a smile. "I'm too far away to hear, though."

"Hon, this little girl here needs a ride into White Leg," Dot said. "How about it? You busy?"

"I hadn't planned on going anywhere from here except my place," said Paco, lifting his coffee cup for a sip. "I've got a bunch of things to do this morning. Can't put them off at all."

"She needs to get to San Antonio, and then on to Austin," Dot said.

"I might could do it this evening, once I finish with my chores. In fact, I could take her all the way into San Antonio, if that's where she's going. I have to go there myself."

Priscilla Arrabal had no intention of going to San Antonio.

"That would be too much trouble," Priscilla said. "White Leg is good enough."

"Wouldn't be but an hour of your time, Paco. Run her into White Leg, and you'll be back to your chores in no time at all," Dot said.

"I know what you mean, Dot," Paco Rangel said. "I got a fresh batch of tomatoes and peppers that I got to pick and box. I don't do it today, I might as well give them to somebody for hog feed. I've got customers who're very picky about what they buy from me. If the young lady can wait until this evening, I can drop her off in San Antonio. My vegetables have to be there at sunup tomorrow. So I guess it won't make any difference if I get them there tonight. It's not out of my way, and it's no trouble."

"That's perfect, honey," Dot said, her face beaming with how pleased she was. "He's got to go there anyway. It'll be easier for you to find a way to Austin in San Antonio. The bus through White Leg is probably already gone by for today. You don't want to spend the night in White Leg. I don't even know if there is a place for you to stay. Why don't you take Paco up on his offer? He's a real nice young man. Everybody around here likes him. He's quiet and respectful. You'll like him."

"I'd hate to be a bother," said Priscilla, turning to look at Paco Rangel. "Are you sure it wouldn't be any trouble?"

At the distance between them, Priscilla saw his light-brown eyes, almost tan in color. They were bright and clear. Cat's eyes, she told herself.

Paco took a good look at her in return. The straight raven hair going down the sides of her face, the full lips bare of lipstick, the bare feet bundled in the sandals below the cuff of her jeans.

"No trouble at all. As I said, all I have to do is finish my chores."

"You can wait here until he comes for you," Dot said. "I have my little house in back. I think we can make you comfortable until Paco comes for you this evening."

Paco was on his feet, walking to the counter, digging into his jeans pocket for the money to pay for his meal.

"Paco Rangel," he said, extending his hand to Priscilla.

Priscilla introduced herself, shook his hand.

Paco placed some crumbled bills on the white Formica counter while he yanked his baseball cap out of his back pocket.

"That about cover it, Dot?" He asked, slipping the baseball cap on his head. It was a Dallas Cowboys logo above the bill.

"Sure does, hon," she said. "Thanks."

"If you want, you can spend the rest of the afternoon at my place," said Paco. "I have a satellite dish. You can watch television while you wait. You can find some great old movies on it."

13

At the Sheriff's Office in Lexington, Brita Mae Mayhew replaced the receiver in its cradle. She closed her eyes to massage them with the tips of her fingers. It was one o'clock in the afternoon. Just three hours more and her workday would be over and she would be free to go home.

The call came in from the manager of the Settler's Motel, a hysterical woman, screaming that the maid had found a dead body in one of the motel rooms. Brita Mae began to worry about her kids. There was little chance that she'd be able to go home at five. She brought her fingers up to her scalp and gently scraped her nails on her forehead. She turned in her metal swivel chair away from the dispatcher's console.

"Is Joe Blue back there in his office?" asked Brita Mae Mayhew.

"I think he's back there," June Akers, the secretary, said. "He's back from lunch."

"What about Sheriff Jim Woodrow? Is he coming back from lunch or not?" asked Brita Mae.

"Brita Mae!" said June Akers, exasperated. "What's got into you?"

"Junie, there's been a murder," Brita Mae said calmly. "Call the sheriff. Tell him to expect a call from Joe Blue in a few minutes."

"He said he was going to play golf this afternoon with Judge Bledsoe," said June Akers.

"Well, then, get him on the cellular."

"He won't carry that telephone with him, Brita Mae," said June Akers. "He gave it to me before he went out. Told me to hold it for him. He said he can't see any reason to carry it around with him."

"Shit!" said Brita Mae. "In that case, send a patrol car to find him and standby. Joe Blue will be calling him."

Brita Mae Mayhew was surprisingly nimble for the large frame that carried her weight. She sprang from the metal swivel chair and made her way through the maze of desks and filing cabinets in the bullpen area of the Sheriff's Office. At the counter where the public was served, she lifted a piece nearest the wall to let herself out. Next to the counter was a green, heavy metal door, which she opened and walked through.

Brita Mae's heavy footfalls on the tile floor echoed on the cinder block walls. Near the end of the hall, she stopped to look in the interrogation room to her right. The room with the long table surrounded by six metal chairs was empty. It was in use most often for meetings between the sheriff and his deputies and less often to question suspects. Occasionally, when his jail-cell office proved too small, Joe Blue used it to do his paperwork.

At the end of the passageway was another, heavier, metal door. In the center of it was a sign, stenciled in red block letters, DO NOT ENTER.

Brita Mae opened the door and went in.

In the first of a row of three jail cells, directly in front of the door, sat Joe Blue behind a scarred, wooden desk. The other jail cells to the right of Joe Blue's office were empty. The door to Joe Blue's office consisted of thick bars welded on a heavy metal frame. It was open, secured with tape to the iron bars of the next jail cell.

A corkboard hung on the wall. Pins with plastic nubs of different colors were neatly arranged in a row across the top of the board. A poster of the Tejano Conjunto Festival, depicting an eerie dancer with chicken feet poking out from the cuffs of his trousers, added the only color to the whitewashed wall. On a nail peg, to the left of the door, hung an off-white straw Resistol and a gun belt. The holster was empty.

Joe Blue sat at his desk with his feet up, reading the *Daily Lexington.*

Joe Blue turned from his newspaper to look at Brita Mae Mayhew. His hair was jet black, coarse, cropped short above his ears. Joe's features were those of the Mexican mestizo; strong and dark, with his skin the color of coffee with a splash of cream in it.

His father, Joe Blue, had married a Mexican woman. Except for Joe, their children had been born with light skin and blonde hair. At an early age, Joe had gone to live with his grandparents on his mother's side. He had learned to speak Spanish and had been raised completely within the Mexican side of his heritage. Unless a precise answer was called for, most people in Lexington referred to Joe Blue as a Mexican. He was comfortable with the reference, preferring it to any other.

"What brings you back here, Brita Mae?" Joe Blue asked, turning back to his newspaper.

"Just visiting the jail where my black ancestors spent so much of their lives, Joe," said Brita Mae, tired, trying to revive her sense of humor in the face of a day that was going to be even longer.

"This building's not more than ten-years old, Brita Mae," said Joe Blue, turning a page of the newspaper. "You want to commune with the spirits of your ancestors, go visit the jail-house museum on the courthouse lawn."

"We got us some town here, Joe," said Brita Mae, laughing brightly. "A damn jailhouse for a museum!"

"You sound tired, Brita Mae," said Joe Blue, putting the newspaper on top of the desk. "I know it's important, so let's have it."

"I just got a call from the Settler's Motel. A white lady. Said she's the manager."

"Pearl Gahagan. What about her?" said Joe Blue.

"Is she the one? Pearl Gahagan? Anyway, she said they found a dead body in one of the rooms."

"When?"

"Just before she called, I guess. She didn't say."

"Anybody we know?"

"She said she couldn't be sure. She didn't want to stay in the room and disturb anything. But, she said it looked like it could be Ralph Mason."

"Orthal Mason's boy? Shit!" said Joe Blue, rising from his chair, reaching for his Resistol.

"The sheriff's playing golf," Brita Mae said. "I sent a patrol car to standby so you can call him."

"Thanks, Brita Mae," Joe Blue said, adjusting the hat on his head.

Joe Blue wore a khaki shirt with blue epaulets. A gold shield was pinned over his left breast pocket. The collar of the shirt was open. He wore denim jeans and maroon lizard boots. The other deputies wore the same shirt with matching khaki trousers that had a blue stripe down the sides.

He took the gun belt from the nail peg. He wrapped it around his lower waist and buckled it.

From his pocket, he took a set of keys to unlock the desk drawer where he kept his .357 magnum. He dropped it into the holster, snapping shut the strap over the hammer. Normally, Joe Blue went unarmed. He wore his gun belt on those occasions when the sight of it made people more cooperative.

When Sheriff Jim had promoted Joe Blue to Chief Deputy, he insisted that Joe Blue not wear the standard issue uniform. The sheriff himself wore a standard issue uniform. Joe Blue had asked the sheriff why he would be the only member of the sheriff's department to not wear the uniform of authority.

"Joe, I need someone to be what you might call the little sheriff under me," Sheriff Jim Woodrow Willow had said. "Run things for me. Take charge of the office and the men. I'm too damned old for that kind of shit anymore. Now, everybody knows who I am because every four years I let them know who I am. That way, they know who to vote for come election time. The uniform is a definite political advantage over my opponents. More than that, I've been on the job so long, nobody alive remembers when there was any other sheriff but me. You, on the other, you have to establish who you are. Make people know that you're more than just a man in a uniform with a badge and a gun. I want people to stand back and say, 'There goes Joe Blue. He runs the Sheriff's Office.'"

Joe Blue walked the length of the cinder block corridor and pushed open the green metal door. Brita Mae Mayhew was back at her dispatcher's console. Joe Blue placed his elbow on the white counter.

"Brita Mae, would you honk at Hank Solís? Tell him to meet me at the Settler's Motel," Joe Blue said, adding, "right away!"

"That's all? Just tell him to meet you there?" Brita Mae was surprised.

"Yeah, and don't go blabbing what it's about to the whole world just yet."

14

Outside, the sun was blazing hot, going into the hottest part of the day. Joe Blue's candy-apple red pickup truck was in the newly-constructed parking lot. Several ancient shade trees had been razed to make way for the parking lot. The contractor, per instructions from the county commissioners had planted trees all around the lot. At the rate they grew, it would be twenty years before they'd give any shade.

Behind the white cinder block building housing the sheriff's office rose the imposing figure of the red-and-cream-colored Lexington County courthouse, built at the turn of the century. It was a landmark that distinguished Lexington from other towns in Texas.

The chrome door handle of the pickup was blistering hot when Joe Blue grabbed it to open the door. He turned on the air conditioner full blast. On the radio, the music from a heavy metal station in San Antonio blasted through the speakers. His kids had been in the truck playing. He punched a button to tune in a Tejano station. La Tropa F, whom he remembered as Los Hermanos Farías, sang "Grítenme piedras del campo."

The steering wheel scorched his hands as he eased the truck out of the parking lot. He drove north on the western side of the town square. There were few vehicles on the streets, and no one walking. Lexington seemed deserted and ghost-like.

As he drove, he picked up the police radio and asked for the sheriff, who responded instantly. Joe Blue simply told the sheriff that he wanted to speak with him at the Settler's Motel. If it's a murder, he told himself, it'll be all over town soon enough.

A mile north of the town square, Joe Blue came to the intersection on top of the hill. Across the divided bypass was the Ligon Wells Saloon. Joe Blue turned his pickup truck to the right, heading east.

When he slowed to turn into the motel parking lot, he saw a sheriff's squad car across the median, coming from the opposite direction. Hank Solís, driving a tan squad car with dark-brown front doors, waved to Joe Blue and pulled into the lot ahead of him, crossing over from the west-bound lanes of the bypass.

Hank Solís stepped out of the squad car, holding his ever-present Styrofoam cup of coffee in his left hand. Hank Solís was tall, over six feet, with a barrel chest that made him appear much larger than he actually was. He'd gotten solid bulk during the six years he'd spent in the Marine Corps. Although he was easy-going and hardly anything ever riled him, Hank Solís had the respect of people in Lexington County. He did not swagger, nor did he try to intimidate anyone, as some of the younger deputies did. Hank Solís was not afraid of people and he didn't want people to be afraid of him. There were enough stories about Hank Solís to make anyone who'd heard them behave in his presence.

"What's up, Joe?" asked Hank, bringing the Styrofoam cup of coffee to his lips.

"Brita Mae says somebody called about a body in one of the rooms here," Joe Blue said, frowning.

"What room?" asked Hank.

"Beats me," said Joe Blue. "Let's go in the office and ask."

They walked under the porte-cochere and opened a glass door leading into the lobby of the Settler's Motel. The lobby and registration area were enclosed in plate glass from floor to ceiling. The drapes were partially drawn to retain the air conditioning. Nevertheless, the lobby was brightly flooded with sunlight. A dandelion chandelier, full of tiny little lights, hung from the ceiling. Scattered about were easy chairs and coffee tables, a few potted plants to break the beige monotony of the color scheme in the lobby.

As they entered the lobby, Joe Blue spotted María Morales at the far end of the lobby, across from the entrance. She sat on a bench upholstered in beige vinyl, holding her hands in her lap. She stared straight ahead, her eyes were red and bright, her eye sockets brimming with tears.

The manager of the Settler's Motel, Pearl Gahagan, came out of her small office in back of the registration desk. She was a tall woman, at the beginning of her fifties, with shoulder-length blonde hair that was probably enhanced with hair color. She wore a coral blouse under a light gray business suit, a string of pearls over her bosom. Her body was well-proportioned, her face smooth and clear, and her demeanor was one of authority.

"I'm sorry to keep you waiting," Pearl Gahagan said, hurrying to intercept Joe Blue and Hank Solís.

She had been watching the entrance to the lobby from her office, waiting for them. She spoke with the narrowly condescending air of someone in complete charge. She took Joe Blue by the arm, intending to lead him to her office.

Joe Blue and Hank Solís looked across the lobby to María Morales, who sat straight and rigid, overcome with sorrow.

"Is she the one who found the body?" Joe Blue asked, nodding his head in the direction of María Morales.

Pearl Gahagan let go of Joe Blue's arm, dropping her hands to her side, as if she didn't know what to do with them. They stood in the middle of the lobby.

"Yes, that's María, one of our maids," said Pearl Gahagan.

"I know who María Morales is," said Joe Blue, pronouncing the name in Spanish. "I didn't know she worked here."

"If you would just come this way, please," said Pearl Gahagan with a sweep of her arm, indicating the registration desk and her office behind it.

Hank Solís continued walking to where María Morales sat. He took a seat on the beige bench next to her. He inclined his head to look at her, maintaining his silence, speaking softly and reassuringly to her.

Joe Blue did not move. He looked into Pearl Gahagan's face. Despite her age, she remained an extraordinarily attractive woman.

"When did María find the body, Miss Gahagan?" asked Joe Blue.

"Twenty minutes ago," said Pearl Gahagan. "I'll show you where it is."

"I believe I'll want to talk to María Morales first," said Joe Blue.

"But, there's no need to talk to María," said Pearl Gahagan, surprised at the breech of her authority. "I'll show you the room."

"Excuse me," he said. "I'll just have a word with her."

Joe Blue walked to where María Morales and Hank Solís sat. She looked up at him with tear-stained cheeks, on the verge of starting to cry again.

"María," said Joe Blue in Spanish, "can you tell me what happened?"

María Morales began to cry in earnest again.

Joe Blue lowered his head, exchanged glances with Hank Solís, and then turned slightly to face Pearl Gahagan. She threw her hands up in the air, upset, indicating there was nothing to be done about María and that Joe Blue should be talking to her and not the maid.

"Miss Gahagan, do you suppose we could have some coffee?" Joe Blue asked, politely. "I expect we'll be here a while. I like mine black. Hank likes his with lots of cream and sugar. We'd be grateful to you."

Pearl Gahagan's face became grim. She turned and walked away without a word.

Hank Solís put his hands on María Morales' shoulders. Joe Blue took a walk to the far end of the lobby and then returned, giving María Morales time to finish crying.

Pearl Gahagan came back carrying two cups of coffee, clattering on their saucers.

"Throwaway cups would've been fine, Miss Gahagan," Joe Blue said. "You didn't have to bother with your china."

Pearl Gahagan ignored the remark.

"Tell us what happened, María," Hank Solís said in Spanish.

"I opened the door of the room and he was lying on the bed," she said in Spanish, in between persistent sniffles.

"María! Speak English!" said Pearl Gahagan forcefully. "We don't understand what you're saying."

María Morales gave up trying to repress her tears and began to cry again in loud, uncontrollable sobs. Joe Blue took a sip from his coffee.

When he had replaced the cup in the saucer, he said, "Miss Gahagan, I wonder if you could come with me."

He walked toward the front desk and turned to face Pearl Gahagan.

"I think we can handle things from here on out, Miss Gahagan," said Joe Blue, speaking softly, almost whispering, but still respectful. "I appreciate your help. I'll be sure and let Sheriff Jim Woodrow know how helpful you've been."

Sheriff Jim Woodrow came through the door, stopping just inside the lobby. He turned his head to look in all directions before continuing forward. He wore his standard issue uniform, with an Army-issue .45 automatic in his holster. He was not a tall man, measuring two or three inches below six feet. Although he had celebrated his seventieth birthday, he had the bearing of a man twenty years younger. His eyes were sharp and penetrating, brooking sass from no one. As he went further into the lobby, his torso sailed placidly through the air, not wavering an inch.

He removed his sunglasses in a sweeping motion. He came up to Joe Blue and Pearl Gahagan. He carried an unlit filter-tipped cigarette in his hand.

"You see the body yet, Joe?" Sheriff Jim Woodrow asked, putting the cigarette to his mouth and lighting it.

"I thought we'd start with María Morales first," Joe Blue said. "She's the one who found body. Right now, she's pretty upset. She's over there with Hank. I was thanking Miss Gahagan here for her cooperation."

"We don't allow smoking in the lobby, Sheriff," said Pearl Gahagan.

"Is that a fact, Pearl?" said Sheriff Jim Woodrow, exhaling cigarette smoke. "Tell me now, you still have that cook of yours? That Bohemian guy, you know the one. He makes those German pastries I like so much, the ones that've got all that streusel stuff on them?"

"He's still with us, Sheriff Willow. You haven't been to dinner with us in a long time, Sheriff," said Pearl Gahagan, becoming cordial as she spoke with one of her social equals. "How is Mrs. Willow?"

"She's fine, Pearl, just fine. And, I'll be sure and pass on to her that you asked about her. I'll be sure and come by, make up for being a stranger, Pearl," the sheriff said amiably.

"I'm expecting you to bring Mrs. Willow for dinner," said Pearl Gahagan.

"You can count on it, Pearl. We'll make a night of it, the wife and I. What's a good night to come, anyway, Pearl? When's your cook gonna do something special?"

"Call me before you come and I'll have him whip up something special just for you."

"I'm sure gonna have to do that, Pearl," the sheriff said.

"I'll see what pastries we have and get you some coffee," said Pearl Gahagan, leaving Joe Blue and the sheriff.

She felt more comfortable, reassured, with Sheriff Jim Woodrow Willow on the scene and in charge of the investigation. The sheriff would be careful about scandal, and he would prevent a circus from erupting. After all, Pearl Gahagan was one of the stalwarts of the Democratic Party of Lexington County and the sheriff depended upon her political support. He would know to protect her interests.

15

Hank Solís began to translate what he'd learned from María Morales as the sheriff and Joe Blue approached.

"María says that she cleans the rooms upstairs in the morning and, in the afternoon, she does the downstairs. How soon she's finished depends on how many guests are registered in the motel. Last night, on account of the rain, they had a lot more guests. That's why it took her until this afternoon to get to the room. She knocked on the door to make sure no one was in the room. Most people check in, get a few hours sleep, and get going pretty early. But she knocks anyway because once in a while somebody stays and sleeps late. When there was no answer to her knock, she opened the door, but didn't go in right away. She turned to get her cleaning trolley ready to drag inside the room. She took a step into the room and saw a naked man lying face down on the bed."

María Morales began to cry again when she heard Hank Solís mention the dead man.

"Thinking that he was asleep, she closed the door right away so as to not wake him up. She was embarrassed to see a naked man. She started to go on to the next room on her list.

There was something she saw that bothered her. She wasn't sure what to do, but she went back to the room and knocked. She knew she might be in trouble if she woke up the guest. She knocked several times and when there was no answer, she opened the door again and stuck her head in. What she saw was blood on the naked man's back. There was blood on the mattress, too. She closed the door and ran here to the lobby to tell Miss Gahagan."

"How did you know it was Ralph Mason, María?" Joe Blue asked in Spanish.

"I don't know who it is that's dead in that room," María Morales said, responding in Spanish.

"Who did you talk to when you came in the lobby?"

"Miss Pearl. She's the one I came to tell right away."

Pearl Gahagan returned to the lobby. In her absence, she had freshened her lipstick, touched up her makeup, appearing even more stunning than before. At her side came one of the kitchen helpers, wearing a chef's white smock and a white stovepipe chef's hat on his head. At waist level, he carried a tray on which were a plate with a pastry on it, a cup of coffee, fork and spoon, napkin, and metal containers of milk and sugar. The helper stood by while the sheriff put milk and sugar in his coffee.

"Tell us what happened when María came to see you," the sheriff said, taking a sip of his coffee.

"She said there was a dead man in one-twelve," Pearl Gahagan said disdainfully, reluctant to recall the unpleasant experience.

"What did you do?"

"I thought it might be a drunk who'd passed out on the floor. Something like that. It's not very likely that we'd have a corpse in any of our rooms."

"So you didn't believe María when she told you she saw a body?" said Joe Blue.

"No, it's not that I didn't believe her," said Pearl Gahagan. "Nobody's ever died in one of our rooms. Not since my husband and I built this motel, and not since I began to manage it. There was a man who had a heart attack a few years ago, but he was removed to the hospital, where he eventually died. He was alive when the ambulance took him away."

"I remember that," said Hank Solís.

"Pearl, what did you do?" asked Sheriff Jim Woodrow, taking a bite of the apple pastry. His face remained firm, with barely a movement of his jaws chewing the pastry.

"Well, I took my keys and went to the room to take account of the situation."

"How did you do that, Miss Gahagan?" asked Joe Blue.

"I went along the sidewalk, unlocked the room and went in. I saw that it was Ralph Mason lying face down on the bed. That's all I can tell you."

"If you don't mind, let's take it from the moment you opened the door," Joe Blue said. "Tell me about every step you took, everything you did, everything you saw."

"Is that important, Sheriff?" asked Pearl Gahagan, ignoring Joe Blue. She became irritated with Joe Blue's forward attitude. Her eyes looked to the sheriff for support. "I told this deputy who it was."

"We'll be through here a lot quicker, Pearl, if you just answer the man's questions. We've got a job to do," said the sheriff, wiping his mouth with the linen napkin. "I promise we won't waste your time by asking anything that's not important."

Pearl Gahagan frowned and lowered her head to speak toward the floor.

"I opened the door and I saw the body, just as María saw it when she tried to go in to clean the room. I saw the blood on his back. I walked in the room, watching the floor so as not to step on anything. I walked around the bed and I saw the blood on the mattress. There was a lot of blood on the mattress."

"Did you touch the body at all? Did you touch anything?"

"No, I didn't touch anything. The face looked familiar, that's why I bent down to get a closer look. I studied the face for a little bit and recognized him as one of the Mason boys. I knew it was Ralph because he dated my daughter when she was in high school. He was on the football team. After I saw who it was, I called your office, Sheriff. I spoke with somebody that sounded like a black woman."

"And, you locked the room when you left?" asked Sheriff Jim Woodrow Willow.

"I certainly did."

"No one has been in there since you left it?" asked Joe Blue.

"Certainly, not!" Pearl Gahagan snapped.

"Let's get a look in the room, see what we've got," said Joe Blue.

"Hank, why don't you go in the company of Miss Pearl here to get a key to the room?" said Sheriff Jim Woodrow.

Joe Blue turned, bending low, to speak to María Morales. He took her hand in his. He gently spoke in Spanish.

"María, you can go back to work. Or, if you're done for the day, you can go home. We may want to talk to you some more. For now, you've been very helpful. We're very grateful to you."

Outside the lobby, in the shade of the port-cochere, Joe Blue and the sheriff waited for Hank Solís to join them with a key to the room.

"What the hell is it with Pearl, Jim Woodrow?" Joe Blue asked the sheriff. "She sure acts like she's got a corn cob stuck somewhere up her ass."

"Maybe you should understand that Pearl's had a pretty good ass-kicking by life itself, Joe," said the sheriff. "Way back, her daddy owned a pretty good spread hereabouts. One day young Robert Gahagan roared into town with a pile of money. Pearl's daddy stumbled all over himself to get Robert Gahagan and young Pearl hitched. It took about half of all he had to get it done, but he got them married. It didn't take too long before everybody in town called young Robert 'Flim-Flam Bob.' Ol' Flim-Flam got Pearl's daddy to invest in some business ideas he had. Some oil-well scheme or other, guaranteed to pay off, leave everybody sick with money. Losing his money never stopped Pearl's daddy. He sure liked Ol' Flim-Flam, right to the end. Never lost confidence in him. In fact, when Pearl's daddy died, her brothers got everything he had; she was left out of the will. He figured Pearl was in good hands with Flim-Flam Bob."

Joe Blue thought for a minute. "I remember Bob Gahagan. When I was a kid, we'd see him speeding down main street in White Leg, riding with the top down in his pink Cadillac. He had some kind of chain, as I remember, along the front grille, like a necklace. Had these glass chunks in the chain, like diamonds. Hell, we all swore they were the biggest diamonds anybody'd ever seen. We were envious, of course. We knew we could never ride in anything like that. And, for damn sure, we'd never own one."

"Well, turns out that Flim-Flam Bob spread money all over the place, lots of investments. All the money he had, and even more that wasn't his. By the time he wrapped the pink Cadillac around a mesquite tree, killing himself and some kind of bar floozy he was with, ol' Bob was flat broke."

"Good-looking woman like Pearl, it don't figure he'd go out with another woman," said Joe Blue.

"No, it don't, Joe," said the sheriff, "but, then, you didn't know ol' Bob. Pearl was managing the motel back then. Ol' Bob had built it because he was convinced Lexington could be a big-time tourist resort. Pearl worked at the motel because it was something she could do to get out of the house, keep her from getting bored. After ol' Bob's demise, his wheeling and dealing came up to the light of day. The creditor that got the motel as a settlement decided to keep ol' Pearl on as manager. She's been at it ever since. Except now, it ain't just something she does to keep from getting bored. She works because otherwise she'd lose that little piece of ranch, the homestead they had when ol' Bob went on to his reward."

"She's a handsome woman. Pretty damn good looking, in fact. How come she never married again, Jim Woodrow, after Bob Gahagan died?"

"I don't know, Joe," said the sheriff, bending down to set the empty plates and cup on the concrete beside the door to the lobby. "There are some things you never know."

Hank Solís came out the plate glass door, jingling a set of keys.

16

Joe Blue took the set of keys from Hank Solís. The three of them walked along the concrete sidewalk to the last room in the barracks-like two-story building. Joe Blue slipped the key into the lock.

"You want me to call for an ambulance, Joe?" asked Hank Solís.

"Yeah, go ahead," said Joe Blue, suddenly fatigued in the face of all the work that lay ahead. He turned the key in the lock and opened the door.

He cast a quick glance at the body on the bed. The sliver of sunlight coming in through the broken window shone directly on the body. The remainder of the room was cast in shadow. Joe Blue flipped a light switch on the wall beside the door.

Joe Blue took notice of the three cans of Miller Lite on the dresser pressed against the wall to his right. He looked slowly and deliberately around the room. Nothing out of the ordinary. No sign of a scuffle, nothing overturned, everything upright and apparently in its place.

Joe Blue stepped into a narrow alcove off to one side of the room. To the right in the alcove there was an open closet with clothes hangers secured to a round chrome bar. Nothing was hanging on the cross bar. He poked his head into the dark bathroom, found the light switch and flicked it on. The towel hanging on the square chrome bar had been used. There was a smudge of red lipstick on it. He nodded his head.

When he came back to the bedroom, the sheriff stood at the foot of the bed, with Hank Solís beside him. Hank's massive body dwarfed that of the sheriff. The sheriff, still wearing his sunglasses, with his arms crossed over his chest, stared at the body.

"You two know those Mason boys? Any idea who's the oldest of the brood?" asked the sheriff.

"I don't know, Jim Woodrow, there's a bunch of them Masons," said Joe Blue. "Too damned many to keep track of."

"Jared, Sheriff," said Hank Solís. "I went to school with him."

"That's right, Hank. Jared. That's the boy's name." The sheriff said.

"That's not Jared lying on the bed, Sheriff," said Hank Solís.

"I know it's not Jared, Hank," the sheriff said, becoming irritable. He removed his sunglasses, stuffing them in his shirt pocket. He stepped back against the wall, leaned back on it.

"I was just thinking back to when Orthal Mason first got married," he said. "This would be to his first wife. Folks around here, we thought he'd gone and married his cousin. Nobody in these parts wanted it said that we were anything like those hillbillies in the mountains of West Virginia. The girl lived with Orthal Mason's uncle, so it was natural to think she was his girl. As far as anybody knew, she was blood kin to Orthal Mason. Turns out, though, that she was a girl who his uncle took in after her momma and her poppa died. It wasn't like them Masons at all to do something decent, but he raised her as his own. Her folks went with the influenza epidemic, back in the twenties. Something like that. Anyway, the truth, it turned out, is that Orthal Mason didn't marry his cousin. She was just raised like his cousin, but she wasn't."

"In the Catholic Church, it amounts to the same thing," said Joe Blue, coming around the bed to look at the body. "She was his cousin, if she was raised that way."

"Well, no offense, Joe, but those of us who talk directly to Jesus Christ Himself, we don't see it that way," said the sheriff.

Hank Solís grinned. Sheriff Jim Woodrow Willow looked at Hank Solís, caught him grinning, and grinned himself.

"Anyway," the sheriff went on, "when Orthal Mason was a young man—he was three, four years younger than I was—we figured he was ripe for the penitentiary. He did a lot of thieving back then. Drank a lot of bootleg during the prohibition. In fact, I believe he tried his hand at making his own bootleg and nearly poisoned himself to death while he was at it."

Joe Blue crouched beside the bed to examine Ralph Mason's body. He dropped his weight on one knee, placed his elbow on the edge of the mattress.

"Orthal Mason's favorite thing to do was to go over to Coon Town to raise hell. Orthal Mason and his cousins. There was a lot more Masons in the county back then than there is now. The thing about Coon Town, it was where folks lived. Mostly peaceable. People stayed in Coon Town, nobody bothered them. It was like an agreement, although no on ever actually agreed to it. Folks mostly stayed out of there. That way the Nigras had their place to live and we had ours. What people did down in Coon Town was their business. The town didn't get mixed up in their business.

"Well, Orthal Mason and his cousins went down to Coon Town one time too many. Them Nigras beat the living shit out of the bunch of them. They came into the sheriff's office to complain about what happened to them. They looked like they'd tangled with a bobcat and got the short end of it. I was just a young deputy then. Anyway, nobody paid any attention because they weren't supposed to be in Coon Town in the first place. When they went back and got the shit kicked out of them again, folks figured them Nigras were doing the county a favor."

Hank Solís became nervous, fidgeting on his feet. Joe Blue was busy examining the body. He felt that the sheriff required him to pay attention.

"The reason, I believe, all this comes to mind, is when I came back from the war and got my job back as deputy sheriff, Orthal Mason had gotten married to that gal everybody thought was his cousin. They had this boy, Jared. I thought to myself, now, that's a good thing. Having a family will settle down Orthal Mason. Make him stop his thieving. Get him to go work for a living. Except, Orthal Mason did no such thing. He never did stop his thieving."

Joe Blue got to his feet beside the bed. He took a small notebook from his hip pocket. He wrote for a few minutes and then closed the notebook and returned it to his pocket. He waited for the sheriff to finish.

"Sure as Thanksgiving comes once a year, Orthal Mason's wife would deliver to him another kid. Jared was one that lived. Maybe one or two more lived, I never kept track of it. The rest of them died at birth. Then, of course, that gal that everybody thought was his cousin, she died, too. Well, when she died, I thought, that's too damn bad, but maybe some good can come out of it. Now that he's got to take care of those kids, he'll stop his thieving. He'll go work for a living. He did no such thing. I don't know where he found her, but quick as anything, Orthal Mason comes to town one day and he's got himself a new wife."

Sheriff Jim Woodrow Willow walked around a corner of the bed and bent down to take a good look at the face of the corpse.

"This is Ralph Mason, all right," said the sheriff. "This Ralph boy is the first of the litter from Orthal Mason's new wife. Ol' Orthal never did stop his thieving. I guess you boys know all about that. I've had him in my jail plenty of times.

Thirty days, here and there. One time, I had to put up with the son of a bitch for six months. The thieving's gone on to this day, except ol' Orthal ain't doing much of the thieving himself anymore. I reckon he got too old. What I know about Orthal Mason is that his kids do the thieving for him now. Whole damn family makes you ashamed to be a Christian white man. None of them's worth a good goddamn."

The sheriff finished his story just as Joe Blue came up to him. He placed his hands on his hips.

"What've you got, Joe? Let's have it," the sheriff said, walking to the wall beside the broken window where there was a chrome and plastic chair. The sheriff sat and began to scratch his chin.

"Looks like somebody else was in the room with Ralph there," said Joe Blue. "There's a towel in the bathroom with lipstick on it."

"He rented a motel room to get his ashes hauled," said the sheriff. "That sound like Ralph Mason to you?"

"Yes and no," said Hank Solís, scratching his chin in imitation of the sheriff. "Ralph's the kind who'll get his fucking done in the cab of his pickup truck. It's not like Ralph to rent a motel room."

"Where's he been working these days?" asked the sheriff.

"He's been working for Porter LaBelle, driving a truck delivering chickens to Houston," said Hank Solís.

Sheriff Jim Woodrow thought for a moment and said, "Hank, look outside and tell me what you see."

Hank Solís looked outside the broken window, turning his head from side to side, surveying the parking lot.

"Parking lot, about empty, not many cars parked," Hank said, looking further out from the parking lot. "Cars going both ways on the bypass. I can see the sign for the Wal-Mart and the parking lot. It's full of cars and trucks. I can make out the roof of the American Legion."

"What kind of vehicle does, or did, Ralph own?"

"Pickup truck," said Hank Solís. "Quarter ton. Big truck, brand new. Just bought it a few months back."

"Hank, you see Ralph Mason's pickup truck out there in the parking lot?"

"You're right, Sheriff," said Hank Solís, embarrassed. "It's not out there."

"Well? Add it up for me, Joe, what you found in this room so far," said the sheriff.

"We've got a six-pack of beer. There's three unopened cans on the dresser. One empty in the wastebasket on the right-hand side of the bed. Could be the lady he was with drank it and threw the empty in the waste basket. I see lipstick on the rim. There's an empty over there on the corner, left-hand side of the bed. Looks like Ralph drank it and didn't bother with the waste basket. And, the third one on the floor, not completely empty. Could be somebody, the girl most likely, was holding it and dropped it all of a sudden."

"That accounts for a standard issue six-pack of beer," said the sheriff, ruminating.

"The towel in the bathroom is smudged with what appears to be lipstick, no mascara or any other smudges. The toilet seat is down, which means someone sat down to take a piss."

"Or ol' Ralph there took a shit, no?" asked Hank Solís. "We'll know from the autopsy."

"Possibility," said Joe Blue. "Last thing, see how the bedspread is pulled back from this corner on the right-hand side. From the position of the body, Ralph Mason stood on the left-hand side, falling forward, as he rests there right now. The left-hand corner of the bedspread is still in place. Somebody was lying on this side of the bed when Ralph got it."

"Any stains on the sheets?"

"No, no stains," said Joe Blue.

"You figure Ralph died with his dick in his hand?" the sheriff asked, a wry smile crossing his face.

"Bed's still made up on Ralph's side," Joe Blue said. "I say, no, he didn't get any."

"That's the way I'd figure it myself," said the sheriff. "How do you see it, Hank?"

"I see it whatever way you want me to see it, Sheriff," said Hank Solís.

"You be God damn right about that, Hank," said the sheriff, shifting his weight in the chair, a wide grin replacing his amused look.

Hank Solís smiled, beaming at the sheriff's comment. Sheriff Jim Woodrow Willow had been a terror in his younger days. As he went past seventy, the sheriff still growled, but it was intended as a reminder of his former self, of the reputation he'd once had.

"The last thing, Sheriff," said Joe Blue. "Did you take a look at the entry wound? I'd say it's small caliber, no more than a .25."

"That's interesting," the sheriff said, getting to his feet and turning to walk out of the room. "I'm going outside. I can't look at Ralph Mason's bare ass anymore. You boys finish up in here."

Joe Blue said, "Hank, stay in here. Johnny's on duty. When he gets here, make sure he bags the beer cans and the towel in the bathroom. I want a separate bag for each can. Tell him to leave the three on the dresser together."

17

Joe Blue and Jim Woodrow Willow stood outside the motel room. They leaned against the fender of Hank Solís' squad car.

"Think we should call in the cavalry?" asked Joe Blue.

"What the hell can they find that we can't?" said the sheriff, spitting between his boots.

"Texas Rangers are pretty good, Jim Woodrow," said Joe Blue. "They've got fancy gear, better'n what we have. They might find something."

"They might at that, Joe," said Jim Woodrow. "I say no. Them boys'll come in here and take over my county. Folks kinda like things to stay the way they are. And, I agree with them."

"If that's the way you want it, Jim Woodrow," said Joe Blue.

"Joe, when I put you to run the office, I meant for you to run the office," the sheriff said. "If you want them sons of bitches to come in, do whatever the hell they do, then, goddamn it, call them in. I'm just telling you, they'll stampede all over you and they'll turn this entire county into their private shithole. But, it ain't up to me, Joe. You decide, and I promise, I'll go along with it."

"You're the High Sheriff, Jim Woodrow," said Joe Blue.

"Damn right!"

Joe Blue leaned inside Hank Solís' squad car to get the microphone. He called the sheriff's office to ask the deputy on duty, Johnny Watkins, to bring an evidence kit, complete with camera.

After the radio call, they heard the ambulance long before it came into view. The driver steered across the median separating the bypass and came into the motel parking lot. He saw where the sheriff stood with Joe Blue, turned in their direction, rapidly bearing down on them. The driver swung the ambulance in a half-circle to back it up to the door.

"We heard you got a stiff, Sheriff," said the ambulance driver. "Where's he at?"

"Where'd you hear that, Elmore?" asked the sheriff.

"Hell, it's all over town, Sheriff," the ambulance driver said.

"Goddamn it!" said Sheriff Jim Woodrow Willow, disgusted.

The ambulance driver's partner came out of the ambulance. The two of them gaped at Sheriff Jim Woodrow Willow.

"You boys have to run that goddamn siren?" the sheriff asked. "Ralph Mason in there don't need CPR and he don't need emergency trauma care. What he needs is a nice, quiet, peaceful drive to the cemetery. But first I want him taken to the hospital so Doc Rivers can perform an autopsy."

"We have our orders, Sheriff, just like you have yours," said the ambulance driver, cocky and insolent.

"What orders?"

"Judge Bledsoe's orders. Came right out of Commissioner's Court," said the ambulance driver. "He got an ordinance requiring that we burn the siren every time we roll out the ambulance."

"Judge Bledsoe did that?" asked Joe Blue, incredulous.

"It's that idiot brother of his," the sheriff said, disgusted, spitting on the paved parking lot.

"Looks like the citizens of our community have spoken through the lips of our county judge," said Joe Blue, sarcastically.

"Jesus Christ!" the sheriff expostulated.

Behind them, the ambulance driver accosted Hank Solís, who stood in the doorway of the motel room.

"Is that where you're keeping the body? We have to get in there to bundle up the body and cart it away, Hank. Move aside," he said.

Hank Solís shifted his wide, solid body to block the door.

"We're not through in here yet, boys," said Hank. "Johnny Watkins is on his way to finish up some stuff in there. You can have the body when he's done."

"Johnny's not even here yet?"

"I said Johnny's on his way," said Hank, shaking his head.

"Shit! What the hell are we doing here anyway?" the ambulance driver asked, of no one in particular. "Is it okay, Sheriff, if we go drive somewhere and get something to eat? We skipped lunch to go on a run to pick up a coronary. We ain't ate."

"Who was it?" asked Joe Blue.

"Old lady Blivens, down at the nursing home."

"Mary Blivens died?" asked the sheriff, incredulous.

"Shit, no, she didn't die! She had chest pains. Thought she was having a heart attack. Nurses thought so, too. We brought her into emergency and all it was, was gas. I bet she ain't had a good fart in twenty years. Doctor said that's all it was. Gas!"

"You boys go on and get something to eat," said Joe Blue. "We'll have everything ready for you when you get back."

The ambulance driver and his assistant returned to the ambulance, cranked the engine and flicked on the siren before driving away.

"Listen to that! Jesus Christ!" the sheriff said, looking up at Joe Blue.

Joe Blue returned the sheriff's look, as if to say, don't blame me.

"What're you thinking, Joe? Any ideas?" asked the sheriff, seeming to be absorbed by the passing traffic on the bypass.

"Nothing I care to put into words just yet, Jim Woodrow."

"You always did hold things close to the vest, Joe," the sheriff said. "You think this split-tail Ralph Mason was with did the shooting?"

"Hard to say," said Joe Blue. "Bullet went in through that window, there. She was probably in the room when it happened. I'd sure like to talk to her."

"You know any gossip about who Ralph's been fucking lately? I know he likes them young, and when he can't get them young, he likes them married," said the sheriff.

"That's what I hear, too," said Joe Blue.

"Either way, he was ripe for being shot," said Sheriff Jim Woodrow.

Deputy Johnny Watkins drove into the parking lot in his squad car. He jumped out, carrying a gray suitcase with blue trim. He came up to where Joe Blue and the sheriff stood.

"Body's in that room there?" he asked.

"Yeah," said Joe Blue. "And, Johnny, the shooter fired through the window from outside. Get some shots of the window. Get some pictures of the broken glass inside the room."

"All of it? Everything?" said Johnny Watkins.

"Yeah, get all of it," said Joe Blue.

Johnny Watkins put the suitcase flat on the concrete beside the door. He squatted on his haunches, opened the suitcase, and took out a camera. From his pants pocket, he took a roll of film and loaded the camera. He got to his feet, walked to the window, and began to figure out the shots he would take.

Joe Blue thought of something and yelled over to Johnny Watkins.

"Johnny, wait up a minute before you do that," Joe Blue said. "You talk any to Georgene last night?"

"I talk to Georgene every night, Joe," said Johnny Watkins. "We try to have a relationship where we communicate."

"What I mean, after she got home from work last night," Joe Blue said, "did she say anything about who was in the Ligon Wells? Something unusual happen, a new face, anything."

"No, to tell you the truth, I was asleep when she came home," said Johnny Watkins, preparing the camera to take his photographs.

"Well, how about this morning, over breakfast?"

"No, sir. She was asleep when I left for work," said Johnny Watkins.

The sheriff let out a sharp bleat, which passed for laughter. He patted Joe Blue on the back.

"Johnny, how the hell do you two communicate if you're asleep when she gets home, and she's asleep when you leave for work?" Sheriff Jim Woodrow asked.

"Georgene says, compared to couples on Oprah, we communicate real well," said Johnny Watkins. "I would trust Georgene on something like that."

"I'm going have to talk to Georgene myself," said Joe Blue.

"I guess so," said the sheriff. "I would say you do."

"Is she over at the saloon, Johnny?" asked Joe Blue.

"She's always at the saloon, if you ask me," said Johnny Watkins.

"I guess I'll run up the hill and talk a little with Georgene, Jim Woodrow," said Joe Blue. "Want to come along?"

"No, you go on, Joe," the sheriff said. "I'll wait here until things finish up."

18

Paco Rangel's red quarter-ton pickup was the last remaining vehicle in the gravel parking lot of Dottie's Cafe. The truck bed was covered by a rectangular shell, much like a camper, in a silver quilted design. Paco unlocked the passenger door and held it open while Priscilla stepped on the running board and climbed inside. He handed her the suitcase, which she positioned in front of her feet on the floorboard.

He went around the back of the truck, coming up on the driver's door, and got in behind the steering wheel. The cab of the truck shook violently when the powerful engine caught fire and Paco floored the gas pedal several times.

He backed the truck into the highway, drove to the intersection and turned on the paved state road. He drove in silence for a few minutes, slowing as he came to the Y intersection by the church with the white steeple. Priscilla's eyes opened wide when he turned on the sandy gravel road. She grew pale and her heart beat faster as they went by the white church, going in the same direction as she had driven hours before.

"Were you born in Austin?" he asked. He reached into a blue plastic basket on the floorboard, rummaging in its contents for a toothpick.

Paco's voice was low, barely audible above the noise inside the truck. He drove slowly because of the washboard ridges that marred the road. The truck clattered beyond what he could stand, and he stepped on the brake to slow the truck even more. He kept his eyes straight ahead, shoulders hunched over the steering wheel, resting both of his forearms on top of it.

"No, I wasn't born in Austin," she said. "I went to school there."

"And, you stayed after you graduated?"

"Yes, that's correct, I got a job there when I finished," Priscilla lied.

"What got you stranded in Larson?"

"Who said I was stranded?"

"Only people in Larson are those who belong here. You got no kin here and you don't have a car. Spells stranded to me. What happened to your car?"

"Listen, I appreciate the help you're giving me," Priscilla said, turning in the bench seat to look at Paco Rangel. "If I want to tell, I'll tell you. When I want to tell, I'll tell you. Until I tell you, don't ask. Please!"

"You're upset," he said.

"I'm not upset!" she said defiantly.

"Have it your way. I wasn't trying to be nosy, you know," he said. The words come out easily, with an unhurried rhythm. "I'm sorry. I thought we might talk a bit. Makes the time go by faster."

"If you'd like to talk, why don't you tell me about yourself, then," she said, turning her head to face the road.

"Okay, I'll tell you about myself, if you can stand to hear it," he said. "There was a time when I liked nothing better than to talk about myself. That was a long time ago. That's when I did my drinking in bars."

"What made you stop?"

"What? Drinking in the bars or talking about myself?"

"Either one."

"Nothing. I just stopped. I'm out of practice, is what I'm trying to say. You want me to talk about myself, where would you like for me to begin? I don't know if I can make myself interesting like I used to. But, I can give it a try."

"You don't have to tell me anything," Priscilla said. "If you'd like a conversation, I thought you could start by telling me something about yourself. I didn't mean any more than that. If you want to, start where you like. What's the most interesting thing you've ever done? That might be a good start."

"The most interesting thing I've ever done? That's a hard one. Before, when I did a lot of talking, I could make everything about me sound interesting, even when it wasn't. I guess it was all in the telling."

"So, you really haven't done any interesting things?"

"That depends. Some things I don't find interesting, other people find fascinating. Absolutely fascinating. And, there's the opposite, too. Things important to me put other people to sleep."

"Well, try one out on me," said Priscilla Arrabal, laughing, surprised that she enjoyed being in the company of Paco Rangel.

Paco Rangel thought for a long moment. Priscilla kept her gaze away from him, looking out of the window.

"Okay, I'll tell you one," he said. "Once, when I was six or seven, I heard some of my cousins talking about a movie star named Errol Flynn. One of my cousins said that Errol Flynn would tie a string to a piece of pork fat and then he'd feed it to one of the ducks they kept in the yard. The duck would gobble up the pork fat, along with the string. The pork fat would go right through the duck, it and the string coming out the other end of the duck. And then he'd feed it to another duck, and so on, until he had the string going through all the ducks in the yard. He tied the ends of the string and he'd have all of them tied in a circle."

"How come you remember it was Errol Flynn?"

"I just remember that my cousins told me it was Errol Flynn. The name stuck in my mind because I'd seen 'The Adventures of Robin Hood.' Anyway, I don't know where they heard it. But, let me finish telling you the story."

"Well, go on. I'm listening."

"My mom and dad and I were staying with my grandparents, out in the country. As you can probably guess, my grandparents had some ducks on their place. Not many, maybe half a dozen or so. They kept them around for pets, mostly. They had a lot of grandchildren and it was nice to keep the ducks on the place. They didn't sell them or eat them. So, the next day, after my cousins told me the story, I got a piece of pork fat and found me a long piece of string and I went out to play with the ducks. It took me a while, but I got that pork and the string through all of the ducks. I tied the two ends together and sat on the porch to watch them."

"What happened then?"

"I had fun watching them, and then I guess I went back in the house and forgot about them. The ducks got tired of my little joke on them. They couldn't go anywhere without dragging themselves in a circle. They made enough of a commotion that my mother came out to see what was the matter. She probably thought it was a neighbor dog or a coyote pestering them. Instead, she saw what I did."

"I bet you got one awful spanking!"

"Well, yeah, I did get a pretty fair beating out of it. I've got a pretty strong memory of that beating, in fact. You see, my mother went to free the ducks, but they were so damn mad that they wouldn't let her get near. They kept flapping their wings and jumping up at her like they were trying to poke out her eyes. At that point, I think, the ducks wanted revenge on a human being; they didn't care who. My mother got scared and went in the house. Forgot about me completely.

Until, that is, my father came home. By then, two of the ducks had died, choked on the string, or they had a heart attack, or something. The others tried to drag the dead ones along. My father saw what I did and he went and got them free. And then he came after me."

"Good for him! Did you learn anything from the experience?"

"After my father gave me the beating, I waited to get my revenge on the ducks. I waited and I waited. One day, when I figured my folks had forgotten about the incident, I went hunting out in back of the place. My grandfather would let me use a little .22 rifle that he had. I went out that day and I shot a couple of rabbits. On the way home, I saw one of the ducks far off from the house. I shot him and left him where he fell. I went out every day until, one by one, I shot every one of those ducks. My folks and my grandparents thought it was the neighbor dogs or varmints that got to the ducks. They never suspected it was me that shot the ducks."

"You killed every one of the ducks?"

"Yeah, I did. But you have to remember that I was only six or seven when it happened. What's a child to know about those things?"

"Didn't you ever regret that you did it?"

"No, not really," he said pensively. "I mean, I shot hundreds of rabbits. I shot pigs for our butchering. I killed my first deer when I was eight or nine. The ducks probably fell in through all that killing without me noticing them."

Paco Rangel turned his head in Priscilla's direction. He gave her a wide smile, revealing white, evenly square teeth. Dimples brightened his cheeks. A fringe of light brown hair on his forehead escaped from the baseball cap.

Priscilla took a good look at his face. His nose was too small, out of proportion to the rest of his features. Everything about his face was regular but undistinguished. He would have had a plain face, neither homely nor handsome, were it not for his eyes. They were bright and searching, never seeming to rest or focus on a single object for very long. As he looked at her, Priscilla could see a telltale flicker in them as they shifted from her own eyes, to her mouth, up to her cheek, back to her eyes, stopping only for a second or two before moving on to something else. Anyone who failed to see the slight flicker would swear that he had an intense stare.

Priscilla also liked his voice, low and even, flowing smoothly with the rhythm of his words. The voice, in fact, was hypnotic. She had not particularly wanted to hear what he had to say about himself. She had intended to listen just enough to make a noncommittal response to keep from being rude. She had much more important things to think about. Mainly, what she would do when he took her to San Antonio and left her there. From what he knew, he'd be leaving her at the bus station. By now, she reasoned, Ralph Mason's body would be in the hands of the police. They would know that she, a woman he picked up at the Ligon Wells Saloon, had been with him and they would be very interested in getting their hands on her. And, then, Paco had begun to tell that silly story about the ducks and Errol Flynn. Just the sound of his voice brought an unexpected relief to her. It was captivating. She'd lost track of her own thoughts and had found herself enjoying his telling of the story.

There was more that Priscilla wanted to know about Paco Rangel. She wanted to hear more of his voice, listen to the wonderfully rhythmic flow of the words as he spoke. Before she could ask or prompt him to say something, Paco turned the truck into a loose-dirt lane, which the rain had turned into a quagmire. Beside the entrance, standing tall as a sentinel, was a lone oak tree with a trunk three feet or more in diameter. Its gnarled branches stretched in all directions, dipping lazily close to the ground.

Ahead, the lane was little more than two ruts separated by a single strip of grass.

"Welcome to my ranch," said Paco Rangel, exaggerating as a way of self-deprecation. "I got my own herd of cattle. All

twelve of them, unless one of them died in the rain last night.
I don't have a bull for breeding. Not the largest herd in all of
Texas, you'll agree. But, then, I'm the lone wrangler. I've got
two horses, a male and a female; except that the male is a
gelding. I guess I didn't look at him close enough when I
bought him. I expected I'd have a litter of little baby horses
every year. Then I figured out the sad truth about my gelding."

Priscilla giggled as the truck bounced easily over the
rough terrain of the road.

"You're making fun of me," she said. "Even I know about
geldings. I was raised on a ranch myself, I'll have you know."

"Don't say any more! Just hold it!" he said, holding his
hand in front of Priscilla. "I would guess you're from South
Texas. That's the easy part. There's a lot about you that says
King Ranch. But, you don't strike me as a *kineño*. I can spot
one of them a mile away."

"What makes *kineños* so easy to identify?" asked Priscilla.
At the University of Texas, she had known several students
whose parents worked on the King Ranch. She, too, could pick
out a *kineños* when she saw one.

"If you've been around enough of them," he said, "it's a
way they have about them. An attitude. Some of the *mexicanos* who work there are descended from people who worked
on that land when it was part of Spain. Or, at least, they
claim to. My guess is this: they've worked on the land for so
long they feel they have a stake in it, like they're part owners.
Not to mention that most of them, and this is especially true
of the *mexicanos,* they think they're better than the rest of us.
They have this snot quality to them that lets me spot them
right away."

"How large is your ranch," asked Priscilla, casting her
eyes about the land that spread out in front of the windshield.

"There's fifteen acres under cultivation behind the house
and forty acres of pasture," said Paco Rangel. "There's a ranch
house on the place. A water well, with the sweetest water in

these parts, comes up clear and cool no matter how hot it gets above ground."

"How many generations has the place been in your family?"

"Generations? I'm the first one," he said. "I bought it about five years ago."

"Are you originally from here? Is that how you decided to come back home and settle down, have your own place?"

"No, I'm not from here at all. Actually, I'm not from any place," he said, keeping his eyes on the road. His voice slipped into the rhythm that she was beginning to like too much. "I was an Army brat. I grew up all over the country, no place for too long. I always felt home was where my grandparents lived, because no matter where my father was stationed, we'd always come back to them. When I went out on my own, I realized that wasn't my home, either. I got tired of the rat race one day. Something about city living just didn't agree with me. I found I had a little money. I looked all over, mostly in South Texas, before this place came up for sale."

"Let me guess now," said Priscilla. "You don't regret one bit that you bought this place, and you're ready to live here happily ever after."

"I don't regret that I bought it. As for the other part, I learned to take life one day at a time. When I get to be a hundred and two, I hope to look back on my life and decide if I lived happily or not."

"What do you suppose your answer will be?"

"I don't know. When I get to be a hundred and two, ask me then."

19

The meandering path on which he maneuvered the pickup truck went through a field of young mesquite. Their spindly limbs and sparse leaves gave the field a pale, delicate, lime color. Scattered among the mesquite were old oak trees, rising stately and dark, towering over the lime-green saplings. From the field of young mesquite, the truck rolled into a dense stand of woods. There were scars on the road where trees had been removed to clear a path.

As soon as the hood of the truck moved into the stand of trees, Priscilla could see straight to the other end where the sunlight shone bright and clear. She caught of a glimpse of the farmhouse. As they came out of the trees, her view of the house expanded to include the black-webbed parabola of the television satellite dish set off from a corner of the house, on the outside of a white picket fence. Beyond the satellite dish, she saw a large outbuilding, which she took to be the barn.

Paco let up on the gas pedal as the truck approached the house. On the other side of the picket fence, Priscilla was dazzled by the array of bright colors rising from a series of flower beds. There was a white statue rising among the flower beds, a figure she faintly recognized but could not identify.

Before she could identify the statue, Priscilla blinked in surprise. She saw a black shape suddenly materialize behind the picket fence. It was a black dog, going up the steps to the porch. The dog stopped, turned, and sat. There was a patch of white fur on its chest. Its four paws were also white. The dog sat on the porch, its clipped ears pointed straight up in the air, watching the truck approach.

Priscilla recognized the unmistakable shape of a pit bull terrier.

Paco stopped the pickup truck five yards in front of the white picket fence under the shade of a tree and shut off the engine. Priscilla opened the passenger door and stepped down onto the moist sandy soil that grew flat tufts of grass in scattered patches.

In an instant, the dog leapt off the porch, sped across the garden, and bounded over the waist-high picket fence. He ran with lightning speed to where Priscilla had stepped down from the truck.

The black pit bull stopped a foot or two in front of Priscilla, and cautiously moved the rest of the way to her. The dog wrapped his body in a semicircle around Priscilla's ankle, straddling her foot with both white paws. She could feel the stiff bristles of fur on his pelt, the rippling muscles of his shoulders. The dog kept its muzzle close to Priscilla's foot, exuding confidence and authority. There was no doubt that he had taken complete control of her.

Paco was down from the truck, on the other side, moving at a running walk around the hood.

"That's Mariachi," Paco said, speaking over the hood of the truck. "Don't be afraid. Stay very still where you are, and don't move. I'll be right there."

Priscilla stood stock still. The pit bull was silent, his head bent down, as if searching for something in the soft sandy soil beyond her foot. His cropped ears were cocked back.

Paco hurried around the hood of the truck. Priscilla moved her free leg forward. When she tried to move the other leg, the dog allowed her to move a little, but his body never lost contact with her ankle. He swerved his body so she'd have to shove his entire weight to move at all. Except for the rippling of the muscles on his shoulders, the pit bull did not threaten or menace, or give any indication that Priscilla was in danger.

"Mariachi!" yelled Paco, approaching, bending low.

Paco came to where Priscilla stood. She was becoming increasingly afraid of the dog, which did not bark, but left little doubt of his abilities. Paco squatted in front of Priscilla, beside the dog. He took the pit bull's face in his hands.

"She's a friend, big fella," Paco said, as if scolding a child. "Come on, Mariachi. Let her go—it's all right. Relax, now."

Paco scrabbled the dog's neck, roughly but with affection. The dog, satisfied that his owner was not in danger, relaxed his body and moved away from Priscilla without a backward look.

"That's a pit bull, isn't it?" she asked. The terror she'd felt moments earlier gradually, reluctantly, ebbed away. She felt a buffeting sensation that she feared might turn into visible trembling.

"He's a registered, bad-ass, mankiller," said Paco, going over to where the dog stopped, shaking the dog's head playfully. "Aren't you, big fella?"

Priscilla moved away from them.

"Where're you going? Come on, come back and make friends with him," Paco said. "He can be friendly, when he wants to."

"You said he was a mankiller," said Priscilla, doubtful, not wishing to get too near the dog.

"Yeah, but only when a stranger threatens me," said Paco. "He's not too keen on strangers, but he won't attack unless he feels he has to."

"What do you call what he just did?"

"Detention. He put you under detention. If I'd've gotten out of the truck first and then opened the door for you, he would've known you're friendly. When you got out on your own, it confused him, so he decided to do what he does best. He put you under detention."

"What if you hadn't been here and I came up to the house? What would he do?"

"Mariachi? Why, he'd do what he did just now. He'd wrapped himself around your leg and you'd have to stay put until I came by."

"You're sure he wouldn't attack?" Priscilla said, still skeptical.

"Not unless he saw somebody attack me, or he sensed I was in some kind of danger. And, of course, if he put you under detention and you tried to get away," Paco said. "Come on, get down here close to him. Touch him between the ears, pet him on the neck. Show him you want to make friends."

"Is he able to make friends with anybody?"

"I don't know," said Paco. "You'll be the first one to try it. I think it should work, though. Come on, try it."

"Well, if he knows when you're in danger," Priscilla said, petting the dog on the neck, "I'd say he must have some kind of intelligence."

"Heck, no! Mariachi's not that smart. In fact, I don't think he's smart at all. He doesn't do dog tricks. He's not interested in learning any of the stupid pet tricks you see on David Letterman. He's not any good when I go hunting. In fact, I live out here all alone and he's not what I'd call good company. He likes to stay under the house. That's all he knows. He comes out only when I feed him. Other than that, I don't think he likes me too much."

"Still, he's trained to protect you," said Priscilla. "He must be pretty smart if he can do that."

"Not even that. You see, I took him to this place in San Antonio where they taught him everything he knows, which is mainly to protect me. The killer instinct, as you probably know, is bred into them. Cost me a bunch of money, too."

Priscilla continued to pet the pit bull, running her hand along the length of his back, smoothing down the rough fur of his pelt. The dog breathed noisily, his belly shaking as he did so. His mouth came open, his tongue hanging out.

20

Paco Rangel got to his feet to return to the truck on the passenger side. He reached inside the pickup cab to get Priscilla's suitcase.

"Let's go in the house," he said, turning to face the ranch house.

"You have many problems with crime around here? Is that why you have the dog?" Priscilla asked.

"Nope, not at all," he said, taking measured steps, the suitcase hardly a nuisance at his side. He led Priscilla by the elbow.

As he pulled up the latch of the gate in the picket fence, he said, "At least, not that I know of. About the dog, I guess I still have a lot of city ways. I'm not a particularly trusting sort. Besides guard duty, Mariachi's not so bad. Just having him around is company enough, even if he doesn't really like me all that much."

Paco opened the gate and held it for Priscilla to walk through. On both sides of a pebbled walkway stretched Paco's garden, extending the length of the house and ten feet beyond on each side. From the corner, she could see that the garden continued along the side of the house. The pathways, covered with tan-colored pebbles, were laid in crisscross patterns among flower beds. Railroad ties served both as containers and pathway borders. Some flowers, all of the same kind and color, were arranged in geometric patterns. Others were tiered, up to three high, with different flowers and shrubs.

To Priscilla's left was a circular pebbled walkway in the center of which was a concrete water fountain. The fountain had a nude sculpture on top. She now recognized it as a not too faithful rendition of the goddess Diana, who held a bow and arrow in her outstretched arms. The nude was perched on a scallop shell that emptied into a round water fountain.

She was awed by the unexpected beauty of the colors that burst forth from the flower beds. Priscilla's face brightened and her eyes lit up. For a brief instant, her troubles faded away.

"This is beautiful," Priscilla said, stopping to admire Paco's handiwork.

Paco went ahead, going up the three steps to the porch, where he set down Priscilla's suitcase. Priscilla looked up at him from the garden, smiling, shaking her head in disbelief.

"It must take all of your time to keep this garden looking so pretty," she said.

"Thanks for saying so. I'm glad you like it," Paco said, returning her smile.

"How long did it take you to do this?"

"Oh, a couple three years," he said, thumping his toe into the wood of the porch. "I got the idea for it, but I found it was too much work. I piddled with it for a little bit, stopped, didn't do anything for weeks, and then I had another go at it. Last year, when I finished the walkabouts, I got serious about putting in the flower beds."

"This is just wonderful. I've never seen anything like it," she said, easing herself forward, continuing to absorb the beauty of the garden. She stopped in front of the steps going up to the porch to turn and take another lingering look.

A sudden chill ran through her spine.

Mariachi stood next to her ankle, his thick fur brushing against the material of her jeans.

"What do I do now?" she asked.

"Get down and pet him," said Paco. "I think it's what he wants. He must've taken a liking to you."

Priscilla lowered herself to rub the pit bull on its neck and run her hand along his spine again. The dog shook himself in a prolonged flutter.

"How are you, Mariachi?" she said. "Are you a good dog? Of course, you're a good dog!"

"That's amazing," Paco said. "He really does like you."

Priscilla stood and walked up the steps to the porch. Mariachi walked alongside. Once on the porch, Mariachi settled on his haunches beside the front door of Paco's house. His mouth was open and he breathed in short, heavy pants.

Priscilla came to stand next to Paco, who stood by the porch railing. At five-eight, Priscilla was accustomed to looking most men in the eye. Paco was a good five inches taller. She took a long, expansive look at the area in front of the house. A tall oak tree rose fat and thick from the ground twenty yards away. A scattering of mesquite trees began a short distance beyond the oak, as if afraid to come too close to it.

"Where do you grow your vegetables, the ones you have to pick today?" Priscilla asked.

Paco extended his arm to its full length and pointed in the direction of the barn, off to the side of the house.

"I do most of it over beyond the barn there," he said, "just a ways off. You can't hardly see it from here. I found other patches of black soil here and there on the place and I've got a few plots more."

"How many people do you have helping you? Working for you?"

"No one—it's just me," Paco said. "I do all the planting, cultivating, harvesting, and delivering. I prefer to do the picking myself. That way, I know exactly what to pick. I have some very knowledgeable customers. It gets me a better price for my produce."

"Must be hard work," Priscilla said, turning to look at Paco. The brightness of his eyes startled her. It was as if she were seeing them for the first time.

"It's getting on to the hottest part of the day," said Paco Rangel. "Come inside and I'll turn on the air conditioner. You'll be more comfortable."

The inside of the house was much larger than her impression from outside had led her to believe. When approaching the house, it had appeared low and compact, swaybacked and squat beside the shade trees next to it on the left. Now that she was inside, Priscilla was impressed with the spaciousness she saw.

Paco stepped lively, going forward across the room. Priscilla stayed by the door, holding her purse in both hands while she looked to her left and right. To the right was a parlor and living room. To the left, judging from the computer, desk, and file cabinets that caught her eye, was Paco's office. From the large windows on the left to the windows on the right, the area stretched for a full thirty feet. It must have been two rooms at one point, she told herself, with maybe an addition to make it larger overall. There was a wall that ran the entire length of the open space, with two doorways. One doorway led to the kitchen and the other to a bedroom.

Priscilla took a few steps forward and to the right to deposit her handbag on a long, navy-blue leather sectional sofa. There was a corner piece and then a shorter extension running under the north windows. A glass-topped coffee table stood in front of the sofa. Paco had placed her suitcase by the sofa.

In the center of the wall across from where she stood was a 35-inch television set, resting on a shelf that came out of the wall and which was supported by a pair of diagonal struts. Immediately to the right of the television were two banks of electronic equipment. There were so many different pieces that Priscilla's eyes opened in a wonder similar to what she'd felt when she saw the garden.

The component stereo system consisted of a tuner, pre-amplifier, amplifier, graphic equalizer, both a carousel and a cartridge compact disc player, two cassette tape decks, a pair of VCRs, a satellite descrambler, a satellite tuner, and a ten-inch reel-to-reel recorder. Priscilla was too far away to discern the brand names, but this was the kind of equipment that her ex, Rene-Chapa, would have loved to have. René would have a fine time bragging all night about what this equipment cost.

Next to the north wall was a speaker, shaped as an out-sized spike, nearly five-feet tall, inclined at a slight angle, resting on a metal pedestal. It's matching companion stood beside the door that led into the bedroom. There were smaller speakers on the shelves, and when she turned her head to look at the ceiling, she noticed the grillwork for more speakers. On shelving sunk into the wall were rows of compact discs, vinyl and cassette albums, and boxes of reel tapes. All of it seemed neat and orderly.

The coffee table sat upon a braided rug, in red, yellow and brown braids. The glass top of the coffee table held several overflowing ashtrays and several empty bottles of Budweiser beer. Cigarette ashes had spilled onto the glass. Paco, who'd slipped out of sight into the bedroom, came back in a rush. He became embarrassed when it was obvious that Priscilla had taken note of the disarray in his living room.

"I guess I wasn't expecting company," he said. "I usually keep the place messy. It looks like I've gone too far in the last few days. Sorry."

"There's nothing to be sorry for, Paco," said Priscilla, wishing to become more familiar with him. "Messy is fine with me. You have an amazing collection of stuff here."

"Yeah, well, I try to keep myself entertained."

"And across the way," Priscilla said, "is that your office?"

"That's it. It's pretty messy, too," he said.

At the other end of the room, in Paco's office, Priscilla could see a large oak roll-top desk in front of which stood a heavy wooden swivel chair on rollers. A leather seating pad was on the chair, held secure by leather straps. There were twin gray file cabinets facing away from the wall. In front of the desk was a rectangular table, about four feet off the ground and five feet in length, on which magazines, books, papers, file trays, seed catalogues, and more overflowing ashtrays were scattered. A brightly polished copper waste basket stood beside the roll-top desk.

Paco approached Priscilla and took her by the arm. Priscilla was overcome by a warm and comfortable feeling as he did so. She felt his presence familiar and welcome.

"Come along, let's go in the kitchen," he said. "I can get you some iced tea, if you'd like. I also have some of that stuff you make lemonade with. I got beer. Lots of beer, because it's what I drink. I got some whiskey, too. And, some sodas. Dr. Pepper, mostly. Might be something else in the refrigerator. What would you like?"

"Iced tea sounds good. Whatever you don't have to make special. I've been too much trouble to you already."

"Don't be silly," Paco said, giving her an abashed smile. "You're no trouble at all."

21

Joe Blue entered the Ligon Wells Saloon. He stopped by the entrance for a moment to allow his eyes to adjust to the darkness. The same elderly men from the day before occupied the slate-topped table pressed against the wall beside the entrance. One of them looked up from the game of dominoes to greet him in Spanish. Joe Blue returned the greeting and met Georgene Henderson, who carried two bottles of beer, bringing them to the two men.

"Joe Blue!" exclaimed Georgene. "What brings you in here?"

"Business, Georgene, sad to say," said Joe Blue, waiting for Georgene to leave the beer and walk ahead of him back to the bar. "I want to ask you a few questions."

"I just put on some fresh coffee, Joe," Georgene Henderson said, going behind the bar, speaking over her shoulder. "This is still breakfast time for me. I still haven't had my fill of coffee for the day. How about joining me for some?"

"Thank you, Georgene. I've had too much damn coffee for one day."

"How about a soda?" she said. "What brings you out here?"

"I'll pass on the soda, Georgene. Ralph Mason's been shot. He's dead."

"Ralph Mason, dead? How did it happen?"

"We're trying to find that out now."

"That's hard to believe, Joe. He was in here just last night. When did it happen?"

"That's what I came to talk to you about, Georgene. Tell me everything you remember about last night, even if it does-n't have to do with Ralph Mason."

"If you want to know about Ralph Mason yesterday evening, I'll have to start in the afternoon, after four, maybe, when he came in. Actually, I'd have to start before that, when the bus to Houston stopped across the road at Tiny's."

"The bus? I don't get it," Joe Blue said. "But, that's good, Georgene. I'm real interested. Just you go on now."

"Well, Joe, it begins when the woman came in," Georgene said. She poured herself some coffee and brought a barstool behind the bar. She made herself comfortable on the barstool to talk to Joe Blue across the bar.

"Tell me about her," said Joe Blue.

"She was on the bus, came in to have a beer," Georgene said in between sips of her coffee. "She had three beers, took one to go. And, not ten minutes later, she came back carrying a suitcase. She let the bus go and told me she decided to stay and do some sightseeing in Lexington. She drank more beer, I sent out for some fried chicken, which she paid for, and we ate. We were eating when Ralph Mason came in."

"Did you introduce them?"

"Hell, no!" Georgene said, her face coloring. "You know how Ralph Mason is. Or was. She appeared to me like a very sweet young lady. I could tell, there was something about her that told me she could take care of herself. In any case, I warned her that Ralph was trouble."

"But, that didn't stop her, did it?"

"Heck, no. We finished eating and visited for a bit longer, and she went up to where Ralph was on the bar yonder and took a seat next to him. They got on real good, right from the start, from what I could tell."

"Any chance, Georgene, that they might've known each other from before? Say, like they were supposed to meet each other, but pretended to be strangers at first?"

"I don't think I could tell you that, Joe. Not one way and not the other. What I can tell you is that they hit it off right away. They laughed and put their heads together and were having a fine time of it. It didn't take too long before they went to sit at a table, over there, by the jukebox."

Joe Blue took a glance in the direction of the jukebox.

"You didn't overhear anything they might've said to each other?"

"Not hardly. Not with the crowd I had in here last night. They got pretty loud as the night wore on."

"Anything else?"

"The two of them got up to dance," Georgene said. "They got pretty horny about it. In fact, I thought about asking them to quit it. Cool it down a little."

"They became romantic with each other?"

"I'd say!" Georgene Henderson said, shaking her head. "For a minute, the way they were dancing, I was afraid they'd get down on the floor and take a go at one another."

"They left together, then. About what time was that?"

"I won't swear to it, but I recall looking at the clock to remind myself that last call was ten minutes away. That would make it eleven-thirty. I do remember, earlier it was, that he pulled on her arm like he wanted her to leave with him. You know Ralph. He got angry about it when she wouldn't do it. He came to the bar and paid me to put a six-pack away for him to take at closing time."

"One last thing, Georgene," said Joe Blue. "Here's what I want you to do. Make a list of everyone who was in here last night. Just put their names on a sheet of paper. If I don't come back for it, drop it off at the Sheriff's office. Or, if you want to, give it to Johnny to bring with him in the morning."

"I don't know if I should tell you this, Joe," Georgene Henderson said, unsure whether she should continue, stammering. "There's something else."

"I need every bit of help I can get on this, Georgene," Joe Blue said. "Anything you tell me, I won't let on where I got it."

"You know Myra Richards?"

"Sure, she's Sam Barkley's girl. What about her?"

"Well, you know she went and married that Richards boy. What's his name? Victor? Walter?"

"Victor. Yeah, I knew they got married."

"I believe they've been having trouble ever since they got married last year. Both of them used to come in once in a while. Lately, they've been coming in a lot. Both of them drink pretty heavy. Once or twice I've had to cut them off, else they'd be too drunk to drive home. A couple other times, I had to ask them to leave because they were arguing too loud. Once, Richards slapped Myra across the face. He might've hit her some more, except some people pulled them apart."

"Go on, Georgene, I'm listening. Do you know why he did it?"

"A cowboy from the Pasó Por Aquí Ranch asked her to dance and she got up like she was going to do it and that's when Richards bashed her. I threw him out right then and there. I told Myra she could stay and I'd drive her home myself, figuring if she waited a while, Richards would cool down, get hold of himself and it'd be safe for her to go home. Myra wouldn't do it, though. She went after him. Good riddance, I told myself. I don't want any trouble in my place."

"I know you're going to get to Ralph Mason. What's this got to do with him?"

"For a couple of months, Myra took to coming in by herself. She said Richards was on the evening shift at the hatchery. She couldn't stand to be at the house by herself and she had to do something with her time. At first, she'd take a table by herself to do her drinking. And, then, Ralph Mason moved in on her one night. I never thought it would go anywhere.

They'd have a few beers together, and then she'd leave by herself and Ralph'd stay behind and try and move in on somebody
else. Pretty soon, though, Myra comes in like she's waiting on
somebody and then Ralph Mason comes in and he sits with
her. He's starts kissing on her, putting his hand up her skirt.
Myra goes along with it. She likes it."

"What about Vic Richards?"

"Myra and Ralph would leave pretty early. A couple of
times, Vic Richards came in looking for her. He asks me if I've
seen her, but I tell him it's up to him to look after his own
wife; don't look to me to do it for him."

"What about Vic Richards and Myra? Were they in here
last night?"

"That's just it, they weren't," Georgene said. "It's been
two-three weeks since I've seen Myra and Ralph together. It
could be it was over between them. Ralph don't last too long
with the same woman."

"Thanks, Georgene, I'll look into it."

"I hope it helps, Joe," said Georgene Henderson, finishing
her cup of coffee.

Joe Blue stood up, tipped his hat to Georgene, and left the
Ligon Wells Saloon.

22

Priscilla Arrabal awoke with a start. She opened her eyes for an instant, becoming momentarily disoriented by the strange surroundings. After taking stock of where she was, she closed her eyes and rested on the navy-blue leather sofa. She was fully clothed, damp with perspiration from head to foot. She had a hollow, buffeted feeling caused by a dream she could not recall.

With her eyes closed, the image came to her as clear as if she were in the motel room again. Ralph Mason's expectant face, the grin disappearing, replaced by contortions of surprise, shock, and pain. Then she saw the barrel of the pistol aiming her way. Behind the pistol was the outline of a face in shadow, framed by the window. The face was too far away in the darkness. There was a glint of light, no more than a fraction of a second. Then her mind went blank.

She tried to fill in the contours of the face, but the shadow was too dark.

Priscilla sat up, swinging her legs to drop her bare feet to the braided rug on the floor. She looked outside the window at the weakening sun of late afternoon. The shadow cast by the barn had lengthened. The day seemed even more lethargic and listless.

Next to the window, the room air conditioner in the wall purred and flushed cool air into the room. Despite the cool air circulating, Priscilla felt hot and uncomfortable, stuffy, as if confined in a shuttered room in summer. There was a pasty taste in her mouth. Her facial muscles were drawn and numb.

She bent lower, her chin between her legs, taking her head in her hands. Her raven hair flowed through her fingers. She moved her thumbs in small circles, massaging her scalp. In front of her, on the glass-topped coffee table, stood the tall glass of iced tea that Paco Rangel had poured for her. The ice in it had melted. Priscilla picked up the glass, which left a ring of water on the table. The cool flowing air in the room kept the tea cold enough to drink. She sloshed the tea in her mouth for a bit to rinse the sleep away, then swallowed.

She rubbed the muscles of her shoulders, twisting and turning her upper body as she did so. The blood began to flow. She made faces and squeezed her cheeks to get rid of the numbness in her face. Rising slowly to her feet, she began to pace slowly in circles on the braided rug around the coffee table, holding her elbows in her hands.

Priscilla finally felt fully awake. She walked out of the parlor area, and into the kitchen. Standing before the sink, she turned the tap on and then bent over, cupping her hands to scoop water and splash it into her face. She wiped herself with a hand towel hanging on a nail peg.

She looked around the kitchen and found it to be surprisingly neat and clean. The kitchen and the neatly arranged things in the parlor indicated that Paco was a good housekeeper. There were a few bare spots on the linoleum covering the floor, but she could tell that he swept often. And yet, there were the overflowing ashtrays and the beer bottles on the coffee table. He had a bad couple of nights, she told herself.

Back in the parlor, she resumed pacing around the coffee table. The remote selector for the satellite receiver lay on the table. She looked at it several times, trying to decide whether she might stand to watch something on television. Instead, she finished the glass of tea and decided to go outside.

She opened the wooden door and stood facing outside through the screen door. A breeze had picked up. The leaves of the trees stirred gently with the lazy swaying branches of the trees. Some fresh air and some exposure to the sun would remove the pall that made her feel dull and insipid, something inside her body that she couldn't shake.

A darting terror went through Priscilla as she paused to consider the monster in black fur with the white chest that lived under the house. How would the black pit bull react to her coming out on the porch without his master close by? Would Mariachi detain her again, block her movements with his body? Or, would he simply go crazy and clamp his jaws shut on her arm, as she'd read about pit bulls and the training they received? Or, did someone train Mariachi to go for the throat once and for all, dig his teeth in, hold them in place with the iron strength of his massive jaws until she collapsed into a lifeless mass?

Nice thoughts, she told herself. Only one way to find out. She turned the doorknob.

Mariachi was already on the porch when she stepped outside. He had sensed her movements even before she made them, anticipating them through the floor of the house, in his lair beneath. The dog pranced in place, his head tilted back to watch her, lifting one foot and then another. He shook his rear, trying to wag the nub of his tail. His mouth was open, his tongue flopped out over his lower jaw. His cropped ears fluttered playfully.

She was unsure of what to do. How friendly should she act? It would be best, she thought, to ignore the dog. Priscilla strolled easily along the porch.

The colors of the flowers in Paco's garden were more radiant now that the sun did not burn so brightly on them. At the north end of the porch, she leaned on the railing to look out past the black parabola to the barn and some smaller out-buildings. A round container, set on a concrete foundation, rose eight feet in the air. Next to it, she recognized the water pump that drew water from the well below. A round water trough made out of concrete was next to it a few feet away.

Mariachi had paced along with her and had dropped to his haunches next to her feet. He, too, scanned the area a short distance away from the house, poised to sense trouble.

Priscilla turned and retraced her steps along the length of the porch, back to the front door. The dog trotted at her side, his nose close to the planks of the porch.

Priscilla knelt in front of Mariachi, taking his face in her hands. She rubbed his pelt. The dog responded by becoming animated, his eyes looking into hers. His eyes were clear and liquid. She wasn't sure what it meant, but so far the dog had been friendly enough.

The nap had restored her sense of balance. The anxious-ness she'd felt earlier had lessened. Paco Rangel's place was off the main roads, secluded enough to prevent anyone from seeing her. It was a perfect place to stay. Not for too long. Per-haps two or three days. Long enough to plan what she would do.

So far as Paco knew, he was to take her to San Antonio later in the evening. There was no point to returning to San Antonio. It wouldn't be too difficult, she hoped, to convince Paco to let her stay in the house a few days.

She liked Paco. It would be easy to spend a few days with him.

She paced to the railing on the porch overlooking Paco's garden. Mariachi sat on his haunches, watching what she watched. She was startled by the sound of Paco Rangel's voice behind her back, sweeping low and rhythmic into the stillness of the air.

"I thought you'd be inside where it's cool, watching televi-sion or something," he said. "You're welcome to roam about the house as you like."

"Oh, as soon as you left, I fell right to sleep. Out like a light. The couch is so soft and comfortable," said Priscilla. "I guess I needed a nap. I'm not much for watching television, anyway. I just woke up a few minutes ago. I thought some fresh air might get the cobwebs out of my eyes."

Paco walked out on the porch, removing brown cotton gloves from his hands. He slapped them against his thigh.

"I'm done with my picking," he said. "I came for the truck. I'll just drive out and load up. When I come back, if it's all right with you, I thought we would eat something and then we can be on our way."

"Will I have time to take a shower?" she asked hurriedly. "I've been in these clothes all day. I'd like to clean up a bit and change into some fresh clothes."

"Sure," said Paco. "There's plenty of time. The bathroom is through the bedroom, straight line to it. You can see the door as you go in the bedroom. I'll put some towels out for you."

Paco disappeared inside the house. Priscilla followed a moment later, Mariachi at her side. She opened the door, and the dog sat as if to wait for her.

"I don't think you're allowed in the house, Mariachi," she said.

"What was that you said?" asked Paco, returning to the parlor. "I left the towels in the bathroom."

"I was talking to Mariachi," she said.

"Well, how about that. You two seem to be getting along," he said.

23

Priscilla picked up her suitcase from where it stood next to the sofa. She carried it into the bedroom and tossed it on the king-sized bed. The bed took up virtually all of the space in the small bedroom. Across the bed was a pair of large windows. There was not more than a foot of space between the edge of the bed and the windows. In front of the bed was a narrow dresser, of the kind sold in unpainted furniture stores. It had been painted in a powder blue, with tiny visible ridges from the bristles of the paintbrush. Paco's clothes hung on the wall from nail pegs, almost all of them in flimsy protective coverings from the laundry.

She took a pair underpants and a clean T-shirt out of the suitcase and went into the bathroom, which she found similarly small and cramped. It had the look of hurried, inexperienced remodeling work. The shower stall was fiberglass, prefabricated in a single piece. She stood in front of the washbasin to scrub her face with soap. She moved her legs apart to lean over, and her calf touched the rim of the toilet bowl. The mirror above the washbasin was stained with water drops and toothpaste splatter. He's clean in some things, and then he's messy in others, she remarked to herself.

She closed the door to the bathroom, instinctively looked for a way to latch or lock it, but found none. She wondered if Paco was still in the house or if he had gone to load his vegetables. He seemed nice enough. What was there to worry about?

Priscilla removed her clothes and showered quickly. The shower revived her body, cleansing her pores, bringing a fresh and tingling sensation to her. She took her time in the waning steam in the shower stall to dry herself, briskly rubbing herself until her skin was red, with a nice glowing feel to it.

After she'd slipped on her underwear, she went into the bedroom to finish dressing. In the bedroom a chill draft came in from the air conditioner. She picked out a white sweatsuit to wear, along with white socks and a pair of running shoes, which she took out of a plastic bag. Out of habit, she was about to return to the bathroom with her makeup kit to finish an essential part of her routine. She decided against it, and instead took a hairbrush with her into the parlor.

She came into the parlor, hugging herself, wagging the hairbrush behind her back. She thought of ways to ask Paco Rangel if she might stay in the house for a few days. The story of difficulties with her boyfriend was good, even though it was only partially true. She could embellish it even more, telling Paco that were she to return to Austin, he'd be there and she didn't want to see him. Was the story good enough to convince Paco?

The death of a redneck in Lexington would not arouse the interest of the television stations or the newspaper in San Antonio. She needn't worry about Paco hearing a news story of Ralph Mason's death while he stayed in the house.

However, if he were to go into town, to Larson or White Leg, it would be big news. In Larson, with Dottie's Cafe as the only gathering place, he'd surely hear about it there. Worse, he'd learn that the police were looking for a woman the murder victim had been with. Could he figure out that it was she that the law looked for? Could he make the connection? And, if he did, what would he do? Again, her head became fuzzy as it filled with questions and unhappy answers that led to more questions until she was unable to think clearly.

Above all, there was a dark foreboding of being caught by the police.

She leaned her head to one side as she began to brush her hair. A smile came to her face as she considered the prospect of asking to stay with Paco. The thought of him warmed her all over. It had been a long time since she'd had such a feeling about a man. Priscilla liked the feeling.

When she first met René Chapa, she knew that he was somebody different from the one-man, one-night experiences she'd been having. René Chapa was lost, childlike in his innocence and drive, perpetually out of his element. She saw right away that he'd always choose the limelight and that she'd be the sanctuary where he could come to regroup and heal his wounds. Sadly, she thought to herself, René Chapa was not made to be in the world that he yearned for so much.

Paco Rangel appeared different in every way to Priscilla. For one thing, he was older than Priscilla by at least fifteen years. There was not enough difference in their ages to make him an older man, but she could not deny that he was older. Fortunately, Paco was young enough to not yet be a confirmed bachelor.

From what she'd seen of him, part of what made him attractive to her was that Paco was settled into his business and into the life he led. What she felt in his presence was his strength and his acceptance of the world he commanded.

Paco could be the sanctuary she needed by providing the place and his presence, himself, so she could regroup and heal her wounds. It would be a nice chance in her life.

Throughout her life, Priscilla had been the strong one, forging ahead with her plans, setting her goals and accomplishing them through hard work and perseverance. She had proceeded apace with her career in a field dominated by men. In the process, she had drawn two men into her life who depended on her strength, who drew from her what they needed if they were to stay afloat in the world.

As she'd been betrayed by one and then the other, she had come to distrust men. She did not completely want to exclude men from her life. After the disastrous three years with René Chapa, she had fully intended to keep men at a distance. One man, one night. Were it not for the trouble she was in, she could easily keep control of her life. Things were too muddled. Paco had appeared when she least expected him, in a place she would never dream of finding herself.

If she were to build her own sanctuary, she would need a long time to heal. She was weak because of the part of herself that she'd surrendered to René Chapa. She would have to recover the strength she lost before she could admit another man into her life.

But there was no denying that Paco Rangel was attractive, coming into her life at the worst possible of times. Although she'd known the feeling only once before, it was unmistakable. She could bring Paco into her life without a second thought. It would take some time to fully know and understand him, of course. Her intuition, though, leapfrogged over the months it would take, and she felt warm and comfortable, safe and protected, in his presence. She thought about his calm and reassuring manner.

It would be a chance, but one she was willing to take. If only things were different. If only she weren't on the run from the law.

What if she were to tell him the truth? What would his reaction be?

Priscilla felt sure that he would offer his help in whatever way she needed it. If she wanted to turn herself in, he would help her. If she wanted to remain in hiding and run away to where she'd never be found, he could arrange it for her.

She looked at the hairbrush in her hand and went back to brushing her hair.

24

Priscilla finished brushing the hair on one side of her head. When she leaned her head over to begin brushing the other side, she was surprised to see Paco in the office area at the other end of the large, rectangular room. She looked at him and smiled, continuing to brush her hair.

"I didn't think you were back," she said. "How long have you been there?"

"You sure make a pretty picture, standing there, brushing your hair," he said, leaning back in his thick wooden swivel chair. "Looked like you were lost in thought."

"You want to offer me a penny each for my thoughts?" she laughed.

"Nope. You said you'd tell me when ready," he said. "That's good enough for me."

"You said you had some beers. I'll take one of those beers now," she said, pausing, then adding, "if you'll drink one with me."

"Sure, I could use a beer," he said, slowly rising from the swivel chair.

Paco walked toward Priscilla, then turned to go into the kitchen. She followed along, still brushing her hair. At the table in the center of the kitchen she sat down, resting an elbow on the table top. She inclined her head to finish brushing her hair.

Paco smiled, turning away from the refrigerator, carrying two bottles of Budweiser longnecks. Standing at the opposite end of the table from Priscilla, he bent low to place a bottle of beer in front of her. He sat down, draping an arm over the backrest of the chair, contemplating her face. Priscilla thoughtfully observed Paco in return. A long moment passed before he raised his bottle in a toast. Priscilla lifted her bottle as well, adding a smile.

"Did you get all your produce in the truck?" she asked, tipping the beer to her lips for a swallow.

"Yeah, sure did," he said. "The thing about farming what they call 'gourmet' vegetables, you can only pick them a few bushels at a time. You don't have to worry about large harvests, and tractor trailers, and lots of pickers. There's never a problem with rain stopping the harvest, or seeing a crop rot on the ground because there's not enough people who want to work picking it. Of course, I don't see thousands of dollars for each crop all at once. This is more like a nine-to-five job. I pick what my customers want, deliver it, and the money trickles in. Sometimes, I get enough by the end of the week in one lump sum to make it feel like it's a real payday."

"You said you don't really have to go to San Antonio tonight," said Priscilla, clasping the beer bottle in both of her hands. Her voice faltered, sounding tentative, as she searched for an opening.

"I told you, I can go tonight, if that's what you want," he said quietly. "It's tomorrow, though, when I really have to go."

"I was thinking, you really don't have to go, not tonight . . . "

"You've changed your mind about going?" he said. "Did you decide to head for the coast, find your boyfriend, kiss and make up with him?"

"You said you weren't listening to Dot and me in the restaurant," she said, mouth open in wonder.

Paco Rangel grinned. "Pretty hard not to, the way sound carries in a small place like that."

Priscilla became pensive.

"No, it's not the coast. I don't want to go to the coast," she said, lifting the beer bottle to her mouth. "There's nothing for me there. By the way, I wasn't kicked out of any car by my boyfriend."

Paco thought for a minute. "What were you doing in Larson, then?"

"I really live in San Antonio. The truth is that my boyfriend decided to move his new girlfriend into the same house where I lived with him."

"Is that so? When did that happen?"

"I don't know. A couple of months ago."

"And, you stayed in the house with them?"

"It's not what you think. It was a two-story house. They stayed in the upstairs and I took a bedroom in the downstairs."

"But, still," he said, trying to find the words to say. "Still, they were in the house. That's pretty damn cold of your boyfriend, if you ask me. Why didn't you just shoot him and put him out of his misery?"

"It wasn't like that," Priscilla said, drinking more of her beer. "At that point, when he moved her in, that is, I just didn't care what he did."

"What about him, and the new girlfriend?" asked Paco. "They didn't care either?"

"I don't know. Maybe they did," said Priscilla. "I know he wanted to keep the house. So, it was up to me to move out. He couldn't afford to pay all of the rent. In fact, the last two months, he didn't pay any of the rent. I paid it all."

"You paid the rent for your boyfriend and his new girlfriend?"

"Don't make fun of me, please," said Priscilla. "It was pretty devastating. I really didn't know what to do. Since there wasn't any urgency to move out, I didn't. I mean, we never discussed me moving out, so I stayed. He was out of work, so I knew if I left, he'd lose the house and be out on the street."

"I don't see where that would be your problem."

"Well, there's more. I let him handle my money. He was spending all of his money along with mine. When he didn't have any money coming in, he kept spending mine. I know it's stupid. I thought he was saving it for when we got married and bought a house of our own. I just didn't think anything of it. I shouldn't have trusted him."

"Meanwhile, he had other plans," said Paco.

"Not at first," said Priscilla. "I couldn't have been that wrong about him. We grew apart, that's all. I saw it building up all along. I saw us going our separate ways and I did nothing about it. It was like it was happening to somebody else and I felt concerned, but there was nothing I could do about it."

"Until it was too late?"

"No, not really. I don't feel I'm a victim here. For instance, I found out what he was doing with my money, and I let him keep doing it. He thought I didn't know, but I did. When I discovered for sure that he had a girlfriend, I'd already given up on him. I had made my decision to leave him. Only, he was out of work again. He was always out of work, it seems now. I didn't feel right leaving him when he was out of work. He wasn't mean, or cruel, or violent. He just wasn't very good at being the kind of person he thought he was—never mind what I wanted him to be. He wasn't very good at being himself. In his work, something always came up and he'd lose his job. He'd tell me that this person was out to get him, or some other person got all the lucky breaks. It was always something. It was never his fault. Even from the very first, I knew that he couldn't handle the jobs he took and that it was only a matter of time before he'd give himself away and they'd have to let him go. So, all the time I was with him, I really felt sorry for him."

"You don't believe he took advantage of you? There are some people who take on a hangdog-helpless attitude as a way to use other people."

Priscilla leaned forward on the kitchen table. Her voice had an edge to it.

"Look, if I put all the facts on the table," she said emphatically, "yes, he took advantage of me. But, that's not the way it was. It wasn't only bare facts on the table. We were two human beings, in love with each other."

"It doesn't sound to me like he was in love with you," said Paco Rangel. "It sounds like he got hooked up to a gravy train and held on to it for dear life."

Priscilla softened, took another sip from the bottle. "I know it's hard for you to understand," she said.

"Because I don't have a wife or a girlfriend?" Paco asked.

"I don't mean that at all," she said. "I cared for René, okay? His name was René. When we moved in together, I decided to give him everything because I felt he was the one man who would bring the fulfillment I wanted in my life. And, I lived up to my part of it."

"What about him, did he give you everything?"

"He did. In his own way, he did," she said, upending the bottle and drinking the last of the beer. "Could I have another of these, please?"

"Sure, let me get it for you," said Paco, rising from his chair.

When he returned to the table with the two beers and had taken his chair, Paco said, "So, you didn't tell me how you ended up in Larson."

"Well, I have a brother who lives in Houston," she said. "I didn't want to stay in San Antonio anymore. It wasn't just because René would be there. I never even liked the people who were his friends. It would be easy to avoid him. In fact, I could probably spend the rest of my life and never run into him or his friends."

"Here's to big cities," said Paco, lifting his beer bottle.

"San Antonio, though, is a very depressing town. It's so smug and self-satisfied. There's all these retired people, military mostly, who think it's an antechamber to heaven. They think it's exactly like heaven, except they don't have to die to go there. It's really sick. Anyway, I decided to leave. Go somewhere else, start over. I had reached what's known as 'the glass ceiling' in my job. Do you know what that is? I'll tell you how it works. There was a man promoted to a job that I knew I had earned and that I had coming to me. The guy wasn't as good as me, but he got it anyway. After that, it was going to be a lot of years before another opening came up. The whole idea of it left me disgusted."

"It's pretty hard to work on a career and then have to leave it," said Paco.

"Don't get me wrong. I love what I do. I felt it was time for me to take on more responsibility; I was ready for it. If I were to stay doing what I was doing, without that promotion, I felt I'd stagnate, become stale and resentful. The challenge I needed was given to someone else. Eventually, I knew, I'd get to hate my job. I didn't want to do that. So, it became time for me to move on to another job. The prospects looked good: more money, responsibility. Day before yesterday, in the morning, while I got ready for work, I thought it might be a good idea to not only move on to another job, but to do it in another city. That's when I thought about my brother in Houston. When I went in to work in the morning, I handed in my resignation."

Paco fingered the bottom of his beer bottle, said nothing.

"I gave my employer a month's notice," Priscilla continued. "By noon that day, even before I went to lunch, they called me in—two of the partners in the firm where I worked. They had a check for a whole month's salary, another check for my vacation time. Someone from Personnel explained how

I could continue my health insurance, and I was counseled on what to do with what I had in the company pension fund. As I sat with them in the conference room, one of the secretaries came in with a box containing my personal belongings from my office. They informed me that the lock had been changed in my office and that I wouldn't be allowed back in there. When we finished, a security guard waited outside to escort me out of the building."

"What the hell did they do that for?" asked Paco, shaking his head from side to side.

"I don't know, they just did it," said Priscilla.

"What did you do?"

"The only thing I could do. I thought about going to get drunk. The only places I knew where I felt safe getting a drink were those my former co-workers would likely come into. I didn't want to see any of them. By the time they left work for the day, the word would be out all over the building. If they ran into me, they'd be nervous. It was best if they didn't see me. Instead, I stopped at the grocery store. I bought dinner and went home. My dinner was some packages of beef jerky, cheese, a loaf of sourdough bread, and a 12-pack of beer."

"Did you have to deal with your boyfriend and his girlfriend?"

"I began to drink early in the day, so I was pretty drunk and in bed before they came in," she said.

"Sounds like it was rough on you," he said sympathetically.

"In the morning, this was yesterday, I went to the bank to deposit the last checks the company gave me. It occurred to me that if I put them in my checking account, my boyfriend would keep spending my money. I got cash and traveler's checks instead. I thought the traveler's checks would be a safe way to keep my cash until I got another checking account. I drove back to the house, packed a bag, went to a friend's house and asked her if I could leave my car in their driveway. From there I took a city bus to downtown, to the bus station. I got there just as the bus to Houston was leaving. I stayed on the bus until it stopped in Lexington. From the time I left the bank to the time I got on the bus, it's all pretty much a blur. I mean, I didn't think about anything. I just did it. On the bus, I tried not to think of anything. At some point, I knew I would put everything together, look over what happened, and then make more definite decisions about my future."

"So you decided to go to Houston on the spur of the moment."

"Not at all. I had already decided that it was where I wanted to start over."

"What about leaving the bus when you got to Lexington?"

"I'm not sure why I did it," Priscilla said, averting Paco's eyes.

25

"What about this man René?" asked Paco Rangel.

"At this point, I can't afford to worry about René anymore," she said. "He's working, so I was going to leave anyway. I didn't expect it to happen in the way it did. The only thing that concerns me at this point are my things. I'll have to go back to the house and get them. My life is a mess!"

"Don't be too hard on yourself," said Paco, patiently. "You've heard, I'm sure, that shit happens."

"Look, those people where I worked were so vicious to me! I never expected them to treat me as they did. I was their colleague. I thought I had their respect. Heck, I even thought they liked me."

"Maybe it wasn't personal," said Paco. "Do you suppose it was a company routine? They do it to everybody?"

"I never heard of it happening to anyone before," said Priscilla.

"Who knows," said Paco. "It does sound strange."

"Anyway. Where was I? So, the bus got into Lexington and I went to this bar across the road from the bus station,"

Priscilla said. "I thought it might be a good idea to go back to San Antonio. Maybe I was taking things too far. I learned that there's not a bus to San Antonio until today, so I decided to drink some beer before finding a motel for the night."

"You went to Ligon Wells," said Paco. "Did you meet Georgene?"

"Yes, she was very nice," said Priscilla. "She introduced me to this man, who I thought was very nice. He said he would take me to San Antonio. He said it wasn't that long of a drive, and we could have some beers on the way. I didn't think there was anything wrong with me taking him up on his offer."

"The way you say that, something bad happened, didn't it?" said Paco. "What was it?"

"Well, I don't know what it was. He did try to force me. So, I guess he tried to rape me, except he didn't," Priscilla said, feeling lightheaded from the beer. "We drove on the highway out of Lexington, I don't know for how long. And, I kept seeing the signs to San Antonio. We came to an intersection, where there's the road going to White Leg. I remember seeing White Leg on the sign. I asked where he was going, seeing that he'd turned away from the road to San Antonio. He said he knew a short cut. And, then he turned on a gravel road, and he stopped the car. He opened up some beers and said there was plenty of time to get to San Antonio. We ought to have some beers first, he said. He tried to put his arm around me and feel me up. I told him I didn't want him to and that we should get going to San Antonio. Then he got kind of ugly and said not before he got what he had coming. He said that I should give it up because otherwise he was going to take it."

"What did you do, then?"

"He'd given me a full can of beer," said Priscilla. "So, I took it and smashed his face with it. He put his arms up, but I hit him again. This time on top of his head. The beer got all foamy and splattered all over the place. I threw the door open and got out. It was raining pretty hard. He started to get out of the car, but decided he didn't want to get wet, the little piss ant son of a bitch! Anyway, he threw my suitcase on the road and he turned the car around and took off. He left me there."

"Do you know who it was? Did Georgene give you his name?"

"No. Well, yeah, she did. Except I forgot it. I'd had too many beers, that's why I can't remember it," said Priscilla.

"We can get his name from Georgene," said Paco, drinking from the bottle. "Tell the sheriff about it."

"He didn't hurt me," said Priscilla. "I was lucky, I guess."

"There's no call for a man to do that to a woman," said Paco. "A man should never force himself on a woman."

"There was no harm done, really. There was a large tree across the fence. I went over the fence and got under the tree. There was a piece of ground that didn't get too wet. I sat on my suitcase until the rain stopped, and then I lay on the ground and went to sleep. In the morning, I got to the highway going to White Leg. I remembered the sign for Larson, and I thought I could walk there and get some help. Which is what I did."

"And here we are!" said Paco, trying to lighten the somber telling of the story. He lifted his beer in salute.

Priscilla lifted hers in return and smiled.

"What do you want to do? You said you didn't want to go back to San Antonio."

"I do, Paco, but not just yet," said Priscilla. "I need some time to think. Get clear on how to get my life in order. My life has been going this way and that way. I really don't even know what I want to do. Maybe if I did nothing, gave myself some time for things to settle...Maybe then I'll know what to do."

"How long do you think you need?" Paco asked.

"Not long. A few days. Could be a week, maybe longer," she said. "Do you think it would be all right for me to stay here? I don't mean for a week. Just a few days until I can get myself going."

"Of course," said Paco. "You can stay as long as you like."

"I can earn my keep. I can clean house, do laundry," Priscilla said. "Except you already keep a pretty clean house."

"It gets messy," he said.

"I can help you pick your vegetables. I'll do anything, except go where anybody will see me. I want to stay out of sight. I've got an aversion to people right now. I want to be completely alone. I can think better that way."

"What about me? I'll be here," said Paco.

"You're different," she said. "I like being with you."

"I like having you here, Priscilla," said Paco Rangel. "I really do."

"I guess I should make dinner," Paco Rangel said, after they'd drunk three beers each. "You must be hungry."

"I am," said Priscilla, nodding her head. The effects of the beer had made her groggy. "Very hungry, in fact."

"I'll get on it," Paco said. "By the way, are we going to drink more beer do you suppose?"

"You're out of beer, I'm sorry," she said. "I don't want any more if you have to go anywhere to get it."

"Well, I have to go outside to get it."

"No, please, I mean it. Don't drive anywhere."

"Who's driving anywhere? I have the beer stored outside. They say beer has a certain shelf life. I think you're supposed to drink it within a week or two of buying it. I don't like to go to town unless I absolutely have to, so I usually buy enough to last me for the whole month, maybe a little more. I don't drink more than a six-pack a day. Sometimes, not even that. Come on along, you can help me with it."

From underneath the sink, directly behind where he sat, Paco brought out a red ice chest with a white top. He carried it outside, going through the side door in the rear of the kitchen to a small sun deck. A platform of two-by-fours had been attached to the porch to hold an ice machine of the kind found in the hallways of hotels. He took the scoop hanging on a piece of chain and layered two inches of ice on the bottom of the ice chest.

"You have your own ice machine?" Priscilla said, wide-eyed in wonder, shaking her head from side to side. "You're really something, Paco."

"Why can't I have an ice machine, if I need one?" Paco said.

"Isn't that just a bit extravagant? An ice machine just so you can ice down your beer?"

"That's not why I got it. Sometimes I have to deliver vegetables so fragile that they won't survive the trip to the city. Other times, in summer especially, it gets so hot my produce would be baked inside the camper shell by the time I got to the restaurants. I can cover them with ice, they stay fresh, and I can get a better price for them. This ice machine is an investment in my business. And, if you don't mind my taking advantage, it comes in handy when I want to ice down my beer."

"Somehow, I knew you were going to tell me something like that," said Priscilla. "I mean, an ice machine, really!"

Paco Rangel smiled. "Now you know for sure."

He walked quickly to a lean-to beside the barn. He went inside and retrieved two six-packs of bottled beer. When he returned to the small porch, he laid the bottles on their sides along the bed of crushed ice. He covered the first layer of bottles with more ice, layered the next six-pack of bottles, and filled the chest to the top with ice.

"You layer the bottles with ice like that, they'll be cold in no time at all," he said. "The trick is to surround each bottle with ice."

"Are you expecting to drink all that beer?" Priscilla asked.

"I hate to run out when I'm drinking," he said. "It's better to have some left over."

Paco lifted the ice chest and carried it back into the kitchen, where he set it on the floor next to the table.

"There we are!" he said. "With the beer right here, we won't have to keep getting up for another round. And, I'm only going to have one more beer. The rest are for you!"

"I think you'll be surprised when you see how many of those beers I can drink," Priscilla said.

Paco went to the refrigerator for the last two beers in there. He opened both of them, handed one to Priscilla, who leaned against the counter beside the sink. He put his bottle on the counter next to the stove across from Priscilla.

"And, now, our thoughts should turn to dinner," he said.

26

"Why do I think you're a gourmet cook?" she said, lifting her eyebrows in a question.

"You would think that, with the fancy vegetables I grow," he said, "that I'd know how to make better use of them."

"And, don't you?"

"Heck, no!" Paco said. "I just don't have the knack for it. I mean, for the fancy cooking. In fact, I'll tell you a story."

"Oh, good," said Priscilla, becoming animated. "I love a story."

"There was a cooking series on the public television station from San Antonio," he said. "Julia Child, it was."

"Oh, I love her," Priscilla said. "I'd never, never try to fix any of the dishes she demonstrated. I just loved watching her. She was something to watch."

"On this series," Paco went on, "she didn't do any of the cooking herself. She introduced new chefs, young ones coming up in the world of cooking. I taped every one of the shows. I made an index of all the recipes, what show it was, and which cassette I taped it on. I mean, I was really all set to learn some serious cooking. The first recipe I tried drove me nuts. I was running constantly from the living room to the kitchen. I watched a little bit of the show, punch the pause button, and run into the kitchen. I'd get the ingredients ready, and then I'd go back to the living room and watch how the chef did everything. I'd come back in here and try to do it in exactly the same way. The dish turned out terrible."

"You didn't have beginner's luck?"

"Beginner's luck! I didn't have any luck at all!" Paco said. "Well, I figured it was all that running back and forth between the kitchen and the living room trying to watch how to do it and running in here to do it. On one of my trips to San Antonio, I bought another television, a small one to fit on the counter over there by the stove. Then, I brought one of the VCR's from the living room and hooked it up to the TV. Now, I was all set. Everything right at my fingertips."

"Let me guess," said Priscilla. "It turned out just as awful as the first time."

"You got it!" said Paco. "That's when I decided I was not, definitely not, cut out to be a gourmet cook. Don't get me wrong. I know how to cook well enough to feed myself. You won't find a single TV dinner in the house."

"Good for you," Priscilla said. "Although, I wouldn't be too hard on TV dinners. Many's the time they've saved my life and kept me from starving. What are you going to fix for us?"

Paco opened the freezer compartment of the refrigerator. He took out a plastic bag and brought it to the sink, where he emptied it and ran the faucet over its contents.

"I got some shrimp here," he said, beginning to peel them. "Not the best, they're farm-raised and frozen. I have to say, though, that they're not bad if there's not a decent restaurant in the neighborhood."

"You'd eat out, if there were places to go?"

"Probably not."

"Don't you get lonely out here?" Priscilla asked.

"Lonely? I wouldn't say that, not lonely," he said.

He finished peeling the shrimp. He found a glass bowl in the cupboard and tossed the shrimp into it. On a cutting board next to the bowl, he chopped three cloves of garlic, which he scraped into the shrimp. He poured olive oil over them. From the refrigerator, he took a bottle of white wine and poured some of that over the shrimp.

"We'll just let these little suckers settle in here for a few minutes, let them marinate."

He came back to his beer, took a long swig of it, and thought for a minute.

"All the years I've been out here," he said, "I've learned to be by myself. It took a while. In fact, I couldn't stand it at first. I mean, I made the decision to be out here. I thought it all through beforehand, including taking into account the loneliness, just the solitary existence I'd have to face here."

"It wasn't what you thought it would be?" she said.

"No, I wouldn't say that. It was exactly as I thought it would be. I never kidded myself about that part of it. What I wasn't prepared for was my reaction to it. I thought I could handle it better than I did."

"What did you do?"

"Well, I went into White Leg a lot. I drank in the only bar there until closing time every night. I went to dances wherever they had one on Friday and Saturday nights. The hangovers hurt like hell every morning when I had to get up and do my work. I realized I was going to have to get used to the hangovers, if I went on the way I was going. Gradually, though, I really did get used to it. Living here, I mean, not the drinking. Many times that first year, I thought about packing it in and getting the hell out."

"Why didn't you?"

"Stubborn, I guess. I'll tell you the truth. I probably stayed because there was no place else for me to go to. There was no one I wanted to be with. No other place I had a particular attachment to. There was not a job I wanted to do or go back to. Nothing. What I wanted was to work with vegetables.

I searched for a long time before I finally found this place here. It's perfect for what I wanted to do. After all the trouble I went through to find it, I couldn't just leave it."

"How'd you get used to being here all by yourself?"

"It was a gradual thing, as I said. It didn't happen overnight, and it wasn't one single thing. It took a combination of things. I bought a stereo, VCR, big-screen TV, satellite, CDs, videos, subscribed to a bunch of magazines and newspapers, joined book clubs, video clubs, CD music clubs. I bought jigsaw puzzles, paint-by-number kits, a stained-glass lamp-making kit. I bought unpainted furniture so I could paint it. It all worked, more or less, until I realized I didn't need any of it. I got used to the solitude here. That's one of the reasons why I could never finish my garden outside. All I needed was to get used to the solitude. Once I got used to it, I could finish the garden because it turned out to be so relaxing to work on it."

"So, you do like it now?"

"Yes, now I do. I wouldn't give it up for anything. It feels good to be living the life I want."

"What about a woman? A companion? Ever think about that?"

"Oh, I think about it all the time," said Paco. "I won't marry just to have somebody in the house. I guess I'm a romantic. I believe there is somebody special for me. When she comes into my life, I'll be ready for her."

"And, what about me being here?"

"You can be a change of pace for me. You're not going to stay for long. Besides, if you don't stay, how am I going to know if you're somebody special or not?"

"Thanks for letting me stay here," said Priscilla, lifting her beer in a toast.

"Well, it's time to get moving on our grub," said Paco. "Let's see if I can't come up with something you can eat."

Paco took a large pot from under the sink and filled it with water, which he set on the stove to boil. They continued to talk until the water turned to a foamy, rolling boil. He brought a package of linguine from the cupboard, measured out enough for two servings, and tossed the linguine into the boiling water. In a few minutes, the linguini was done. He poured out the boiling water and set the pasta aside in a bowl of cold water.

Paco cut half a stick of butter into a large cast-iron skillet, after which he shook in a dash of peanut oil. The butter sizzled and almost immediately settled into a bubbling mass in the skillet. He tossed in the shrimp, stirring them quickly, until they lost their translucence. Paco removed the shrimp from the skillet and tossed in some garlic he'd chopped, to briefly sauté it. He poured in some wine to deglaze the pan, and then he poured a container of heavy cream into it. After bringing it to a boil, he lowered the heat to reduce the mixture to a sauce consistency.

While the sauce thickened in the skillet, Paco cut a head of lettuce and two tomatoes in quarters. He arranged a quarter of the lettuce and the tomato quarters on salad plates. He brought the plates to the table with a commercial Caesar's dressing. He returned the shrimp to the sauce, adding the cold linguine. He seasoned it only with white pepper. He waited a minute for the linguine to heat through and divided up the contents of the skillet on two plates.

Paco served Priscilla her plate and then sat down. He leaned over in his chair, dragged the ice chest to his side, and took out two more beers.

"I guess we're ready to eat," he said.

27

Paco and Priscilla sat quietly at the kitchen table, drinking the last of the beer in the ice chest. Several times, they had called it a last round, but ended up having another. They had finished eating two hours earlier. Priscilla insisted on doing the dishes, which she accomplished quickly and efficiently, and then returned to her chair at the table.

"You know we're drinking the last two beers," said Paco.

"Do you want to go out and get some more?"

"Not unless you want to drink more," he said.

"I don't want this evening to end," Priscilla said. "But, I really don't want any more beer."

"Good, it worked out," he said. "There were just enough beers to last for a pleasant evening."

They left the kitchen, their arms around each other's waists, their hips touching. They stopped in front of the door leading to the bedroom.

"You sleep on the bed, I'll take the couch," Paco said.

"I tried the couch this afternoon," she said. "It's fine. I'll sleep there."

Paco placed his hands on her shoulders, turned her to face into the bedroom.

"You're my guest," said Paco, his speech slurred. "It's the bed for you. I insist."

"No, I insist on taking the sofa," said Priscilla.

"How about a compromise?" asked Paco. "The bed is way big enough for two. We can both sleep on it. We can do what Clark Gable and Claudette Colbert did in 'It Happened One Night.' We'll put up a sheet to divide the bed in two."

"The two of us on the bed?" she said, turning to face Paco.

Priscilla raised her arms and embraced Paco around the neck. She tilted her head, raising herself on tiptoe, bringing her face up to his for a kiss. Paco lowered his head a little, just enough to meet her lips.

A shudder went through Priscilla's body. She tightened her embrace around Paco's neck, thrusting her body forward to squeeze her breasts against his chest. She opened her mouth in the kiss, swallowing his lips, trying to slip her tongue into his mouth. She lifted her pelvis to press it against his lower body.

Paco remained passive, his body still and unyielding.

He brought his hands up to her shoulders and pushed her gently away. His buoyant mood quickly changed to an expression of pain on his face.

"Don't," he said, turning his face away.

"It's okay," Priscilla whispered hoarsely. "It's okay."

"Please," he said, "not this way."

Priscilla looked into his eyes, touching his cheek with her hand.

"What's the matter?" she asked.

"Having you in the house makes me feel good," Paco said. "Makes me feel as good as I've felt in many years. I don't want to spoil it."

"What's there to spoil, Paco?"

Priscilla raised up on tiptoe again. She placed her hands on his chest, bent her head, bringing her hands to cover his ears, and kissed him lightly on the lips. As she did so, she slid her hand down, got it between his legs, and found his penis. As she had expected, it was semi-stiff. She gave it a squeeze and began to kiss him harder.

Paco again broke away from her searching mouth, turning his face away from her again. His fingers gripped her wrist, removing her hand from his crotch.

"Don't you want to?" she asked. "I thought we might . . . "

"I do want to, more than anything," he said. "But not like this. You're in my house; you're in trouble. I don't want you to feel that you're obliged to do it. I don't feel right about it. Not just now."

"Is that what's bothering you?" Priscilla said, smiling, touched by his sweetness. "I drink a few beers and I always get horny. It's all I can to keep myself from jumping on the first man I see."

"If you don't mind," Paco said, his voice thick in his throat, "I'd prefer to wait until it means something between us. Something special, maybe. I think it's possible that we have something here."

"That's very sweet of you, Paco," she said, trying not to sound disappointed. "I guess I'll sleep on the couch."

"You can still sleep on the bed with me," he said. "I won't bother you."

"We'd better not," she said.

28

Sheriff Jim Woodrow Willow came into Joe Blue's jail-cell office. He stood in front of the desk, watching Joe Blue, who sat in his straight-back chair, elbows on the desk, resting his head in his hands. The sheriff took the chair in front of the desk and put his feet up.

"Been a long damned day," said Sheriff Jim Woodrow.

"Way too long, Jim Woodrow," said Joe Blue, glancing at his wristwatch

"I say, pack it in for the night, Joe," said the sheriff. "Let's all go on home."

"I'd feel a lot better if we had this thing wrapped up," Joe Blue said.

"You gonna finish up for today?" said the sheriff. "Or you want me to send out for something to eat? It's getting late."

"I'm about through here," said Joe Blue. "I was just going over some things here. I should go home."

"How about a nightcap, Joe?" said Sheriff Jim Woodrow, taking out a silver flask out of his hip pocket and placing it on the desk.

"Just a short one, Jim Woodrow, I ain't much for drinking," said Joe Blue, picking up the telephone and dialing a number.

"Junie, would you bring the sheriff and me some coffee?"

The sheriff said, "You have to call through the telephone company to get somebody out front to bring you coffee, Joe?"

"Nope, I get up and go get it myself, most times," he said.

"Didn't I approve an intercom system for in here? Hook up me, you, and the front desk?"

"I sent the request in months ago, Jim Woodrow," Joe Blue said. "County's holding it up."

"Nitwits! How about Georgene? How'd your talk with her go? Anything?" the sheriff asked.

June Akers came in carrying two white Styrofoam cups of coffee. She set them side by side on the desk. When she finished, she stood by the desk with her hands behind her back, expectantly.

"Thank you, honey," said the sheriff. "You're a joy to behold. If you don't mind my asking, what are you doing here this late?"

"I stayed because we've never had a real murder before, Sheriff," said June Akers. "It's exciting! And, then, Brita Mae asked me to cover for her because she had to go home. It's okay if I'm here, isn't it, Sheriff?"

"Of course it is, darling," said Sheriff Jim Woodrow. "But, you better go home and see about your momma and your poppa. They'll be worried about you."

"Brita Mae told me to stay until Joe Blue says it's okay to leave."

"Go home, Junie," said Joe Blue. "We're finished for the day. Thanks for helping out."

With that, June Akers left. The sheriff twisted the cap of the flask, poured whiskey into the Styrofoam cups. He handed one to Joe Blue.

"The woman's name is Priscilla. Gave no last name," said Joe Blue, grimacing after sampling the coffee and whiskey. "I got a description of her that'll fit just about any woman in her twenties, about five seven, five eight, black hair, busty. Real white skin, dressed in black. Of course, we can narrow it down to only those women who wear scarlet lipstick."

"That's all you got on the description?"

"She's a looker," said Joe Blue. "Now, here's something for you. According to Georgene, she made the first approach on Ralph Mason. They spent the evening drinking. At closing time, they left together."

"Is she a professional in the art of picking up men?"

"I didn't think to ask Georgene," said Joe Blue. "Georgene would've spotted her if she was in the trade. My guess is, not."

"You put out an alert for the pickup truck?"

"Yeah, Brita Mae got the license plate number and she's called out the alert. I put in the description that Georgene gave me as a possible driver."

"There's nothing more to do on that angle, Joe," said the sheriff. "I expect the T-Rangers will get wind of it and start sniffing around here, trying to horn in on things."

"They can't do shit unless we ask them," said Joe Blue.

"Yeah, you're right, the hell with them," said the sheriff, taking a sip of the coffee, and after freshening it with another splash of whiskey, he asked, "Did Johnny find anything we can use in the room?"

"No," said Joe Blue wearily. "We wait and see what comes in. We got some prints off the beer cans. We wait to see if we get a match, tell us who the woman is we're looking for, provided her prints are on record."

"Any chance we can catch up to her?"

"I've been working on a hunch, Jim Woodrow. From what I can see, on the surface, anyway, the woman was passing through town. Ralph Mason gets a shot in the back and she gets in a panic. First thing she does is get away. Everything points to her being long gone."

"Looks like she's got Ralph Mason's fancy new truck to get long gone in," said the sheriff.

"Suppose, Jim Woodrow, she isn't. This is my hunch," said Joe Blue. "Suppose she's still in these parts."

"How do figure that, Joe?"

"Let's say she's not a bar floozy at all, dumb as they come," said Joe Blue, leaning forward on the desk, his eyes bright. "Ralph and her are in the motel. Ralph gets shot. The woman gets her things together real quick and runs off in his truck. Where's she gonna go?"

"Same distance as there is between Lexington and half-way to hell, I'd say," said the sheriff.

"That's right. That's what it looks like, as far as it goes," said Joe Blue. "But, what if she figured out the easiest thing is for us to find the truck? What if she knew every lawman in the state was out looking for the truck, with her driving it? What would she do then?"

"She'd get rid of it, of course" said the sheriff, tossing his head over the backrest of the chair to look at the ceiling. "Which, and I bet you a Hershey bar on this, she's already done. The fact is, that young lady had a good twelve-hours head start on us. That's enough time to drive to the other side of Lubbock. That says to me she could be anywhere."

"I've got a feeling on this, Jim Woodrow," said Joe Blue. "My hunch tells me she's not far from here."

"How you figure that, Joe?"

"It's nothing I can put my finger on," said Joe Blue. "My hunch says that she wasn't too far from here before she figured out we'd be on her tail. I think she got rid of the truck before she went too far. She'll have to be cautious about hitching a ride out of the county. I think it'll be a day or two before she has the nerve to get moving."

"That reminds me about the old days, Joe," said Sheriff Jim Woodrow, lapsing into a mellow, relaxed state, holding the Styrofoam cup over his chest. He'd finished the coffee and was sipping straight whiskey.

"There was a time when we got ourselves a murder and we could go look over the situation and the killer'd be standing over the corpse with his pistol in hand, ready to surrender. Or, we could come back to the office and the killer would be waiting for us. Turn himself in. Or, somebody'd walk in and say, 'Go pick up so-and-so, he did it.' And we go to so-and-so and ask'im 'Did you do it?' and he'd say, 'Yep, I did. And, I ain't sorry about it, neither.' There'd be a pretty damn big commotion. It'd stay with you so you thought it'd never be over. People'd be scared at their own shadows for weeks and months. The murder victim was somebody everybody knew. You don't forget people that quickly. The fact that there was a murder sobered people up. It would be a long damn time before somebody'd go and commit another murder."

"Times have changed, Jim Woodrow," said Joe Blue. "The world is a more complicated place these days."

"I disagree with you, Joe," Jim Woodrow Willow said. "It's been my experience that the world is always complicated. People just never seem to know what their place in it is. You no sooner think you understand the way things are, when something comes along that tells you it ain't that simple. Most people take it for granted that things change and they try to get along as best they can. Others get confused; they go a little crazy. It used to be when someone went a little crazy, somebody'd talk to them. It doesn't seem like people much do that anymore. Things go a little haywire and there's no telling what'll happen. That's where we come in. The job we have is to put things back in their place."

"How do you account for all the crime we have to deal with?" Joe Blue asked. "Why are people committing more crime these days? Why isn't it safe for people to go out of their homes? I've heard that in the big cities, people are afraid to even go to the store for groceries. It's just not safe at all. It's a hell of a thing, Jim Woodrow."

"There's not that problem here in Lexington. Not in my county."

"Not yet there isn't. But, it's coming. It's on its way. There's been more crime in Lexington. I've been compiling the numbers, Jim Woodrow. There's more crime we have to deal with."

"I know you've been putting some numbers together, Joe. It's that college training in you. In my day, you didn't need college and you didn't have to add up any numbers. There's more people, and the more people you have, the more they commit crimes. You don't have to add up the numbers. All you have to do is drive around town. You can feel it in your bones. It may not seem to you that people committed crimes in the good old days, but they did. It was part of those good old days."

"How come it feels different now?" Joe Blue asked.

"It feels different to you, but not to me. You're just starting out, Joe," Sheriff Jim Woodrow said.

"Can you give me any explanation for it?"

"Sure, I can tell you, but you won't understand it. You have to hold on. Live for another thirty years," he said. "That's when it'll make sense to you."

A glint of light caught in the sheriff's eye as he grinned. Joe Blue began with a slow grin and then broke out in laughter.

29

Orthal Mason sent the metal door at the end of the
passageway slamming against the cinder block
wall. The crashing sound echoed in Joe Blue's jail-
cell office. Sheriff Jim Woodrow rose to his feet from the chair
in front of Joe Blue's desk. He stepped out in the passageway.
Joe Blue came up behind him.

A young deputy sheriff tried to hold Orthal Mason back
by yanking on his arm. Johnny Watkins came running and
grabbed Orthal Mason's other arm. Orthal Mason continued
shoving his feet forward, bringing the two deputies along with
him.

Johnny Watkins yelled, "You can't go back in there,
Orthal! Goddamn it!"

"The hell I can't," said Orthal Mason. "I want to see Jim
Woodrow."

"You ain't allowed, Orthal! Not until the sheriff says so!"

"He'll talk to me!"

Johnny Watkins caught a glimpse of the sheriff and
released Orthal Mason's arm. He huffed and puffed, and said,
"We tried to stop him at the counter, Sheriff, but he wouldn't

listen. He just went on through like he had the walk of the place."

"I want to talk to you, Jim Woodrow," said Orthal Mason, shaking his arms, taking another step forward.

"Let him go, boys," the sheriff said, holding his coffee cup.

"That's more like it, Jim Woodrow," Orthal Mason said, squaring his shoulders, walking forward until he stood a few feet away from the sheriff.

Jim Woodrow planted his feet firmly on the tile floor. When Orthal Mason was three feet in front of him, Sheriff Jim Woodrow Willow took a step forward and brought his right arm in a roundhouse that slammed his fist into Orthal Mason's jaw.

Orthal Mason's knees buckled and he crumbled to the floor.

Sheriff Jim Woodrow Willow looked at the prone body of Orthal Mason. A look of distaste crossed his face as he took a sip of the whiskey coffee.

"Pick him up, boys," the sheriff said to the two deputies, "and put him in the cell next to Joe Blue. When he comes to, let him go. If he says one goddamned word, lock the son of a bitch up."

The two deputies scurried to lift Orthal Mason up by the arms and drag him to the jail cells.

"I'm going home," said the sheriff. "There's been enough excitement around here for one day."

30

Priscilla awoke with a fierce headache that raged at her temples with the dense thumping of a kettle drum. She was afraid to move for fear that the heavy liquid in her head would explode. She pulled away the blanket that covered her from head to toe. Her body felt sweaty and clammy inside the sweatsuit she'd slept in. Summoning strength that surprised her, she swung her feet away from the sofa and placed them on the braided rug on the floor. The air in the room was humid and sticky. Her wristwatch said 7:30.

She walked into Paco's bedroom. The bed was made and Paco was gone.

In the bathroom, she washed her face, brushed her teeth, and combed her hair. In her head, her brain felt as if it wobbled in some kind of heavy liquid. Her morning wash improved her condition a bit, but she still felt like shit.

She returned to the parlor. It took an effort to bend down to get her suitcase and place it on the sofa. She opened and brought out a fresh T-shirt. She removed the top of the sweatsuit and slipped on the T-shirt. The coolness of the cotton material made her feel a little better. She drifted on unsteady feet into the kitchen.

There was a note on the kitchen table, written in a crude, hurried scrawl.

Off to Big City. Fresh pot coffee. (Made 6 a.m.) Look stove. Breakfast. Reheat. Be back abt 10. PR.

Priscilla smiled.

The drip coffee maker was on the counter next to the stove. There was a large Dallas Cowboys coffee mug beside it. She poured herself a cup, lifting it with both hands to take a first sip. The coffee was old but good enough. She lifted the cover of a pan on the stove and saw eggs scrambled with tomatoes, onions, green peppers, and little red discs that looked like pepperoni. She wrinkled her nose at the sight of it. She'd never thought of pepperoni for breakfast.

She sat in a chair before the table. A steaming hot shower would help, but she decided the coffee would help more, for the time being. She would have to take things slow until she recovered the full sense of a living body.

She sat drinking coffee for nearly an hour. The stiffness she felt, from sleeping on the sofa and the hangover, relaxed after her blood seemed to flow more freely. The headache persisted. As did a feeling of utter exhaustion.

When Priscilla felt she could move easily, she went back to the bathroom for a shower. Not wishing to fully dress as yet, she put on a clean pair of underpants and the same T-shirt. In the medicine cabinet, she found a jar of aspirin, took two of them. She gripped the sides of the lavatory and waited to feel better, but she didn't.

She turned on the burner under the pan with the scrambled eggs. On the small piece of counter between the stove and refrigerator was a toaster, and beside it, a loaf of bread. She toasted two slices. She found the butter dish in the refrigerator empty. After rummaging on the shelves, moving things around, Priscilla decided it was probably better to forego the butter when she couldn't find any more.

She did find a small pitcher of orange juice, and poured herself a glass. The large breakfast did not immediately restore her normal condition, but she did have a clear indication that the hangover would not be permanent and that her physical misery would soon go away. When she finished eating, she made a fresh pot of coffee and washed all of the dirty dishes in the kitchen.

With the coffee mug nestled in her hands, she walked to the front door, which she opened to let in some fresh air. She stood in front of the door, looking through the screen at the pale gold of the sun spread upon the geometric patterns of Paco's garden. Beyond the white picket fence there was the expanse of sandy soil, dark with the morning dew, spotted here and there with large patches of crab grass.

Beneath the house, Mariachi sensed that Priscilla was at the door. Suddenly, with slow, fluid motions, the black pit bull came up the steps of the porch, swaying from side to side as if carrying troublesome weight. Once he was on the porch, it was a graceful glide that brought him to the screen door, where he lay down, his black face on his white paws.

Priscilla felt goose bumps rising on her forearms as she watched the dog lying on the other side of the screen door. Paco Rangel and the pickup truck were gone. There was no doubt in her mind that the dog was eighty pounds of pure menace. Lying on the porch was a simple gesture on the part of the dog, probably friendly, for all she knew.

And yet, she couldn't help but fear the dog. It was more than the training Paco had told her about. Generations of breeding, selecting and cultivating the killer instinct were bundled up in the taut, rippling muscles of the animal. The dog lay on the planks of the porch, his eyes drooping slightly, looking at an aluminum plate on the screen door. On the other side of the door were her feet. She wondered if Paco had fed him.

Paco Rangel told her that the dog was taken with her. Mariachi had accepted Priscilla with a friendly manner that

Paco said he had never seen before. But, that was yesterday, when Paco was close by. The dog would know. Now, with Paco gone, she couldn't be sure. The smart thing to do was stay in the house until Paco returned from San Antonio, to be on the safe side.

The morning was so still and quiet just beyond the white picket fence. It was warm and damp as the sun rose higher on the horizon. Priscilla decided to take the chance. At the worst, the dog would detain her and she'd have to stay put for a couple of hours until Paco returned.

She pushed the screen door, which was obstructed by Mariachi's body. The dog lumbered to his feet in exaggerated slowness, not unduly upset by the disturbance. Priscilla stepped out on the porch. The dog moved close to her, the stiff hairs of his pelt touching her bare calves. He made no move to wrap his body around her leg. So far, so good, she told herself.

Far off, she could hear the cry of a killdeer and an answer from another one coming from somewhere on the other side of the house.

She sipped her coffee, enjoying the peacefulness that she saw all around her. All that had happened the night before had been nagging at Priscilla all morning. There were the things she and Paco had discussed in conversation that she would like to reassess, and there was the mortification of her failed attempt to seduce Paco. She'd felt so rotten all morning that she couldn't bring herself to face up to it and think about it.

For one thing, in her predicament, she couldn't afford thoughts of romance, much less a romantic entanglement. Until she was cleared of any but an unlucky involvement in Ralph Mason's murder, it was much too chancy to lose her head in romance. Whatever might come of it, she could not deny her attraction to Paco Rangel. At some point, she would have to take account of the feelings she had for him.

She'd had the same feelings before, in the chance encounters of her sex life, but always she had suppressed them.

Either the feelings had not been strong enough, or she had been too strong to submit to them. In any case, she had turned them away.

René Chapa had come along at a time when Priscilla was ready to establish an enduring relationship. Up to the day she met René, her life had been a series of accomplishments for which she'd prepared herself and planned. Having taken things in order and having waited until she knew more about herself, René Chapa struck at precisely the moment when she could methodically apply herself to a relationship.

She asked herself, had René been such a bad mistake?

In a perfect world, the world of her mother and her aunts and their mothers before them, René Chapa certainly had been a bad mistake. For one thing, he had not been established in a trade or career. He had not been prepared to take care of a wife and the family that would follow. Even so, a woman of her mother's generation would still take a chance on a young man. The family would be close and would help to make life bearable. If the young man turned out to be a bounder, then you lived with the mistake.

In Priscilla's generation, there were no such mistakes to be made. It was a generation of no-fault relationships. When it became evident that you couldn't live with somebody, you left. It was as simple as that. Say good-bye to one another, and each went a separate way with no hard feelings. For a woman of Priscilla's generation, there was always the next guy and the hope that next time things would work out.

Priscilla recalled the words of her best friend in college, Chavela Prieto. In our time, Chavela said, there are no unions such as the unions of our mothers and fathers. Today, there are only relationships that last only as long as the good times. We are better prepared for our relationships when we recognize that the good times are ephemeral. Nothing is permanent, nor is it meant to be.

A union brought together a man and a woman to cement ties that went back for generations and served as foundations for a continuation of the family line, the *estirpe*. In a relationship, there was only a commonality of mutual and mutable interests. The relationship lasted only as long as the interests held fast and were deemed worthwhile.

People change, of course, and their interests evolve. Different stages of personal evolution sometimes require a different partner. One partner must always bring a set of interests to match those of the other. In some instances, one partner could possibly deny a personal interest in favor of the other. In that case, the relationship lasts only because the personal evolution of the one partner meets little or no resistance from the other. There is a sense of growth and continued commitment, at least for the one partner.

To Priscilla's friend, Chavela Prieto, subordination to the male spelled doom for women. The need for vertical power remained the bane of modern women. It was a male-dominated world in which women were still expected to subordinate their personal evolution in favor of their male partner.

Human beings, she said, were not meant by nature to remain in lifelong pairs. To remain so served only the interests of men. The ideal relationship, predicated on the self-interest of both partners, brought a measure of true equality because women, just as easily as men, could discard the relationship whenever it became unsatisfactory.

The relationship she saw was a modern version of necessary pairings in our primitive ancestors. It was preferable to the union of the previous generation in which a union depended upon women entering marriage as the property of the man they married. Women come to relationships as equals, and thus relationships provided women with the means of choice. They, too, are free to go their way once their personal interests do not coincide with those of their partners.

Priscilla, reflecting on her friend's analysis, did not agree entirely. Her first experience with Jaime, her high school boy friend, and then recently with René Chapa, showed her that there was much truth in what Chavela Prieto said. Of course, she had not begun with the intention that they be relation-ships of the kind Chavela described. Each time, Priscilla had fully intended that it be a union in the tradition of her mother.

After the first betrayal by Jaime, she had spent two years finishing her university studies, dating rarely, and only satis-fying her physical need for sex when it suited her. Her one-man, one-night stance served her well because it precluded, in the most stringent terms possible, emotional complications. Moreover, it gave Priscilla the freedom to pursue her own interests without regard to anyone else's.

She recognized the selfishness in what she did. However, the men she dated, and who spent a few hours or a night with her, were fully aware of her intentions. She gave neither more than she promised nor would she accept more than she gave. Even when the sex was so good that she felt a blistering readi-ness to have a second go at it, she had restrained herself. She held on to the course she'd set for herself. She would not date anyone seriously until she finished her studies and had set-tled in a job leading to career advancement.

The accomplishments she intended to pursue proceeded on schedule. Soon after receiving a major promotion in the company she worked for, she'd met René Chapa. It had not been a propitious beginning. René had been pleasant, interest-ing, but not particularly sexual. She'd brought him to her apartment, having selected him for the evening as part of her one-man, one-night set of experiences.

René Chapa behaved as if she were his conquest.

In the morning, there was not the awkward moment of the past when the man made the overture for a genuine date, or more sex. René made himself at home as if he were meant to do so.

She had planned a day of shopping with a sister coming up from Laredo. They were to meet at one of the malls. René Chapa had been clumsy and inarticulate that first morning, far from the ideal she had set for herself. It had begun with the foolishness where he'd taken a shower first thing upon waking and then had paraded into her bedroom wearing a black silk robe she'd brought for herself. The robe, other than around his protruding middle, was much too large for him. Oblivious to the spectacle he made of himself, he had traipsed into her kitchen to fix awful omelettes.

René turned out to be really sweet, totally without guile. He was a creature who gave freely of himself, demanding as much in return, and maybe a little bit more. His disappointments came when his demands went unanswered or he received less than he expected. In many ways, René was a man-child, innocent and trusting, woefully dependent upon the guidance of an adult.

His attempts at the manipulation of others were really nothing more than a plea for help, an expression of his need to be taken care of. Had René had a genuine cutthroat personality to go along with his ambition, he would have been lethal.

As it was, René was harmless. Many people could not look beyond his bravado and see the defenseless creature that he was. But in her kitchen, on that first morning-after, with him wearing her robe that was too big, making her breakfast, Priscilla saw right through him. She saw the desperate attempt to project a masculinity that he couldn't sustain and that, were he able to, she would have despised.

By the time her sister called from the mall, demanding to know if Priscilla was coming to meet her, she had discerned almost all that there was to know about René Chapa. Lamentably, considering how it worked out, she had not asked him to leave. Priscilla yielded to her need for a sense of order and René Chapa became a fixture in her life.

René and she returned to bed and had laid together, their bodies entangled, until early afternoon. She had made her decision about René, but more importantly, about herself. She had agreed to meet her sister for dinner, and when she returned that evening, René was sitting in his car in the parking lot of the apartment complex where she lived.

"What are you doing here?" Priscilla asked.

"I was waiting for you," René said.

It was end of her one-man, one-night rule.

Priscilla had agreed with her friend, Chavela Prieto, that her dating habits were nothing more than relationships stripped down to bare essentials. There was a fear in Priscilla that she would be abandoned, as she had been when she wholeheartedly expected Jaime to marry her. She wished for a union that would be long-lasting, bear children, and would end in the quiet companionship of old age.

She wanted a continuation of the life that her parents had, and that her older brothers and sisters were on their way to having. With her career settled into what she well knew would be predictable advancements and increased responsibilities, with few surprises in the certainty of her achievements, Priscilla settled in with René Chapa.

They had leased the two-story house to which she could easily contribute half the rent, but which more often than not was beyond René's means. She was on her way to a six-figure salary in five to seven years, according to her schedule. René Chapa would need considerable help and a great deal of good luck if he was ever to maintain a salary to match hers by even one half. She did not hold the disparity in salaries against him. After all, it wasn't his fault that social-service work, noble as it was, paid only half of what a good accountant earned. She was willing to contribute more than her share because what mattered most to her was being with him.

Money was a source of discomfort from the beginning. Almost immediately, Priscilla experienced several instances where René was caught in what he called a cash crunch, and she had to pay for movies and dinner, and once, she loaned him fifty dollars. But when they moved in together, René assured her with his broad and expansive gestures that he would be able to take care of the rent and all their expenses. He was able and willing to provide for both of them. By the time they shared habitation, she knew René well enough to face the fact that she'd be lucky if he paid his half of their agreed-upon division of expenses.

She believed René the first time when he abruptly quit his job. He told Priscilla that he had done so because he already had another job waiting. It was a very lucrative change in jobs. He needed only to wait until the position was authorized. He would go through the sham of interviews, and then he'd be on the payroll. He explained that it was in the bag as he had been a prime mover in the election campaign of the agency head's brother. It was a political payback that he had earned. It was the way to do things in San Antonio. René waited and nothing happened. The story, with changes in agencies and favors called in, was the same over and over again. René simply could not make any headway with his career.

A year or so into the relationship, René had suggested that they share a bank account. They were pooling their money to pay rent each month. Many times, René had been short. At other times, he had asked her for loans of as much as two hundred dollars. Priscilla saw through the ruse without much difficulty. With a shared bank account, René could simply help himself to her money without having to ask. She agreed to it cheerfully, bolstered his ego by telling him that it was a very good idea, especially helpful to her since all she did at work was handle money and numbers and she positively hated to do it in her personal life.

She had rescued the relationship from a potential trouble spot by agreeing to the shared bank account. However, René, who was basically a decent and fair man, could not restrain the ambition that he could not realize. He began to feel shame at having to take her money. He expressed his discomfort in a variety of ways that indicated a mounting sense of personal inferiority in the face of her promotions, salary increases, and bonuses.

While she was comfortable sharing her money with him, he was not happy having to take it. He was the first to reach the breaking point. He disengaged emotionally from her long before she could bring herself to face the inevitable. It reached the stage where the time they spent together was cold, with a rumbling of discontent below the surface as the tension between them increased.

She began to notice it first in their sex life. René had been an avid, but inexperienced lover, who took his pleasure as quickly as he could without regard for his partner. Priscilla taught him to take his time, to take pleasure from the enjoyment of his partner. René improved, delaying his release until he was certain that she had hers.

But towards the end, René returned to his selfish performance where only his own pleasure mattered. When she brought it up for discussion, mindful that she could easily bruise his ego, René spewed forth the resentment he'd been building up.

"I'm not your fucking slave," René said.

She knew it was over between them.

31

Priscilla finished her coffee while she stood before the railing on the porch. The sun began to rise higher on the horizon, bathing the peaceful quiet with a heavy and hot stillness. She enjoyed the silence, which was broken only by the birds twittering gaily and flitting about in the branches of the trees.

Mariachi's bulk lay at her feet throughout the time she took to think about what to do with her feelings for Paco Rangel. She was startled out of her reverie when Mariachi got to his feet, walked a short distance away and shook himself violently. He then returned to lie at her feet.

Priscilla remembered telling Paco that she got horny after drinking a few beers. His reaction had not been quite what she had expected. To her, it was permissible to have sex without more than a passing acquaintance with one's partner. There were times when sex assumed a higher priority than a relationship. Reflecting upon his nervous but polite refusal, she was charmed that Paco had preferred to wait. She liked the idea that he had chosen to build upon the anticipation. She took it to be a denial of themselves until it could be an important, special moment for the both of them. It had been sweet of him to refuse her advances.

She remembered Paco saying that it had been a year or two since he'd been out to the dances. She could interpret the statement as a confession that he hadn't been laid in that long. Maybe he was anxious that after masturbating so much— he must masturbate, she told herself— he would be anxious about his ability to have intercourse. She'd read somewhere that too many hand jobs dull the sensitive areas of a man's penis. Perhaps, too, he was afraid that all the beer he'd had would keep him from getting an erection. She'd dated older men to whom it had happened. In those instances, she had been able to solve the problem with oral sex.

A flush of mortification rushed through her body. She tossed the dregs of the coffee over the porch railing and into the garden. A shudder of embarrassment went through her shoulders as she thought about it.

Paco had been a perfect gentleman throughout the time they drank beer. Not one suggestive comment and not once did he try to put his hands on her. Had she blown it? How had he reacted to the forwardness of the offer of her body? He had gone off to bed quickly, before she could fully assess his reaction. Thinking about it at the moment, she realized she'd drunk too many beers to remember with much clarity. Had there been more to his reaction than his polite and charming refusal?

There were men who cringed when confronted with women who took the initiative in sex—men who found themselves inhibited and intimidated by the usurpation of what they felt was a male prerogative. The demand for sex, for some men, was strictly a male domain.

Or, was there a moral angle to it. Could a religious upbringing prevent him from engaging in illicit sex? No, she told herself, that couldn't be it. The way he spoke and drank his beer, the clearness in his eyes, the sureness of his physical gestures, all of it indicated little fanaticism in anything, much less in his religion.

Priscilla tapped the empty coffee cup against her bare leg. It was madness to go on thinking as she was.

The pleasant surroundings of the farm and the warm possibility of falling in love with Paco Rangel made the matter of Ralph Mason's murder seem distant and not quite so threatening. Her life, nevertheless, had suddenly become too complicated, fraught with a danger whose depth she couldn't gauge. There was nothing she could have done to avert it. A simple afternoon and evening in a strange town had unsettled a life already disastrously off-balance.

There was a chance the police would find Ralph Mason's killer. There was the very slight possibility that she would not be implicated in the murder at all. If she could keep herself out of it altogether, and if the police were any good in their investigation, the killer would surely be found and brought to justice without involving her. Afterward, maybe she could come back to see if Paco was still interested, and maybe the feelings flooding over her would still be as strong.

In the meantime, it would be best if she left Paco Rangel alone. She would have to shut him out of her life. Saying so to herself was one thing. Actually accomplishing it would be another.

It was time to go inside the house. The sun outside had become more intense, signaling the remainder of the hot day to come. She made another tour of the porch before going back inside. The open suitcase on the sofa reminded her to finish dressing. She picked out a pair of faded blue jeans to put on.

She turned on the air conditioner. Using the remote control, she clicked on the television, pressing the scan button on the remote control to skip over the channels. The morning news and talk shows were too tedious to hold her attention. There were reruns of baseball games, home shopping shows, cartoons and exercise programs.

A tap of the remote control landed the television on *American Movie Classics*, just as the opening credits of "Call Northside 777" rolled on the screen. She'd seen it before at a film-society screening at the university. She especially recalled the scene when James Stewart meets the immigrant charwoman who tries to convince him that her son in prison is innocent and was wrongly convicted.

Priscilla recalled the group discussion following the movie. Jimmy Stewart kicks his trademark earnestness into high gear to bring about a measure of justice to people, immigrants, which the rest of society would rather have stay in the shadows until they can fit in as true Americans. Not much has changed, Priscilla thought to herself.

Priscilla had little patience or desire to sit through the movie. The few minutes she spent watching the images flicker in black and white on the large-screen television were a sign of the hangover fatigue. She pressed the 'off' button, turning the television to black, and began to pace around the coffee table.

Across the elongated room, in Paco Rangel's office, above the roll-top desk she found an entire wall of shelving lined with books. Most of the books were paperbacks, but some were hardbacks. He must have bought them during the Book-of-the-Month Club phase he'd mentioned to her.

There was another bookshelf against the outside wall, next to the window ledge. Beside it stood a computer on a narrow stand. It was a mass-market computer with enough power to perform most home and small office computing chores. It was nothing like the powerhouse computer she'd worked with at her last job.

On this bookshelf, she found a length of trade paperbacks by authors she'd never heard of: Jim Thompson, David Goodis, Cornell Woolrich, and Charles Williams. She ran her fingertip along the spines of the books before she stopped at random and picked one of them to sample. It was The Killer Inside Me, by Jim Thompson.

Standing beside the bookcase, she read the first page and then the second. Several pages later, she was still reading. She only stopped reading to pinch the bridge of her nose. She remembered one of the failed promises she'd made to herself upon finishing her studies. She had been so single-minded in the course work that would prepare her for a career that she only read textbooks. Movies were easier to fit in, especially when a discussion followed and the artist-critic types came forward with their comments, explaining the deeper meanings of the films. She could sit passively, absorb the comments, and come away fairly knowledgeable about the movie she'd seen.

Books were another matter. They required an effort from the reader. It was time and effort which she felt would short-change the important studies that led to success in life. It was turning her back on the twelve years of schooling during which reading was stressed. To make up for it, she had made a solemn promise to herself that once she graduated, she'd devote more time to reading. She'd catch up, she told herself, on what she had missed during those years.

Of course, upon beginning her job she'd discovered that the demands of the workplace were even more brutal than the pace she had set for herself in college. Again, she made herself the promise that she would devote a few years to firmly establishing her career and then she would find the time for entertainment, hobbies, and self-improvement. Reading would be at the top of the list. She had yet to begin a steady regimen of reading, as she had promised herself.

She continued reading Thompson's book, inching over until the wooden swivel chair in front of the desk was behind her, and she sat.

After a little more than an hour, she'd read nearly half the book. Her eyes became tired. Her hangover headache had returned, but she had been oblivious to it as she read. She felt thirsty.

She went into the bathroom and took two more aspirins. In the kitchen, she poured herself another glass of orange juice, which she brought back into the parlor, setting it on the glass-top coffee table. She lay on the sofa, positioning herself to get the best sunlight coming in through the window, and she went on reading. An hour later, she finished the book. She sat up on the sofa, stunned at the plot developments and at the hard, cold voice of the killer who narrated the story.

She took the book into Paco Rangel's office and slipped it back into the slot left gaping when she'd taken it out. She sat down at the roll-top desk and leaned back in the fat wooden swivel chair. She took a good look at the slots, cubby holes, and designs on the roll-top desk. This is not unpainted furniture, she told herself. The roll-top desk was old and worn and, from its well-cared-for appearance, she guessed that Paco had bought it in its restored condition. Everything on the desk seemed to have a conscious arrangement. It was the part of Paco Rangel that was neat.

He had shot glasses full of paper clips and fasteners. A taller bar glass, one for old fashioneds, was full of pencils. Neatly aligned parallel to each other were a hole puncher, a stapler, a tape dispenser, and an adding machine. In a dark corner was a stack of colored note paper and several stick'em note pads. Next to them was a metal eyeglass case with the silver earpieces visible.

In the slots on the left-hand side of the desk she saw a stack of bills and invoices. In another, below it, she found his receivables, bills where he scribbled dates on which to send second overdue notices.

Priscilla Arrabal became excited. As she looked at the clipped bundles of bills, invoices, and receipts, she saw a way to help Paco in return for his helping her. From the look of things, he did his own bookkeeping, all of it by hand. She opened drawers along the sides of the desk and saw files, all with neat, handwritten labels. As the arrangement of items on the desk suggested, Paco was organized and thorough.

With her mind racing, she flipped the "on" switch of the computer, but nothing happened. She looked closer and saw that she had in fact flipped it off. Below, on the floor, was a power strip and surge suppressor. With the tip of her toe, she tapped the "on" switch of the power strip and the computer began to roll and grind.

In the program directory she found a checkbook program which computer manufacturers included as part of the software package pre-loaded on their machines. She quickly debated the invasion of privacy as she contemplated loading up the checkbook program. She really shouldn't. At least, not without his knowledge and permission.

But, she was too excited to wait for Paco to come back from San Antonio. If she was going to help organize his bookkeeping, which is what she planned to do, she'd have to know if he'd already made some use of the program. If so, she'd have to determine how he'd been using it. In all probability, and this she had learned from her clients, Paco would have to unlearn what he already knew and learn the proper way to use the program. It was the only way to get him to handle all of his financial transactions himself, efficiently and accurately.

She clicked on the checkbook icon and it flashed a setup screen, which told her the program had never been used. Good, she told herself, I can start him from scratch. There wouldn't be any nasty, bad habits to unlearn. Priscilla smiled, satisfied with herself that she would give Paco some high-powered accounting help.

She would discuss it with him on his return from delivering his vegetables. She didn't want to pry into his business affairs without his permission. It would be a small thing for her to set up his books. After that she would teach him what he needed to know. She didn't think it would take more than a day to get things organized in the computer, and maybe another day to train Paco in how to input and maintain the data. It would be a productive way to keep herself occupied.

Back in the parlor, she turned on the radio and got a station from Austin that played country music. Hank Williams,

Jr., one of her favorites, belted out a song. She walked up to the window, feeling the cold rush of air from the air conditioning. She gazed outside, her arms crossed over her chest.

She was engrossed in her thoughts so much that she did not hear Paco come in. He walked in the door silently, almost stealthily. He was already halfway across the parlor, when she jumped with a start, sensing his presence.

Paco was on his way to the kitchen, several plastic grocery store bags dangling from his arms.

32

It took me a little longer in town than I expected," Paco Rangel said, going into the kitchen. "And, then I had to stop at the grocery store. But here I am. When did you get up? Been keeping yourself busy?"

Following him, Priscilla said, "I tried to watch your television for a little bit. It was an old movie I saw in college, but I couldn't concentrate on it. Too hung over, or too worried about my troubles, I guess. Besides, every time I start to watch a movie on television, I fall asleep. I don't feel well when I sleep too much. I picked up one of your books. It had an interesting title and I wanted to read through the first page and I ended up reading the whole thing. It wasn't too long. I finished it a few minutes ago."

"Good, you have been busy," Paco said. He placed the white plastic bags on the counter. "I got some extra groceries, since you'll be here a few days. I didn't know what you like to eat."

"I can't think of anything special that I like to eat," she replied.

"Well, I was in the store, trying to figure out what to get," Paco said, putting the groceries away. "This is the idea I came up with. I sometimes get a craving for a certain dish and I begin to get things together to make it, and it occurs to me that it's a dish for two people. I look at everything and I say, this is no good for one person."

"Like the shrimp you fixed last night?"

"Yeah, that's right. I would've fixed that dish and sat by myself to eat it. It wouldn't have tasted the same," he said. "The missing ingredient would be someone to eat with."

"That's very sweet of you to say something like that, Paco," Priscilla said. "I don't think I've ever looked at food that way, that food tastes better when you eat with someone else."

Paco became embarrassed. "Yeah, well, maybe I've been cooped up in this place for too long. I'm thinking too damn much."

"I was going to make lunch for you," she said, to change the subject, "but I didn't know when you'd be back. I didn't want it to get cold."

"Help yourself," he said.

He had finished with putting the groceries away. He took a deep breath, stood to one side of the counter. "You want to fix lunch, go ahead and make lunch."

"I'll get started then," Priscilla said, getting up from the table.

"If you don't mind, I'll just sit here and watch," said Paco. "I've been on the run since six this morning. I'm a little dogged."

"Aren't you hung over?" she asked.

"I don't get hangovers, at least not to where I pay attention to them. Can't afford to. Mostly, I don't drink that much. Last night was an exception."

"There are times when I drink too much, too often," she said, the tip of her forefinger touching her chin.

"Anything you need to fix lunch, ask me," Paco said. "What are you going to make, anyway?"

"I thought I'd make some crispy tacos?"

"Love'm," he said. "You'll want some hamburger. Good thing I thought to buy some this morning. I didn't think to buy taco shells."

"That's all right," she said. "It's been years, but I think I can fry the shells myself."

"Fry them yourself!" he said, surprise in his voice. "Did you learn to cook from your mother?"

"I wouldn't say that," said Priscilla, opening the refrigerator. "I mean, you can't help but learn a few things growing up, passing through your mother's kitchen. Ever since I was a little girl, I decided I would not be a housewife, like my mother. It was fun to be with my mother in the kitchen, but I never took too seriously what she did in there. I wanted to be a doctor or a lawyer, just like my brothers said they were going to be."

"And, did you?" asked Paco. "Did you become a doctor or a lawyer?"

"No, I didn't, and neither did my brothers," Priscilla said, smiling.

She held a package of hamburger in her hand. She found a frying pan beneath the counter and put it on the stove. When the fire under the pan got going, she unwrapped the package to slide the meat from the Styrofoam tray onto the frying pan. She used a wooden spoon, which she took from a coffee-mug container beside the stove, to break up the slab of meat.

"What did you study in college, if you didn't become a doctor or a lawyer?"

"Accounting. I decided to become an accountant."

"Accounting? Isn't that a boring job?"

"No, not at all," said Priscilla. "You have these companies that create an image, both for the public and for themselves. You know, a fancy office, nice furniture, men and women all dressed up moving quietly and efficiently all over the place. If you're a client, the image of confidence and success is overwhelming."

"It's all show, no substance?"

"Not exactly. I go in to audit their books. This is where you get to see behind the image. I can actually see the company as it really is. You can see what the company does, how it works. You can see whether it's strong or weak, and not just in terms of the money. The money tells a lot about the personality of the people who spend it. You'd be surprised about accounting. Sometimes it's pretty exciting."

While the hamburger turned to a gray color in the pan, Priscilla chopped some onion, garlic, and green pepper, which she tossed into the skillet. She shook cumin, black pepper, and oregano into the mixture.

In another pan, she began to fry the corn tortillas, folding them in half with a pair of tongs to make taco shells. Finally, she shredded lettuce and cheese, and chopped tomato. She poured a commercial picante sauce into a small bowl, and the meal was ready.

Paco brought two Dr. Peppers from the refrigerator.

"That was quick," said Paco Rangel, rubbing his hands together.

They ate hurriedly, without speaking, breaking the silence only to laugh when Priscilla bit into a crispy taco shell and it disintegrated, falling through her fingers onto the plate.

When they were finished eating, Paco cleared the dishes from the table and scraped what they didn't eat onto a plate to give to Mariachi later. He placed the dishes in the sink to wash later. He returned to the table to finish drinking his Dr. Pepper.

"I'll do the dishes in a minute," he said, leaning forward on the table. He looked as if he were trying to bring up a subject he was uncomfortable with.

"Listen, about last night," he said.

Before he could say more, she stopped him, raising a hand, palm toward him, saying "You don't have to say anything," she said. "It was my fault. I drank too much. I should've behaved better."

"The loneliness still comes back," he said softly, staring at the top of the table. "I don't know if I can explain it very well. I know all about sex and how it can be physical and it doesn't have to mean more than that. I don't know if that's what you had in mind last night."

"It's my liberated city ways," she said. "Maybe I shouldn't have come on so strong."

"We hardly know each other," said Paco Rangel. "I've been through the one-night-stand business before, the casual sex. I'm interested in something that will last, Priscilla. What I wish for most of all is for someone to live with me and share my life. What I'm thinking is that you can spend a few days here and see if you'll get to like it. Maybe then you'll decide that it's worth it to stay longer."

"My life is a mess of shit right now, Paco," she said, truthfully. She cautioned him, "I wouldn't want you to get the wrong idea about me."

"That's what I'm getting at," Paco said. "Right now, I don't have any idea of what all of this means. I need some time. We both need some time."

"Listen, Paco," she said earnestly, leaning over to get closer to him. She wanted to stay as close to the truth as possible. But, she couldn't bring herself to tell him everything. Not yet. "I'm not going to deny my attraction to you. Last night, it was more than just something physical. But, we've got to be careful."

"How so?"

"You've got a nice little setup here. You've got your own farm, a nice little business going. And, you're probably right, you need somebody to share it with. I'm not sure I can be the one you need to share it with. Not right now at least. There's too much going on in my life just now. I don't understand all of it yet. Until I do, there's the chance that I'll make a decision that isn't right. Not right for me or you. I don't want either of us to get hurt."

"Don't be so quick to shut me off," he said, a look of wonder on his face. "Why don't we give it some time? Then, we'll see what develops."

"Listen to what I'm saying," she said, an edge to her voice. It was not going the way she had intended. She would have to be blunt in holding him at a distance. "It isn't a matter of anything developing between us. I don't have very good luck with men. That's the truth. At least, it's been true so far. Maybe it's the men who are attracted to me, or maybe I attract a certain kind of man that brings out someone in me who's a regular shit. I don't know. In any case, much as I'd like nothing better, I don't see anything good coming out of this. Not right now, and not with the way things stand. I have to settle some things in my life first."

"If this place is too remote for you, we could always live in town, you know," he said. "I mean, don't let this place put you off. White Leg is not far away. It's small, but it's got all the conveniences."

"Oh, my God, you're already rearranging your life for me, Paco! That's what I mean! Don't!"

"I'm sorry," he said. "Sometimes being here gets to be too much for me. I get so maybe I don't know what I'm saying. Just forget it!"

Priscilla remained silent. There was a look of pain in Paco Rangel's face.

"I'm sorry," he said, again.

Priscilla stood up, pushing the chair backwards with the back of her knees. She strode forward and around the table, coming up behind him. She lowered her body, placing her arms around his chest. She kissed the back of his neck, then kissed him again a little higher up behind his ear.

"Come on, let's get in the bedroom," she spoke into his ear.

"I think there should be some feelings between us before we . . . "

"There are feelings, Paco," she said. "You just now showed them to me. Promise me that you'll hold on to those feelings for the time being. I have some issues I have to resolve. I don't want to see you get hurt."

33

In the bedroom, standing beside his king-size bed, Priscilla took the strap of his belt and unhooked it from the large rodeo buckle. She undid the top button of his Levi's jeans, pulled down on the zipper. She yanked the bottom of his T-shirt, out of his pants. Her arms went around his neck and she touched her forehead to his for a moment. Paco held his arms loose at his sides.

Priscilla raised her head to look into his eyes as she ran her hands up the sides of his ribcage. The T-shirt became bunched at his upper chest. She slipped her hands into it and brought them out through the neck opening, clasping his face, rising on tiptoe to kiss him on the mouth. Paco could not hide his willingness.

The reluctance of the night before was gone.

They kissed for a long moment. She slid her hands along his back, thrusting them into his underwear, fanning her fingers, squeezing first one buttock and then the other. A moan erupted from inside Paco's chest and he wrapped his arms around her waist. She began to slide his shorts and jeans down his thighs. They dropped as far as his knees, where they bunched up.

His member was shriveled and tiny, hanging loosely over his wrinkled testicles. Priscilla sank to her knees, bringing her face to his crotch, pressing her closed mouth against him. His member began to swell with blood.

It took but a minute for Paco's penis to harden and point straight up toward the ceiling. Priscilla parted her lips and took him inside her mouth. She felt it throb, and Paco thrust forward, pushing against her palate. His breathing came in short quick pants, beginning the unmistakable throes of an orgasm.

Quickly, Priscilla took her thumb and forefinger and wrapped them around the base of his penis, squeezing tightly. The head of his dick swelled with blood, turning purple. Paco groaned, jackknifing his body, grabbing the top of her head, groaning as if he'd been punched in the stomach. Priscilla tightened the ring she made of her thumb and forefinger, squeezing harder at the base of Paco's penis.

"Lie down on the bed," she said.

Paco did as bidden. Priscilla pulled off his boots and socks, and then his shorts and Levi's. She sat on the edge of the bed, running her hands, fingers outspread, along his thighs. She stopped to pull her T-shirt over her head, letting it drop to the floor at her feet. Her large breasts were starkly white, alabaster mounds around the dark circles of her nipples. She turned sideways to grab each of Paco's heels and pulled his legs apart.

She climbed on the bed, on her hands and knees. She crawled forward, dropping her large breasts over Paco's groin. Priscilla dropped down, mashing her breasts against him, while she brought her hands up to his chest to pinch his nipples. She began to take little bites of the soft skin on his belly, just below his belly button.

When Paco began to hump urgently, grinding himself against her soft breasts, Priscilla raised up on her hands, breaking the contact of their bodies. She jumped off the bed to

remove her jeans. When she was completely naked, she got
back on the bed, straddling him, her body over his lower body.

Paco could feel the wetness of her sex pressing down over
his throbbing member. Priscilla raised herself up a little, and
then pressed down again. Paco reached his hand between
them to guide his member in, but she pulled his arm away.
She repeated the up-and-down movement in rhythmic cycles
without taking him inside.

All the while, she gazed into his face, as if studying its
shape, texture, contours.

There was something familiar about Paco's face, but she
couldn't place it.

She began to kiss his chest, nibbling on his nipples, making one long continuous kiss over his chest, up to his neck, on
the underside of his chin, over the chin, and finally she got to
his lips, forcing his mouth open with her tongue.

Paco grabbed Priscilla's face in an urgent, rough manner
that startled Priscilla because of its suddenness. He shoved
his tongue into her mouth, kissing her hard, gripping her neck
tightly with his arms. She returned the kiss with equal
urgency, despite the hurt from his arms. She shook her head
loose from the grip of his arms and raised her chest until only
her nipples made contact with his body.

She raised her bottom, bringing it forward until the tip of
his penis was at the center of her wetness. She swivelled her
body over him until the head of his penis found her opening.
She then slid downward, taking in all of it. Paco sighed and
trembled, the sound coming from deep inside his chest cavity,
ending in a whine of pain and anticipation.

She could hear Paco's heart racing under her as he thrust
upward to meet the downward pressure of her body. He thrust
to meet her movements in perfect rhythm. His mounting
desire outpaced hers, overtaking his efforts to control himself.
He was unable to wait for Priscilla, desperate though he was
to come in a mutual orgasm.

Suddenly, as he began to vibrate with an orgasm beyond his control, Paco's movements became more intense. Her inside muscles began to throb in practiced moves, grasping him tightly as he shoved himself into her.

"It's okay," she purred over him, "come. Don't hold it in. I want you to come."

"I love you, Priscilla," he said in a weak, little boy's voice.

"Come, Paco, come in me," she whispered hoarsely into his ear.

"I want so much more for us," he whispered in anguish.

"Come," she repeated.

Paco was on a downward spiral, unable to contain himself, thrusting violently. Priscilla grasped his hips, trying to hurry her own orgasm in the vain hope of catching up with him. There was nothing Paco could do to delay the flow of himself that rushed from his body. The more Priscilla tried to speed her orgasm, the more it retreated.

He groaned loudly in release. His hips under her body moved furiously up and down, as if he were bouncing her on his lap. Suddenly, he held her tightly, suspended in the air, a grimace on his face. After a long moment, he relaxed his hold. He shuddered a few more times in the last spasms to complete his release. Paco gasped loudly and erratically. Soon enough, the interval of his breathing increased as it was restored to normal.

When he was finished, he lifted one of his hips and Priscilla rolled over to lie beside him. Paco turned on his side, lifted himself up on an elbow. He first kissed her mouth, and then he kissed her nipples. Priscilla began to rub her hands over his back. When she rubbed along his spine, close to his buttocks, she felt his body tremble.

She felt a draft of cool air wafting in from the air conditioner. It brushed over her breasts and her belly, producing a slight chill on the film of sweat that covered her. Priscilla stared straight up at the ceiling. Beside her, Paco breathed deeply, but not as labored as before.

Priscilla began to draw circles at the edges of her nipples. In a moment, the fire between her legs, momentarily dampened, was rekindled. She squeezed her breasts, pinching her nipples, her pelvis thrusting upward. She brought her thighs close together.

She took Paco's hand and placed it on her wet, glistening pubic hair.

"I thought you came," he said.

"A little bitty one," she lied. "I have several of those before I get the big one."

His fingers moved between her legs, into the slime of his own release and the sex juices she excreted.

"Will this help?" he asked.

"Hmmmm!" she purred.

"I have a better idea," he said, rolling over her.

Priscilla reached between them and took his limp dick in her hands. She rubbed her clitoris with the head of it until she couldn't wait any longer. It took some effort, but she managed to get it inside, and Paco thrust forward to shove the rest of it in.

34

Orthal Mason regained consciousness lying on the thin mattress in the cell next to Joe Blue's jail-cell office. He shook his head several times before he sat up on the bunk. Joe Blue sat behind his desk, hunched over a report he'd received. Orthal Mason glared at Joe Blue through the bars that separated them.

Orthal Mason massaged his jaw, trying to rid it of the soreness left by the sheriff's fist. On his head, his white hair sprouted in thick irregular tufts from his scalp. His long angular face was bloodless, his skin stretched tightly over the bones, giving Orthal Mason a translucent, cadaverous look. His face was filled with an anger that took a lifetime to build. His thin lips were pressed together into a hairline between his chin and nose.

Orthal Mason stood up on his feet, swaying a little from side to side, holding on to his jaw.

"Why'd that son of a bitch Jim Woodrow Willow hit me for?" he growled. "He didn't have no call to do that!"

"You'll have to ask him, Mr. Mason," said Joe Blue, bent over his desk, taking notes on a legal pad as he read the report. "He's gone home for the day, but you'll see him again."

"I'm asking you, Mexican!" said Orthal Mason. "You answer me when I talk to you!"

"Mr. Mason, let me tell you something," said Joe Blue, turning to face the old man, a stern expression on his face. "We are going to get along a lot better if you just watch your mouth. It takes a lot to piss me off. The fact is, right now you distract me when you run off at the mouth."

"Just cause you're a deputy and you carry a gun don't make you more than the Mexican you are," said Orthal Mason, clearing his throat and spitting over his shoulder. "There was a time when Mexicans knew their place in this county."

"Have it your way," said Joe Blue, picking up the telephone. He dialed the number at the front desk. There was a pause before he spoke.

"Brita Mae, send Hank in here to my office," Joe Blue said, replacing the receiver.

Hank Solís came into Joe Blue's jail-cell office.

"Hank, Mr. Mason over there seems to think Mexicans are a lower form of human life than other people. I think he means himself, mostly," Joe Blue said, leaning back in his chair. "I wonder if you might tell Mr. Mason how it was that you joined the Marine Corps and how it was that you were decorated with a Silver Star."

Hank Solís hooked his thumbs into his gun belt and approached the bars separating the two jail cells. He looked into Orthal Mason's eyes, his own eyes hard and narrow. His lip on the right side of his mouth curled up in a sneer.

"When I look at people like Orthal Mason, all I see is shit yellow," said Hank Solís. "Sorry, Joe. I don't have anything to prove to a redneck peckerwood like Orthal Mason!"

"You'd best be careful how you talk to me, Mexican!" said Orthal Mason, stepping back from the bars.

"You're twenty years behind the times, you sick stupid old man," said Hank Solís, shaking his head in disgust. "There's more respect between people than there used to be. Joe, you think I should go in there and teach this old fool some respect? Apparently, he's so far behind the times he needs to learn a few things."

"It wouldn't do any good, Hank. Not with somebody like him," said Joe Blue, his face clear and serene. "Besides, it would be a case of police brutality."

"Not if there's nobody to see it," said Hank Solís. "Who do you think is going to believe anything this old fool says? I'd say, just from looking at the son of a bitch, he's gone loco, Joe. Look at him! I've seen it before. He's ready to start banging his head on the walls of that cell in there. From the looks of him, I predict that he is so unstable and upset that he'll break his fucking arm in there. In fact, I can just about guarantee that a man in his condition will very likely end up with a broken arm. If he had any fucking teeth, he'd probably lose some of them, too!"

"You two are goddamn crazy," said Orthal Mason. "You wouldn't dare lay a hand on me."

Joe Blue and Hank Solís began to laugh. The brawny deputy, still grinning, walked out of the jail-cell office and went up the hall to the main reception area.

Orthal Mason stepped back and sat on the thin mattress covering an iron bunk. His fear subsided and his face turned petulant.

"Sons of bitches! I only came in here to find out about my boy's killing," he said. "You got no call to treat a white man like this. I want to know what you're doing about finding my boy's killer."

"We're investigating, Mr. Mason," said Joe Blue, returning to his notes on the yellow legal pad.

"Well, let's hear it," said Orthal Mason.

"Hear what?"

"I want to know everything you got so far," the old man said. "I got a right to know."

"All I can tell you is we're investigating, Mr. Mason."

"The hell you say. You're going to do better than that. Get that son of a bitch Jim Woodrow in here! We'll see if you're gonna give me that information or not!"

"Mr. Mason, what I want you to do is come out of that cell. It's not locked. Go through this door in front of me, and head on out the passageway until you get to the main office. There's a door up the steps that'll get you outside into the fresh air. Once you get your scrawny ass outside, you mind what I say and you go on home."

"Hell, I can drive right up to Jim Woodrow's house myself, ask the son of a bitch to his face!" Orthal Mason said.

"Mr. Mason, if you don't follow my instructions, I will arrest you for trespassing," said Joe Blue calmly, without looking up from his notes. "Then, I'll put you back in that cell and this time I will lock it."

"I've been in jail before."

"You are trying my patience."

"You'd like it just fine to lock up a white man, wouldn't you?"

"It's all the same to me, Mr. Mason," said Joe Blue, turning to look at his adversary. "The way I figure it, you ain't smart enough to piss me off. You can talk all you want about what you want to do, that doesn't interest me. You do something, and that something is against the law, then you will have my interest."

"Listen, boy, be reasonable," said Orthal Mason, with less malice in his voice. "We're after the same thing here, you and me. I want my boy's killer, and I want him a lot more than you do. Let me have what information you got. Tell me who you suspect. I can make, me and my boys can, that is, we can make a lot more headway with somebody that don't want to talk. The way I see it, we can help each other out. Me and my boys get to the son of a bitch who did this first, and I can save the county time and money bringing him to trial. You won't have to feed the son of a bitch till he gets the needle up in Huntsville."

"Sheriff Jim Woodrow wouldn't want any vigilante justice in his county. He is peculiar about that," said Joe Blue, a kinder tone coming into his voice. "Best thing, Mr. Mason, you let us handle it. We'll find who did it, and you'll get your justice."

"I believe justice will be done, boy," said Orthal Mason, "but not by you and not by no court. We Masons take care of our own. There ain't gonna be no trial, I'll tell you that."

35

Orthal Mason opened the jail cell and moved on wobbly feet past Joe Blue, who still sat behind his desk. He walked through the heavy metal door and along the passageway. He passed by Hank Solís coming in the opposite direction. Hank grinned at Orthal Mason.

"You got something to say about Mexicans, Orthal?" Hank Solís prodded him.

Orthal Mason ignored the deputy and kept walking.

"I didn't think you did," said Hank Solís.

In Joe Blue's jail-cell office, Hank Solís said, "We got an ID on the prints from those beer cans, Joe.

He set a massive haunch on the edge of Joe Blue's desk.

"Priscilla Arrabal, Certified Public Accountant," said Joe Blue, reading the sheet that Hank Solís had placed in his hand. "We got the prints from the state licensing outfit, otherwise, she's never been in trouble. Last known address, it says there, is in San Antonio. She's clean as a whistle."

"What do you make of it, Joe?" asked Hank Solís.

"It's more or less what I expected. Young woman gets off the bus, has a few too many beers, gets picked up by one of our citizens. He gets shot, she runs. Takes his pickup to make her escape."

"Is she the shooter, you think? Remember that case in Florida, those two women who picked up men in bars, and then shot them."

"You mean, could this be a serial killer? I don't think so."

"What about if Ralph Mason got a little rough on her? She decides that teasing is better than going through with giving it up all the way. Ralph won't take no for an answer. And, she just happens to have one of those ladies' small-caliber pistols in her purse?"

"Not much likelihood that she did, Hank," said Joe Blue. "If we put together what we found in that motel room, she'd have to go outside and shoot him through the window. Why not just shoot him inside the room where they were together? Besides, there was no sign of a struggle."

"Let's just say she got cold-blooded about it. She wants to make it look like a third party was involved. Runs outside so she can shoot him, throw us off the track."

"Maybe, Hank, but still not likely. Wouldn't Ralph have run after her if she went out of the room? Is he going to stay in the room with his back to the window?"

"Okay, Joe, she didn't shoot him," said Hank Solís. "If she was just in the room when the shot was fired, why'd she run? That's the part I can't figure out. She could just tell the truth and she's in the clear."

"She got scared. It's a town she doesn't know. There's a body in the room. Local boy. Maybe she figured we'd arrest her because she's closest to the body. Ready-made suspect. Why look for somebody else?"

"Or, she got a good look at the shooter," said Hank Solís. "Figures he'll come back for her."

"She could have, at that. It's a real possibility, Hank," said Joe Blue. "That's one of the main reasons I want us to get our hands on her. I think there's a good chance she might know something."

"I still don't get why she ran, Joe," Hank Solís said. "Why? It just don't figure to me."

"I don't know. My guess is, she panicked," Joe Blue said. "She saw Ralph Mason fall dead on the bed and she went into shock, or something. Let's say she's a normal young woman, out to have a good time. A thing like this happens. No telling what she's liable to do."

"Bottom line, you don't think she's involved in the murder at all," said Hank Solís. "She's just a witness."

"That's the way I see it where she's concerned. Somebody wanted Ralph Mason dead," said Joe Blue. "Let's check into Ralph Mason; let's find out what we can about him. I think that's where our answer lies."

36

"I got something from Georgene about Ralph Mason. It's probably nothing more than gossip," said Joe Blue. "Anyhow, I think I'll check it out."

"It's probably the same rumor I heard." Hank Solís said.

"Yeah, I'm sure it is," Joe Blue said. "Ralph was messing around with Victor Richards' wife."

"That's an old rumor, Joe," said Hank Solís. "The way that happened, I believe Myra Richards got a powerful itch and went out looking for somebody to scratch it. Ralph Mason was one, but there were some others, too. She's back to home now, not straying anymore. Victor's forgiven her and from what I hear, they're trying to make a go of it. Start over brand new. No hard feelings."

"How long ago did you hear this?"

"I don't know. Not long. Weeks, maybe more."

Joe Blue gave Hank Solís a confused look.

"So you've got another rumor that you heard. What is it?"

"I hear Ralph Mason was moving a little dope," said Hank Solís.

"Here in town?"

"Don't know," said Hank. "I haven't been able to get my hands on anything solid. We haven't caught anyone with any of it that we might trace back to him. So far, people just say he was moving it, as if it's common knowledge. If he was moving it in town, it couldn't be much. As I said, I haven't been able to connect him with it."

"How long have you known about this?"

"A year, maybe."

"What do you make of it?"

"Well, Joe, when I heard about it, first thing I asked myself is, where's he getting the stuff?"

"You think he was growing it?"

"No, sir, not on you life," Hank snorted. "None of them Masons ever farmed worth a shit. They know how to work hard when they have to, but they just can't pay attention to what crops need. Not enough to farm, anyway They'd rather let somebody else worry about what's in the ground coming up."

"They could just plant the stuff. It grows wild, doesn't it? They wouldn't have to care for it much. All they'd have to do is go harvest."

"I thought about that, too, Joe. Orthal Mason's got three of his boys still living with him. Two of them go to high school. Third one's not married yet, so he lives in the house with him, too. Ralph stayed with his brother, McCoy, who's married and lives out on the road to the interstate. There's three more of Orthal's boys scattered all over the county. None of them live in town. What I did, I got together with Carter Vinson. Using the cover of him being the game warden, we went looking for poachers."

"Poachers?"

"Yeah, poachers. It was funny as hell," Hank said, laughing. "We went on that place that Orthal rents. He comes out and says, 'What the hell you doing on my place?' Carter Vinson tells him we're looking for poachers and we have permission from the owner to take a look on the property. Ol' Orthal don't like it one bit. He says he don't care who gave permission, nobody's trespassing on his place. That's when I stepped forward and I looked Orthal Mason right in the eye and told Carter Vinson that he could look all he wanted and I'd make sure nobody bothered him."

Joe Blue grinned. "No wonder Orthal loves you so much."

"Anyway, that's how Orthal Mason feeds that brood of his. They just go out and shoot deer any time they want some red meat. We found plenty of evidence of it. Hell, they don't even bother to bury the hides and heads."

"I never could figure out," said Joe Blue, "if those Masons are dumb, or if they have such a profound disrespect for the law that they just don't give a shit."

"Probably a little of both," said Hank Solís. "We were after something else, though. The upshot of it is that we didn't find anything. We looked everywhere that a marijuana patch could be hidden on that place. Then, after Orthal Mason's place, we went out to pay a visit on the places where the rest of his brood lives. Nothing there, either."

"So, if the rumors are true, Ralph Mason was importing it from somewhere?"

"No, not necessarily," said Hank, scratching the back of his head. "The way I heard the rumors, it sounds like Ralph Mason was in on a delivery system of some kind. He was hauling pretty large shipments. I mean large, like a felony's worth of large. There would have to be somebody else behind it. I'm pretty sure of that. Else, I'd've caught the son of a bitch. As it stands, I can't prove any of it, though."

"You have any ideas?"

"You know Porter Labelle?" asked Hank, shifting his weight as something else came to mind.

"Chicken-farmer fella, corporate type? Moved here from Arkansas a few years ago?"

"That's the one. They say he's a personal friend of Bill Clinton."

"I've never met him. I've seen him in town, though. I know him by sight."

"He's got a bunch of chicken farms all over the place. He's also gone into the range-fed chicken business. Calls them 'Ranger Chick.' Lots of people with more money than brains think you let chickens run loose and you got yourself a better-tasting chicken. The exercise the chickens get is supposed to make them taste better."

"I heard about that operations he runs."

"Ol' Porter Labelle's figured out how to do it, too. He runs it top to bottom. He's got his own egg hatchery on the place. He's got three, four places where he runs thousands of chickens out on the loose. He's also got a packing-house operation going. Dresses the chickens right on the place. He can't freeze them, because then nobody'll buy them, so he packs them in cardboard boxes filled with ice. Right now, with the size of his operation, he's got about six refrigerator trucks, bobcats, to make his deliveries. They're ready and rolling every morning."

"I knew all that," said Joe Blue. "Maybe not as thorough as you know it, Hank, but I knew it."

"Let me go about telling you in my own way, Joe," said Hank Solís. "You're kind of testy at the end of the day. I'm almost done, anyhow."

"Go on, Hank. I'm sorry," said Joe Blue.

"Four of those refrigerated bobcats go to San Antonio and Houston every day of the week. Monday and Thursday, there's one bobcat goes to Austin and another goes to Corpus Christi. Rest of the week, they go to San Antonio and Houston, too."

"Go on, I'm getting the picture," said Joe Blue.

"I figure there's dope moving on those bobcat trucks," said Hank Solís. "What do you think of that?"

"You think a friend of the President of the United States is mixed up in drug trafficking?"

"No, I didn't say that, Joe," said Hank Solís, tossing back his straw cowboy hat. "I mean, Porter Labelle's got big money in that chicken operation of his. It ain't all his money, neither.

He's got backing from some investors all over the country. You wouldn't think he'd put all that in danger just to run a few bales of marijuana."

"Where does that leave us? I mean, where does Porter Labelle come in on this?"

"He doesn't. It's the drivers," Hank Solís said. "They're the key to it."

"Ralph Mason was driving one of those delivery trucks?"

"He most certainly was, Joe," said Hank Solís. "Most times, he made deliveries to Houston. He'd make a run to San Antonio or one of the other cities when a driver didn't show up for his run."

"How do you know all this?"

"I talked to some of the people who work out on Porter Labelle's chicken ranches, not the drivers. I didn't get too deep into it because I was just having a beer with them, you know. Shooting the shit, listening while they unloaded themselves of their job troubles. It pays to be a good listener."

"So, you think Ralph Mason was delivering marijuana, using Porter Labelle's delivery trucks?

"I'd almost bet on it. But, there's one more thing, Joe."

"Tell me."

"About a month ago, Ralph Mason quit driving a truck for Porter Labelle. Johnny Watkins told me he's been hanging out at the Ligon Wells Saloon, spreading a lot of cash around, just like he was still working. What I'm asking myself is where does he get all that money? I was thinking of looking into it when Ralph Mason got shot."

"Let's say he saved up his money, just in case he finds himself out of work."

"You and me might do that, since we're law-abiding citizens when we're not out enforcing the law. But not them Masons. According to the Ligon Wells gang, the boys that make a home there every day, Ralph bragged to them that he'd got himself into something that don't take up too much of his time, pays him plenty of money. They say he's been buying plenty of rounds for the house."

"If he's not driving the trucks, either for wages or for delivering the dope, where's the money coming from?"

"Hard to say," said Hank Solís.

"But, you don't think the rest of the Mason clan is in on it?"

"I wouldn't swear to it. You never know with them Masons. Just when you'd say they don't know anything about it, they're in it up to their necks. So, I couldn't tell you, either way."

"Suppose they're not involved, but Ralph has a few beers and starts to brag to his brothers..." said Joe Blue.

"Now, there's a definite possibility," said Hank Solís.

"You think he'd tell his brothers a little more about his business than he would the gang at the Ligon Wells?"

"You might have something there, Joe. Although, I don't think any of those Mason boys'll talk. They've been raised by their pappy to keep their mouths shut around the law."

Joe Blue touched the tip of his nose.

"You say you and Carter Vinson found evidence of those Mason boys taking deer out of season?"

"Yeah, we did," Hank Solís said, narrowing his eyes while he looked at Joe Blue. "Carter said all they probably eat most times is grease gravy and biscuits. So, what if they shoot a deer every now and then. They need the protein."

"You know the two boys that Orthal Mason's got in high school?"

"Sure," said Hank Solís. "I know them boys. I went to high school with their mother. I never could figure out what got into her to marry Orthal Mason, a man twice her age. She was always a decent sort, Joe. Maybe with her influence those boys haven't grown up all Mason. There might just be a spark of good in them."

"Pick those boys up when school lets out, Hank," said Joe Blue. "I want to put a little scare into them. I'm going to tell them there's a fine for poaching and if they can't pay the fine, they have to serve time in jail. See what shakes out."

37

Priscilla slid out of bed quietly, so as to not disturb
Paco, who slept soundly. Her clothes were on the
floor beside the bed. She put on her T-shirt and
underpants and went to wash her face in the bathroom. The
nap she took after the lovemaking renewed her vigor, dissipat-
ing the effects of the beer from the night before.

She went into the kitchen and poured a glass of ice water
from a jar in the refrigerator. Then she went outside to stand
on the porch. A soft breeze of warm air swirled over her bare
legs, flapping the skirt of her T-shirt. She moved on her bare
feet to the porch railing. The afternoon lay wilted and lazy in
front of her, with an oppressive stillness that tugged at the
energy she had recuperated with the nap.

Paco's garden, spreading out from the porch, was less
green than it had been earlier in the day, having lost the
sheen of the morning dew. The flowers were still bright and
colorful, but they now had a barely perceptible wilt to them, a
slight drooping. The flowers no longer stood straight and
proud on their stems. Beyond the garden, the branches of the
trees seemed to droop with a listless heaviness. The tufts of

grass, so green and bright in the morning, were now flat and lifeless, as if covered with a gray dust.

Even Mariachi took his time sauntering up the porch steps from his lair beneath the house. He came up the steps reluctantly, doing so out of an obligation that compelled him, a habit perhaps that he could not break. He sat on his haunches in front of Priscilla, expectant, waiting for something to make his dislocation in the hottest part of the day worthwhile. His tongue flopped over the side of his jaw.

Priscilla stooped down, poured a little of the ice water into her hand and offered it to Mariachi, who lapped it up. She touched the lip of the glass to her palm and poured a slow trickle into it for Mariachi to drink. When the glass was empty, Mariachi went into his two-step, lifting his paws one at a time while remaining in place.

Paco Rangel came out on the porch, behind Priscilla, wearing only his striped boxer shorts. He came up behind her and slipped his arms around her middle, squeezing gently, nuzzling her on the side of the neck. Priscilla returned his gesture of affection, raised her face to kiss him on the cheek.

"Aren't you going to work today?" she asked.

"I haven't had a vacation in years," Paco said, speaking into the flesh of her neck. "I could use a day or two off."

"Listen to me," she said. "I sound like I'm nagging already."

"Nag all you want," he said. "It's kind of nice to have someone on the place concerned enough about me to nag."

"I just don't want to disrupt things for you," she said, lowering her head so her chin rested on her chest.

"What shall we do on my day off?" he asked, taking away his arms and moving up against the porch railing. "You know, we could drive into Lexington. Look around. There's not much to do in Lexington, but there's lots to see. We could get some barbecue at Henry Terrazas' Meat Market, best barbecue there is, and we could take it with us and have a picnic by the river. We could sit, eat, and watch the water flow by."

"I don't feel like going anywhere," Priscilla said, a chill going through her spine at the thought of returning to Lexington. "Let's stay here. Why don't you show me the place here."

Paco seemed relieved.

"Can you ride a horse?" he asked.

"Not for many years," she said. "Not since I was a little girl, before the family left the ranch and moved into Laredo."

"If you knew how to ride once, you'll see it's like riding a bicycle. You never forget how to do it," he said, smiling. "Come on, let's get dressed."

They dressed and went through the kitchen and out the back door. They walked hand in hand to the barn, a large structure with a peaked roof. Just inside the barn, next to the entrance, were two horse stalls. One of the animals lay on the ground, while the other helped itself to the feed trough.

Paco took a bridle from a stanchion and opened the first horse stall. He slipped the bridle over the horse's head and led him a short way to the entrance to the barn. The other horse got to its feet, waiting for Paco to come into the stall with the bridle.

Paco led the horses outside of the barn to a utility shed attached to the side of the barn. He brought out a saddle blanket and saddle from the shed, draping the blanket over the horse and then tossing the saddle high in the air and letting it drop over the horse's back. It landed perfectly. He pulled the saddlehorn several times to make sure the saddle was positioned properly, after which he reached under the horse's belly for the cinch. When he finished with the cinch, he handed the reins to Priscilla.

"He's all yours," he said, going inside the tack shed again to fetch the other saddle.

Once the horse was saddled, Paco grabbed the saddlehorn with two hands and leaped in the air, swinging his right leg over the saddle. He got enough of his leg over the saddle to pull himself up the rest of way. Priscilla slipped her left toe into the stirrup, rising straight up in the air, and gracefully mounted the horse. A flutter of muscles rippled through the horse's body.

The horses stood face to face.

"We should've gotten you a hat," said Paco, adjusting his Dallas Cowboys gimme cap.

"I'll be all right," said Priscilla.

Paco pulled on the reins to the left and nudged the horse with his heels. Priscilla slackened the reins and her horse followed. They headed toward the edge of the house, going past the satellite dish, veering left past the truck with the silver camper shell on it. Priscilla's horse became animated once past the house. The horse leaped forward several times, as if to take off at a run. Priscilla reined in the animal to remain apace with Paco.

They entered the stand of oak trees in front of the house, where only streaks of sunlight penetrated through the tangle of branches. The air was cool and there was a dampness that rose from the ground. They followed the ruts of the road until they came out on the grassy pasture at the other end. They left the road and moved at an easy gallop through the young mesquite. The horses avoided the branches of mesquite trees as best they could, but several times Priscilla felt the stinging whip of the thin branches.

They came upon a barbed-wire fence. On the other side, running parallel to it, was the sandy gravel road to Larson. They followed the length of the barbed-wire fence for a few minutes. In the distance, two solitary oak trees loomed large and dark above the shoulder-high lime green of the mesquite. Paco held out his arm, and they reined in their horses. A handful of cattle was grouped under the oaks, taking in the shade.

"That's my herd," Paco Rangel said, tossing back the brim of his gimme cap. "I breed them every year and sell the calves. I put away the money I make and buy another cow or two, depending on the market for calves. Most cows I can safely handle on this piece of land is about twenty. More than that means I'd have to buy feed for them. But even so, I think I can still make some money on them. Later, if I want more cattle, I'll have to buy more land, or lease it. I haven't figured out whether I can do it financially. I'd have to wait and see. And another thing, I'd have to get me a hired man to help. With my produce and the cattle, it'd be too much for me to do all of it alone. If I'm going to put a lot of work into something, I'd like to make a profit from it."

"So, the animals you have now are just a hobby for you?" asked Priscilla. "Like your garden?"

"With the animals, sort of. To tell you the truth, I started the garden because I was watching the news on CNN one evening," he said. "The news report said that the eating public was going to flowers. Latest fad was eating flowers. I got to thinking. I already sell my zucchini with the flowers attached. I don't know if the people eat the flowers or not, but I know chefs use them to pretty up the dishes. But, there's other flowers that are used for presenting the plates, and they're edible. So I began my garden thinking it would be a hobby that I could make some money on."

"And did you?"

"Shit, no! I made the suggestion, took some samples to the chefs I deal with and they laughed. People in New York and up East like adventure when they eat. They'll try anything. People in San Antonio are different. They'd be scared to death of eating something like a flower. But, I was already thinking about a garden, so I went ahead with it."

They rode on until they reached the fields of produce. The rows were short, divided every few feet by pathways. Paco alternated several rows of one vegetable with rows of a different sort. They dismounted next to a shed, covered on three sides in aluminum siding. Running from the shed was a slanted roof set on top of cedar poles, about eight feet high. Under the roof were long plywood tables.

"That's a water well inside the shed, over there," he said, pointing. "I had it put in because once we get a dry spell, I can't afford to lose my crop. Digging that well cost me a lot of money, since I had to go deep to get to the water table where I won't run out of water. I wanted to put in a drip system, so that each plant gets just so much moisture. But, it was too expensive. I settled for those black hoses that you see there, running along the rows. In a good year, I won't have to water but three or four times. I haven't been through a heavy drought yet. If there's ever one, I'm ready for it."

"You like to plan ahead, then," Priscilla said.

"Over here," he said, excited that she was interested, "is the packing shed. Most days, I have orders from my customers. They'll tell me what they want for next time when I make a delivery. Sometimes, they'll call on the phone to give me an order. Or, if I see that I've got something that one of the chefs particularly likes, I'll make the call to see if I can get an order out of him. Anyway, as I'm picking, I keep an eye out for the kind of produce that my customers want. I try to sample whatever I'm picking to make sure the flavor's right. Size and color are very important, too."

"There's more to this business than I'd've expected," said Priscilla.

"I bring what I've picked here to the packing shed. I go through it one more time to make sure each and every piece is up to the standard of quality that my customers have come to expect from me. It takes more time that way. When I think about it, there's no other way to do it. It's the only way I can stay in business."

Paco stayed under the shade in the packing shed as Priscilla went for a walk among the rows of tomato bushes. She saw a tomato on the ground and picked it up. She brought it back to where Paco stood.

"It was on the ground," she said.

"Give it here," he said. "I'll rinse it off and you can eat it."

They mounted their horses again and rode for a short distance at a canter. Priscilla drew up on the reins to slow her horse and turned away from the direction that Paco followed.

When Paco saw her, he flapped his elbows against his ribs, kicking both his heels roughly into the sides of his horse. He yanked on the reins to turn the horse's head to chase after Priscilla. The horse sped forward at a fast run. Paco caught up with her just as she entered a darkened wood of more oak trees. Paco leaned over on his saddle to grab the reins of her horse.

"Where are you going?" he asked, pulling on the reins to stop both their horses.

"We haven't been this way yet," she said. "I thought we could ride through here and swing around and come back to the house on the other side."

"No," he said, edging his horse parallel to hers, leaning over to kiss her. "Let's just get back to the house. This way's the shortest."

"I'll race you," Priscilla shouted, giving her horse full rein.

Paco was well behind when Priscilla reached the barn. She jumped down from the horse and had the cinch loosened by the time Paco rode up. She yanked off the saddle, grabbed the saddle blanket, and took them inside the utility shed next to the barn. There was the beginnings of lather on the horse's withers. Priscilla took the reins and began to walk the horse in a wide circle in front of the barn. Paco unsaddled his horse and did the same.

"You do know something about horses," said Paco.

When they had finished cooling down the horses, they went into the house. Paco lifted the front of his shirt, poking his nose into it.

"I sure stink," he said.

"I do, too," Priscilla said, wrinkling her nose. "Let's get in the shower."

They undressed quickly and went into the shower together. The fiberglass stall was too small and narrow for both of them. In the cramped space, their bodies touched. Priscilla took the plastic bottle of shampoo and poured a little of it over Paco's head, after which she poured some on her own head.

She brought her arms up and began to rub his scalp, working up a lather, and then she brought his head under the shower spray to rinse away the shampoo.

Priscilla turned her back to Paco to wash her own hair. Paco soaped himself, his chest brushing against her back as he did so. She could feel his rock-hard penis poking at her backside. He began to soap her back. When he soaped below her waist, he lingered over the curves of her buttocks, taking special care to work up a lather in the valley between them.

Suddenly, he was spreading her lower cheeks, opening them wide, and she felt the tip of his penis find the puckered entrance of her anus. From the roll of his knuckles brushing against her buttocks, Priscilla knew that he was applying soap to the head of his dick. Priscilla became tense as he thrust upward, forcing the opening of her anus without penetrating.

When he placed his hands on her hips for leverage in forcing himself inside her anus, Priscilla moved her buttocks sideways, making a half-turn.

She looked up in Paco's eyes, placing her hands flat on his chest.

"Please," she said, "not that way."

Paco's body tensed, his lips tightened, forming a grim line across his face. When she peered into this eyes, they'd gone from their normal tan color to something closer to yellow, with a hard glint to them.

The grimness in his face softened. Paco's face relaxed as he expelled a long, labored breath.

"I'm sorry," he said. "Sometimes I get too playful."

Priscilla raised up on tiptoes and kissed him lightly, a mere brushing of her full lips over his.

"Let's finish in here," she said. "We can get on the bed."

38

Once out of the shower, they left the bathroom hand in hand, with Priscilla leading the way. She had interpreted the brief tension between them to Paco's being horny. The poor guy, she thought to herself, he hasn't had any for who knows how long.

He had been anxious back there in the shower, that's all.

Priscilla sat on the edge of the bed, holding Paco by the hips. His member had softened considerably and drooped in a curve over his testicles. She placed her right hand under his balls. Paco gripped her shoulders and pushed Priscilla onto her back on the bed. The lower half of her body was over the edge of the bed, her feet planted squarely on the floor. He dropped himself over her body, his mouth immediately going for her right nipple. He pressed himself urgently between her legs, and Priscilla felt the resurgence of his erection.

Priscilla pressed her hands against his chest, pushing him away from her.

"Here," she said, patting the bed next to her, "lie down here, next to me. You're very horny. I can take care of that."

"What about you?" he said.

"Later," she said. "Let's do something about you being so horny."

Priscilla slid off the bed, turning on one knee, positioning herself on her knees between his legs. She gripped the shaft of his penis with her hands, pulling down tightly. Slowly, using her tongue, she spread saliva over the head of it before sliding it into her mouth, pressing down with her lips. Paco dug his fingers into her hair as her head bobbed up and down over his crotch, his penis sliding in and out of her mouth.

He began to thrash violently as he orgasmed. He moaned and gasped, emitting the sounds of a wounded animal. Priscilla held on to him, alternately increasing and relaxing the suction of her mouth. Paco finally swooned, and he began to relax. He expelled a long soothing breath, and then he lay quietly, peacefully, as if succumbing to the inertness of late afternoon.

After several minutes of stillness and quiet, Paco said, "I've had a very nice day today. How about you?"

"I have, too," Priscilla said. "When I came here, I had a lot of things on my mind. They don't seem so important right now."

Paco Rangel kissed the top of her head as she lay nestled in the crook of his arm.

"I wish you would tell me what's wrong that upsets you so much," he said. "Makes me feel that you don't trust me."

Priscilla squeezed his hand tightly.

"I trust you, Paco," she said. "I can't tell you anything, just yet. Mainly because I don't know myself what's going on."

"I'm ready to listen to you whenever you want to tell me," he said. "I promise I'll do everything in my power to help you. In the meantime, I can't help you if I don't know what's troubling you."

"You're already helping me tremendously just by letting me stay here," she said.

"Come, it's getting late, " he said, sitting up on the bed. "I think it's time for us to have a beer."

They dressed and went into the kitchen. Paco took the red ice chest outside, drained the water out of it, filled it with more ice and beer. Once he was back in the kitchen, he twisted the caps from two beer bottles and set them on top of the kitchen table. Priscilla leaned forward on her elbows.

"I want to do something for you," said Priscilla, smiling, anxious to give away her secret.

"You already did," he said, grinning, with a mock maniacal look on his face.

"I'm serious. Listen. Tell me how you handle your bookkeeping," she said.

"Couldn't we discuss something more romantic," he said, becoming suspicious, giving her a grin that bared his teeth. There was no masking his discomfort. "Bookkeeping makes me nervous. Besides, I take everything to an accountant in White Leg. She looks over what I give to her and tells me how much I can spend on myself and how much to leave aside for the business."

In the cursory look she'd taken at his bills and invoices, she'd not seen anything to indicate he was getting professional help with his books.

"It probably costs you an arm and a leg to get all that bookkeeping done if you don't have all your paper in the right order. How I can help you is, I can fix up a system so that you just make an entry into the checkbook program you have in the computer. Presto! The machine does the rest for you. You make one entry in the program, and then you can file your paper and forget about it. The computer can do the work of your professional accountant. You'll not only save some money, but you won't have to scramble every quarter or every end of the year to get your papers in order."

"How do you mean?"

"Well, for the size of your business, we can set up the checkbook program to give you a profit and loss statement, set up a pop-up menu for everyone you do business with—just click on the one you want, make up categories of expenditures and income, flag certain items for tax purposes, and so on. The program will interface very nicely with just about any computer income-tax program. All you have to do is answer the questions that the tax program asks you, and when you're finished, you click the button on your mouse and out comes your income-tax forms, all ready to mail. All you do is write a check to the Internal Revenue Service, or wait for your refund, whichever. No muss, no fuss."

Paco became interested, leaning forward on the table, taking a sip of the beer.

"Tell me more," he said. "This sounds interesting."

"Which part of it did you find interesting?"

"The part about sorting through the paper, getting things in order. I hate doing that. My accountant in town says I could save a lot of money if I did it myself instead of dumping everything on her. She takes me for a healthy chunk of money to get it done."

"I thought I might get your attention. The main thing is to place all your expenditures and your income into categories. Some of it will be personal. Some of it will be expenses directly related to your production of income. Label everything with the proper category. Each time you write a check, just click on the category of expenditure. At the end of the year, the computer will automatically group the expenditures, total them, and report out a profit-and-loss statement. When you load your income-tax program after the end of your business year, it will automatically fill in that category into your Schedule C. You don't do anything. Your income, as it goes out, will be divided between personal and business expenses. You put money into an IRA, the program will do the computations for you. It'll give you reports on a monthly, quarterly, or annual basis, however you need it."

"How long will it take you to install the program in the computer and get me started."

"Not long," she said. "When I thought of doing this for you, I took the liberty of turning on your computer. The checkbook program is already installed. All we have to do is set it up and customize it for your business. All I need to do is look over your bills, invoices, and so on for the past year. From there, I can have your expense and income categories set up, and everything'll be ready to punch into the computer. After you enter all of the transactions for the current tax year, all you have to do from that point on is just enter them as they come in."

"That sounds pretty neat," he said. "You say it's idiot-proof?"

"Nothing is idiot-proof, Paco," Priscilla said. "This first year, to make sure you're on the right track, you can take the printouts to your accountant, along with the paper, and have her do an audit for you. If everything checks out and you get the green light, after that you're on your own."

"Looks like I'll be depressing the economy of White Leg by not paying my accountant."

"Whoever she is, she will survive, I'm sure," Priscilla said.

"I'll try it," said Paco. "You know, I bought the computer with just such a purpose in mind. I must've played with it for months and I never could get the hang of it. I gave it up when I came to the conclusion that I am destined to remain a computer illiterate."

"There's no such thing," she said.

"Wait until you try to teach me on the computer," he said. "You'll change your mind."

"I've worked with people scared to death of those machines," said Priscilla. "All you need is patience and the determination to keep at it until you get it right. After that, you'll do fine."

Paco opened two more beers. They agreed that while Priscilla fixed dinner, Paco would go into his office and begin to put together the bills and invoices Priscilla needed in order to devise his accounting system.

Priscilla butterflied two chicken breasts, dusting them with seasoned flour, and tossed them into a skillet to fry. In another frying pan, she browned new potatoes with garlic, black pepper, and rosemary leaves.

When Paco finished in his office, he returned to the kitchen.

"I've gone through everything I have," he said. "It's in a manila folder on top of my desk. If I forgot anything, or you need more information, just let me know. If there's anything you don't understand, let me know that, too."

"Okay, good, I'll get on it tomorrow," said Priscilla.

He opened two more beers under Priscilla's protest that she still had her bottle half-full. He placed the cold bottle next to her on the counter where she tore bits of lettuce to toss into a salad bowl. He slipped his hands inside her T-shirt, bringing them up to her breasts, lightly pinching her nipples.

"Your hands are cold!" she squealed in laughter.

39

For the third morning in a row, Priscilla awoke with a hangover. They had not had as many beers as their first night together, but she did drink far more than she was accustomed to drinking. After they had finished with their dinner, Paco washed dishes while Priscilla sat at the table and drank her beer. Paco had joined her when finished with the dishes and they'd sat in the kitchen, drinking more beer and enjoying each other's company. The time passed by quickly until Paco looked at his watch and observed that it was after midnight.

As Priscilla opened her eyes in the chill of the morning, she felt the weight of Paco's body silently rising from the bed. A moment later, she heard the roar of the shower spray and she drifted back to the twilight of sleep. The absence of his warm body next to her made Priscilla aware of how cold it was in the bedroom. She had slept in only her underpants. She pulled the sheet over her and tried to sleep some more.

They'd gotten into bed and she fully expected to have sex, but Paco had punned that he was too drunk to hold up his end of it. The day they had spent together had left her peaceful and rested and she went right to sleep, nestled in his arms.

Upon awakening, even though the effects of her hangover were unavoidable, the pleasantness of the previous day was enough to preserve a light and buoyant feeling in Priscilla.

She heard Paco putting on his clothes beside the bed. Priscilla rolled over and reached for his hand. He took it and squeezed.

"I got coffee going," said Paco. "Are you going to sleep some more, or should I pour some for you?"

Priscilla sighed deeply. "Pour me a cup," she purred. "I want to look at you in the morning. I haven't done that yet."

She found her T-shirt on the floor, put it on and brushed her teeth. She hurried into the kitchen to join Paco.

When he saw her standing in the kitchen doorway, Paco's face lit up with joy.

"I didn't really think you'd get up," he said.

"I told you I wanted to have coffee with you," she said, scratching her scalp and running her fingers through her hair, yawning daintily.

"Coffee's almost ready," he said, looking at her with a gentle face, his bright tan eyes sparkling.

She walked over to where Paco stood beside the counter, waiting for the coffee pot to complete its brewing cycle. She took his face in her hands, her hair falling over his chest, and kissed him passionately. She turned and pressed her bottom against his lower body, reaching her arms above her head to wrap them around his neck.

"How're you this morning?" she whispered into his ear.

"Good. Very good," he said. "You feel up to eating something? I'm going to make breakfast."

"I'll eat a little bit of whatever you're having," she said. "Don't fix me anything."

Paco turned to the counter next to the stove and poured coffee into two mugs that sat ready beside the drip coffee maker. He brought them to the table and sat down. Priscilla came over, kissed the top of his head and walked around to take a chair. Once seated, she leaned forward, took his hand, and squeezed it.

"Are you working today, or will you loaf as you did yesterday?" she asked.

"I have to work today," he said. "I've got some plants in the greenhouse nursery ready to take outdoors. I'll be doing that most of the day. And, I have to pick some produce to take into San Antonio tomorrow. I'll pick today and have it ready to go in the morning. What about you? What're you going to do today?"

"I'll work on your books, as I promised," Priscilla said. "It shouldn't take me more than a few hours this morning. This afternoon, maybe I'll saddle up one of the horses and go for a ride. It's been so many years since I've been on a horse. I never realized I like it so much. What time will you be coming for lunch? I'll get it ready."

"I'll be in and out all day," he said. "By the way, I thought you weren't the domestic type."

"I'm not," she said, smiling. "There's nothing wrong with timing my lunch to yours. And, while I'm at it, there's no harm in making lunch for two."

Priscilla made another pot of coffee after Paco Rangel left for work. She washed the breakfast dishes and then went outside to stand on the porch for a few minutes to finish drinking her coffee in the cool and quiet of the morning. Mariachi came out of his lair beneath the house, hanging his head low, coming silently with determined steps up to the porch.

Priscilla sat on her heels to rub Mariachi's head and to run her hands along the thick, bristly pelt along his spine.

"How are you, Mariachi? How are you this morning?" she cooed. "Did you have a nice night's sleep? I bet you did!"

The black pit bull remained on his four legs until she finished petting him. When Priscilla stood up, Mariachi sauntered over to the porch railing and curled up beside her feet and fell asleep.

Priscilla finished her coffee, turned, and went into Paco's office area adjacent to the parlor.

The sun cast bright rays of blinding light into the room. She adjusted the drapes and, having done so, found that it was too dark to work. She found a lamp and turned it on. The manila folder that Paco had prepared for her was on top of the desk. She reached below the computer desk and switched on the power distributor. The machine roared to life.

She organized the bills and invoices. It was standard stuff, not very complicated. She separated everything into its proper categories, and in two hours was ready to set up the program, customize it, and input what she had at hand. Paco would have to worry about the paper already filed away.

In one of the slots of the roll-top desk, she noticed the unmistakable cloth covering of a small ledger. Absent-mindedly, as she sipped her coffee, she took it out of the slot, opened it, and began to leaf through the pages.

It was a record of something, written in pencil— a tally of some sort. Priscilla assumed that it might be a record of Paco's sales that he kept for quick reference, as a reminder when he prepared his invoices, something he could carry in his hip pocket.

The entries went back three years. She fanned the pages until she was midway through it, where the entries stopped. She came back to the first page. There were five columns. The first column was made up of dates. The next column was a listing of names, the same four names repeated in order, penciled in over and over again. As she went through the pages, one of the four names would disappear to be replaced by another. Next to the names were two columns of numbers. The last column was nothing more than hurried check marks.

She looked through the invoices he'd submitted to his customers, the chefs and purchasing agents of several restaurants in San Antonio. None of the names matched those on the ledger she thumbed through.

Priscilla turned to the last few pages of the entries. The last entry was penciled in just the week before. Her eyes opened wide. She brought her face closer to the page.

One of the names, repeated over and over again, was Ralph Mason.

She blinked to clear her eyes and sharpen her focus. She shook her head to clear it, certain that it would show that she was mistaken. The name, though, would not go away. There it was: RALPH MASON.

It was written in Paco's clean block letters.

She flipped the pages back, going faster and faster, seeing Ralph Mason's name over and over, check marks next to it every time. There was an urgent, desperate motion in the way that her fingers moved. She went back to the end of the entries. On the last page, all the entries were checked off, except on two dates for Ralph Mason.

Ralph Mason.

The last two entries without a check mark were dated nearly a month before Priscilla's arrival in Lexington.

A chill ran up Priscilla Arrabal's spine.

40

Joe Blue drove his candy-apple-red pickup truck out of Lexington. He drove south on the road that eventually dead-ends on the coast of the Gulf of Mexico. He punched a button on the truck's radio to listen to a Tejano station in San Antonio. Emilio Navaira sang a country tune.

Mexicans, he thought, we're all shitkickers at heart.

He roared past the twin bridges over the Lexington River. A mile further up, he took the west fork of the road, where it veered toward White Leg. After another two miles, he turned on a paved farm road going to Killdeer. He could see the house as soon as he turned on the road. It sat on a bare piece of ground a short distance from a pair of chicken houses, each some five-hundred feet in length, with aluminum roofs glistening in the afternoon sun.

Joe Blue eased the truck into a lane graded down to the caliche bed. The lane went straight to the openings at the end of the chicken houses. He followed the caliche road until a spur of soft black soil angled to the right going up to a small block house badly needing a coat of paint. Next to the house sat a silver butane tank, oblong and fat, with streaks of rust. A garage, leaning to one side, was set off from the house on the left. In front of the house were parked an old Toyota sedan and a pickup truck. The truck was old, but well-kept, washed and waxed.

Joe Blue stopped his truck in front of the house, next to Victor Richards' pickup truck. He sat and waited.

Shortly, through the screen door, he saw a young woman in shadow, an indistinct shape behind the screen door. Joe Blue recognized Myra Richards. She wore a white T-shirt and denim cutoffs. She held a white plastic bowl against her belly. She stared at Joe Blue, who sat behind the tinted glass of the windshield.

Myra Richards stepped out on the porch.

Joe Blue popped a stick of gum into his mouth and opened the door of the pickup. He walked up to the house and placed a boot on the single step going up to the porch.

"Is your husband home, Myra?" Joe Blue said, removing his straw hat, running his fingers through his hair.

"He's asleep, Joe," Myra Richards said, stirring the contents of the white plastic bowl that she held against her belly.

"Wake him up, would you, Myra?" Joe Blue said. "Tell him I want to talk to him. After I talk to him, I'll want to talk to you, too."

Without a word, Myra disappeared inside the house. A few minutes later, Victor Richards came out on the porch, wearing starched Levi's, his feet and his chest bare. He yawned, wide and loud, scratched his lower belly.

"What can I do for you, Joe," said Victor Richards, lifting his arm in the air, scratching his armpit.

"I have to talk to you about something, Victor," said Joe Blue. "Get something on your feet and walk with me a bit. It won't take long."

"Damn, Joe, you couldn't've picked a worse time," said Victor Richards, yawning again. "One of the heaters went out over at the hatchery last night. Son of a bitch went out just when my shift was over. I was out there till four, five this morning getting it to work again."

"I'm sorry to put you out, Victor, but this is important."

"After I finished at work, I came home to find Myra was sick. We're going to have a baby," said Victor Richards. "So, I had to go and gather eggs for her. Myra gathers eggs in those two chicken houses over there twice a day. We get to stay in the house without paying rent, and she brings in a little pay-check, too. With the baby coming, I can't afford either of us not working."

"Sure, Victor," said Joe Blue, bending to the ground, picking up a grass shoot to chew on. "I know how it is."

"Let me get my boots on," he said. "You gonna tell me what it's all about?"

"I'll tell you when you walk with me," said Joe Blue.

Victor Richards returned, having put on his boots and a light-blue checked shirt, which he had not buttoned. They walked away from the house, toward the silver butane tank, and further away amidst ankle-high Johnson grass.

"Ralph Mason got shot last night," Joe Blue said.

"I can't say I'm sorry to hear about that, Joe," said Victor Richards, turning away to stare into the distance. He shifted his gaze to the ground and said, "The reason you're here is, you think I did it."

"I don't know, Victor," Joe Blue said. "People talk. You know that much. It's my job to check into things when people talk."

"Hell, I can't blame you for thinking I might've had some-thing to do with it, Joe," said Victor Richards. "I know all about Ralph and Myra. Shithooks, when I found out about them, I was mad enough to do it. Shoot the son of a bitch, you know? I won't lie about that. Look, Joe, Myra and me, we had a rough time for a while back there. She went out and she did some things. I was out doing things I oughtn't to do myself. We just woke up one day and saw what it was doing to us, the both of us. And, we decided to quit it, give it a chance, work things out. We got our heads together and patched things up. I want you to know that. I don't like to say it, but in a way it looks like Ralph probably did me a favor. Else, I wouldn't've seen what I got right here at home with Myra."

"You say you were at the hatchery until four or five this morning?"

"I sure was, Joe," said Victor Richards. "It was me and Seferino, that guy from Mexico. I don't know if you know him."

"Okay, Victor," said Joe Blue. "I had to check into it just the same."

"Sure, you're just doing your job, Joe," said Victor Richards. "I know that."

"Now, I've got to talk to Myra," Joe Blue said. "You don't suppose you could wait out here until I finish?"

"Do I have a choice?"

"When's your baby due, Victor?"

"January or February, sometime in there."

41

It was a useless trip, but one that Joe Blue had to make. Myra Richards agreed with her husband that he'd come home after five in the morning. She was certain because she'd had a terrible night vomiting and feeling miserable, and she kept looking at the clock in the bedroom wondering where Victor was. She thought he might be out tomcatting as before, but it turned out that he had work to do at his job.

On the way back into Lexington, Joe Blue met one of the yellow school buses that fanned out all over the county every morning and afternoon. Hank Solís should have picked up Orthal Mason's two boys. He wondered what he might learn from them. They'd be defensive and tight-lipped. If they knew anything, he'd only get it if he could put enough of a scare into them.

Orthal Mason's two youngest sons sat on a wooden bench adjacent to the entrance just inside the Sheriff's Office. Both of them had dark blond hair, shaved up one side and cut to flow over the forehead. Hank Solís pointed to them, motioned them to stand up when Joe Blue came down the steps. They were dressed almost identically. Baggy pants and polo shirts designed to fit men twice as large. The hem of the shirts reached midway down the thighs. Their scuffed running shoes were not laced.

Joe Blue signaled to Hank Solís to follow him as he walked past them into the long corridor leading to his jail-cell office. He reached the office in long strides, went around the scarred wooden desk and dropped his straw hat on the nail peg on the wall. He sat in the straight-back chair as Hank Solís entered, the two boys in front of him. Hank steered them with a massive hand on each of the boys' necks.

The boys displayed a defiant attitude as they pushed their backs against the iron bars that separated the jail cells. They took note of the Tejano Conjunto Festival poster. Hank Solís dropped a haunch on a corner of the desk. He stared at their eyes and they shifted their gaze to the floor.

"Well, boys," said Joe Blue, leaning back in his chair, lifting the two front legs of it off the floor. "Look at me when I talk to you!"

Joe Blue caught the look in their eyes for a moment with a stern expression on his face, compressing the fullness of his lips.

The boys looked up, trying to stare down Joe Blue. It was a practiced look, betrayed by tics and twitches and uncontrollable blinking. In the end, they couldn't sustain the defiance. They broke the stare and lowered their heads to look at the floor once more. Joe Blue did not speak for a moment. The boys shifted their weight on their feet.

"Deputy Solís says you boys've been shooting deer out of season. Even in season, he doubts you boys bother to get a hunting license," Joe Blue said.

"We didn't do nothing and you can't prove we did it, neither," one of them said.

"You boys are careless," said Joe Blue. "Wasn't like that when I was a boy. We buried what was left of our crime before we ate it. According to the report I have from Deputy Solís, you didn't get rid of the evidence. He and Carter Vinson saw more than one deer carcass out on that place where you live with your daddy. Heads, antlers, skins, everything. They're convinced somebody's been poaching out there."

"I told you, we didn't do nothing," the same boy repeated.

"What you did or didn't do is up to the judge," said Joe Blue. "I expect that when the judge sees the evidence, he'll fine both of you."

"It's your word against ours, fuckhead!" the other boy said.

Joe Blue smiled, raising his hands, palms facing them. "It's not me, boys," he said. "It's the game warden and Deputy Solís. They're the ones who caught you and they're going to press charges against the two of you."

The boys fidgeted to hide their trembling. Joe Blue kept silent, waiting patiently until one of the boys spoke.

"Instead of trying to find out who killed a fucking deer, what you oughta be doing is finding out who killed our brother," one of the boys said.

The other one said, "Yeah, why ain't you out finding that son-of-a-bitch killer who murdered my brother?"

"Well, now that you mention it," Joe Blue said, nodding his head, "there is something concerning your brother's death that you can help me with."

"We don't know nothing."

"Maybe you don't. Then, again, maybe you do," said Joe Blue, leaning forward on the desk. "Did Ralph ever talk to you about where he got his money, by any chance? After he quit his job, he was still getting money from somewhere. I want to know where he got it. Did he ever mention anything about that?"

"He worked for it, just like everybody else! That's where he got it!"

"I know he worked for Porter Labelle, but he quit that job a month ago. Thing is, there's people who say he still had plenty of money. I bet he gave you boys some of it, didn't he? I think Ralph was real nice to you that way. How about it?"

The two boys exchanged glances. Joe Blue dropped the chair behind the desk to the floor.

"Look, boys, Ralph's dead. Whatever he was doing, if it was against the law and you know not to say anything about it, well, your brother Ralph's gone. The law can't touch him. You can help me find his killer. Did he ever mention somebody, anybody, that could've been paying him for something that maybe he shouldn't've been doing?"

The boys cast their eyes downward, refusing to look Joe Blue in the face. One of them squirmed.

"He said he had a deal going with some Mexican," one of the boys said. "He never said what it was."

"It was just a deal that paid him some money," the other one said.

"You don't have any idea who it was paying him or what they were doing?" asked Joe Blue.

"I don't know. All he said is that it was a Mexican. He said it was a deal so sweet he was never gonna have to work again for a real long time."

"Did he say where this Mexican lived?"

"No."

"Anything different about Ralph that you might've noticed?"

"Like what?"

"Oh, I don't know," said Joe Blue. "Anything he did that he never done before."

"A couple of times, when Ralph came to give money to daddy, he brought momma vegetables, okra and squash, some other stuff."

"And he never did that before?"

"No."

"Did he say where he got it?"

"He didn't have to. We know where he got it. At the grocery, like everybody else."

Joe Blue nodded his head pensively and got to his feet.

"Hank, get somebody to take these boys home, will you?"

42

Joe Blue put on his straw hat. He took his gun belt from the nail peg, strapped it around his waist. He unlocked the desk drawer where he kept his pistol, picked it up, checked to see that it was loaded, and slipped it into the holster. Hank Solís returned to the stand in front of the desk.

"Where are we off to?"

"You know that truck farmer, Vietnam-vet fella, came out here a few years ago?"

"Paco Rangel? Sure. He bought a place out by Larson."

"What do you know about him?"

"Nothing much. He grows fancy vegetables for some restaurants in San Antonio. Makes pretty good money at it, people say. Mostly, he keeps to himself."

"He's not very sociable, is he? I've only seen him a few times in White Leg."

"Yeah, he's pretty much of a loner. I know he was going out with one of Sam Richards' girls, Myra's older sister. What was her name?"

"Jamie, if it's the one I'm thinking about," said Joe Blue.

"She's the one," said Hank Solís. "Yeah, I remember now. She wouldn't go out with anybody unless they were Mexican. You remember that?"

"I heard about it, Hank. Was that true? I never believed it," Joe Blue said.

"I'm sure it wasn't. At least, not at first," Hank Solís said. "The way it is, a white girl goes out with a Mexican and every white boy thinks she's got to be addled in the head. At least, that's what a lot of these peckerwoods around here think. I guess they're saying if she goes out with one Mexican, then no self-respecting white boy ought to get near to her. Limits her choices to only Mexicans."

Joe Blue thought for a minute, then he said, "There's a story about Paco Rangel that I remember now. Seems he was parked at the Dairy Queen in White Leg one morning. Had the bed of his pickup truck filled with cardboard boxes full of vegetables. Herman Whiteside, who never did know any better, picks up a banana pepper from one of the boxes in the truck and walks into the Dairy Queen with it. Paco Rangel is in there to have a donut and a cup of coffee, on his way to the big city to deliver his vegetables. Well, it seems ol' Herman mistakes Paco for a roadside vendor. He walks up and starts to shake that banana pepper in Paco's face. Ol' Herman says, 'What you get for these, boy? I want some for my wife.' Paco yanks the pepper out of ol' Herman's hand and says, 'You ain't got the money to buy any of these. Don't go snooping in my truck again.'"

"What is it they say about people who have the knack to grow things?"

"Green thumb."

"You think Paco Rangel's got his green thumb on some loco weed out there on that place of his?"

"I don't know what to think about that, Hank," said Joe Blue. "I do think we ought to go out there and pay him a visit. Have a little talk with him. Nice and friendly."

"I got my kids coming over about five, Joe," said Hank Solís, looking at his wristwatch. "It's already four-thirty. I was going to knock off for the day."

"I'll go by myself. It's on the way home, anyway. There's probably nothing to it, Hank," said Joe Blue. "I'll just go out there, friendly like, and have a little conversation with him. I just want to check it out, make sure there's no loose ends."

"No, Joe," said Hank Solís, a look of concern flashing over his face. "Let's wait. I want to go with you."

"What the hell can he do, Hank?" said Joe Blue, irritated.

"Listen, you go out to talk to Victor Richards, that's one thing," said Hank Solís. "We watched that boy grow up. His wife, too. We know both their folks. Hell, even those Masons, none of them's worth a shit, but I wouldn't be afraid to go out there to their place by myself. They talk mean, but that's about all they are, nothing but talk. There's not much to be afraid of with them. This fella out there in Larson, he's new. We don't know anything about him. He keeps to himself. There's something funny about that. I don't like it."

"Just because a man's quiet and private, Hank, that doesn't mean he's dangerous," said Joe Blue.

"I didn't say he was dangerous, Joe," said Hank Solís. "I said we don't know anything about him. Unless we know, there's no use taking any chances. That's all I'm saying. Besides, what's the damned rush? I'll meet you in White Leg tomorrow morning and we'll go out to his place from there."

"Okay Hank, you win," said Joe Blue, letting out a deep breath. "I'm tired anyway. I should go home myself."

Hank Solís left, saying he was going to pick up a mess of fried chicken to feed his children. Their mother was taking them to the video store to rent movies before bringing them over.

Joe Blue stood outside the Sheriff's Office, his hands in his jeans pockets. The late afternoon sun was pale and mild, the shadows of the day lengthening. He got into his candy-apple-red pickup truck and drove out to White Leg, where he lived. listened to Tejano music on the radio as he drove.

43

They threatened you with a fine for shooting God-damned deer out of season?" barked Orthal Mason.

His two youngest boys cowered in front of him.

"That Mexican deputy, not the big one, the other one, he said he'd forget about the deer if we told him what Ralph was up to before he got killed," one of the boys said, almost in tears. "Joe Blue said we could help him catch Ralph's killer."

"Yeah, Pa, that's what you said yourself. You said you wanted Ralph's killer found," the other boy said.

"Useless little shits! Looks like nothing I ever taught you done any damn good. I want that son of a bitch for myself, don't you understand? I'm going to kill the son of a bitch myself."

"Well, we didn't tell who did it because we don't know, Pa."

"Well, what in the goddamn hell did you tell him?"

"Nothing, Pa. We just told him that Ralph brung okra and green beans a couple of times when he brought you some money. That's all we said to him, Pa. Honest."

"Yeah," said the other boy. "Let that son of a bitch deputy think Ralph was working at the grocery store."

Orthal Mason calmed himself. He tousled his son's hair, speaking gently. "Don't let you momma hear you curse, boy."

He walked off by himself, going a short distance to a dilapidated wooden fence with rotting fence posts. He put his toe on one of the slats, curled his thumb and began to bang it against his forehead.

Suddenly, he stopped and turned. There was a wide-eyed look on his face. He walked in rapid strides across the open space and went into his house. Moments later he was outside again, carrying a Winchester 30-30 and a box of shells.

"You boys go on in the house," he said. "Do your chores. You have homework from school, don't you?"

"Where you going, Pa?"

"I think you boys done give that half-breed Mexican, Joe Blue, your brother's killer."

"We never done no such thing, Pa."

"You boys didn't mean to do it, I know that," said Orthal Mason. "But, you did it just the same. I just hope that half-breed Mexican don't catch on to it too quick. I got to get there to him before Joe Blue does."

"Who is it, Pa."

"Get in the damn house!" he said. "Tell your ma I'm going hunting. I might be back late."

44

Priscilla Arrabal pushed back the heavy wooden swivel chair. The palms of her hands felt clammy with sweat as she placed them on the edge of the roll-top desk. The green ledger was open, lying flat on the desk. She had looked carefully through every page. It was the last pages, dating back a little more than a year, that contained the name of Ralph Mason.

She looked through the bills and invoices Paco Rangel had placed in the manila folder for her to review. There was no record of any business done with Ralph Mason. She pulled out the desk drawers to look through the other files, looking for something that would connect Ralph Mason and Paco Rangel in business. She found nothing.

She replaced the files and pushed the drawer shut. She got to her feet and began to tap the desk with the knuckle of her forefinger. Finally, she picked up the green ledger and replaced it in the slot where she'd found it. She walked away, going into the parlor, as the truth sank in.

The image in the window of the motel room came back to her. The image had been nagging at her, skirting the edges of her consciousness, mocking her. She'd seen the image, a man's face, for only a fraction of a second. Through the haze of the aluminum-mesh screen, she could not make out the image cloaked in shadow. She brought her mind back to the motel, trying to bring every instant back to life, forcing herself to sharpen the image of everything that happened, everything she'd seen.

There was Ralph Mason, the redneck she'd picked up at Ligon Wells Saloon on the hill. He had his foot on the edge of the bed. His dick was in his hand. He said something—the words were not important. Her gaze went from Ralph Mason's face down his chest to his lower abdomen. His shoulder tilted, giving her a full view of the window behind him.

The windowpane crashed. Ralph Mason's body jerked, blocking her view of the window. It was a long moment after the crash of the broken glass before Ralph Mason wobbled and fell face first to the bed. With his body out of the way, her eyes went straight to the window.

She'd caught a glimpse of the face outside, framed by the window, the sharpness of it masked by the window screen. She had seen it for only a fraction of a second.

Priscilla closed her eyes, pressing down on them, to sharpen the image in the window.

Before she could focus on the outline of the face, she had noticed his hand and the pistol. He aimed the gun at her. She distinctly remembered that when Ralph Mason fell face first onto the bed, she screamed. As it became clear in Priscilla's mind, she had screamed when she saw the gun aimed at her.

It was the scream that blocked the image in the window.

It all came back to her. The fraction of a second in which she caught the brief glimpse of the face in the window. She saw enough of it to make out a determined face, wearing a Navy watch cap, black in the shadow of night.

And, something else.

Her mind returned to her present surroundings in the parlor. It was on the roll-top desk. She rushed back to the Paco's office. Beside the neatly arranged desk supplies, she saw it, in a corner of the desk. A metal case for eyeglasses. The silver earpiece of the eyeglasses was on the outside of the lid. She opened it. There they were.

When she took out the steel-rimmed glasses, she knew right away that she'd seen them in the instant before the glint of light caught them. They were on the face of the man outside the window in the motel. The face now came into focus.

It was the face of Paco Rangel.

It was his hand that held the gun.

It was his gun aiming at her.

45

Priscilla ran back to the parlor. Her suitcase lay open on the navy-blue leather sectional sofa. She hurried to the bedroom, gathered up the clothes she'd left piled on the floor and threw them on the bed. From the bathroom, she grabbed her toilet articles and stuffed them into a plastic bag. She scooped up the clothes and brought them quickly to the suitcase. She stuffed them in with the clean clothes and hurriedly zipped up the bag.

Oh shit! she thought in a panic.

She'd never be able to get away carrying the suitcase.

It was cumbersome, too much weight.

Priscilla had to run, get away from Paco's place as fast as possible. She would worry about clothes later.

Running was no good, either. There was no telling when Paco would come back. She looked at her watch. It was thirty minutes to twelve. They'd agreed that she'd have lunch ready at noon. That didn't leave much time.

She had to get away!

The horses! It was her only chance. On a horse, she might have a chance.

She ran out to the front porch, stopped at the edge of it, looking in all directions for a sign of Paco. Everything was quiet.

The black pit bull, Mariachi, came up the steps to stand alongside her. She could feel his pelt against her calves. A shiver ran through her body. Dogs can sense fear!

She moved the leg that touched the dog. Nothing happened. She lowered first one foot to the porch step, then the other. She took two more steps before she was on the ground. The dog followed her, his face serious, keeping his snout close to the ground.

She ran along a diagonal path to the barn and opened the large doors. She found the bridle and went into the stall to slip it over the horse's head. The horse became anxious, knowing that it was going out for a ride, sensing the urgency of Priscilla's movements.

She led the horse outside, dropping the reins beneath the horse's head. The horse stood still while she went inside the tack shed for the saddle. The saddle felt heavy and unwieldy.

After she had cinched up the saddle, she got on the horse and turned away from the barn. The horse was anxious to get going, jumping, lifting his hind legs and kicking in short bursts into the air.

Priscilla opened her legs wide, and brought them in a slapping motion against the sides of the horse. The animal lifted his head in the air and galloped for a short space until she clapped her legs against the sides again, and the horse took off at a fast run.

In seconds, she had gone past the house and beyond the pickup truck with the silver camper shell. The horse was running in the cool shade of the oak stand in front of the house. They cleared it, and the horse increased his speed along the meandering ruts of the sandy road going in the direction of the entrance to the farm. To the side, the scrub mesquite breezed by in a blur. The black blur moving on the ground next to the horse, she realized, was Mariachi running along-side at full speed.

She saw the lone oak tree that grew beside the gate.

So far, so good. If she could only get past the gate and onto the gravel road.

It would be another three or four miles before she got into Larson. She could be there in no time at all.

Once she got to Larson, there was only one thing to do. Call the police. Turn herself in. Tell them about Paco. Let them handle it.

The horse saw the cattle guard before she did. The horse tried to come to a dead stop, seeming to try and gallop back-ward. The horse's brake of movement was so sudden that Priscilla lifted off the saddle and was propelled forward. She was on her way over the horse's head when she grabbed the saddlehorn and pulled herself back.

The horse turned, going in a full circle in front of the cat-tle guard, frightened, desperate to avoid it. Priscilla pulled up on the reins to control the animal. She jumped down from the saddle.

She took the reins and began to walk quickly in front of the horse. She would lead the horse carefully over the cattle guard, hoping the horse had sense enough to hop over it.

When she got to the cattle guard, Paco Rangel stepped out from behind the oak tree to the right, about ten yards.

He carried an M-14 rifle cradled in his left arm. His right hand gripped the stock, finger on the trigger.

"Going somewhere?" asked Paco Rangel, calm and pleas-ant.

Priscilla looked at him. Her jaw slackened, her mouth fell open. She stopped in midstep, opening her hand to let the reins fall to the ground. Her shoulders slumped in defeat.

Mariachi stood beside Priscilla, unable to understand what was going on. The fast run had winded him, leaving him gasping for breath. Mariachi coughed several times.

Paco Rangel extended his left hand out to Priscilla, shouldering the rifle.

"Give me the reins, Priscilla," he said.

She surrendered the reins. Paco took them, slipped them over the horse's neck and got on the horse.

"Now, walk back to the house," he said. "I don't want anybody passing by to get a look at you."

Priscilla began to walk back to the house.

Mariachi trotted in front of her, his tongue hanging out.

Paco Rangel followed on horseback, the stock of the M-14 resting on his thigh, barrel pointing into the air.

46

When they returned to the house, Paco Rangel dismounted and tied the reins to a fence post of the white picket fence. He kept the rifle pointed at Priscilla's back. He stepped close behind her as they went through his garden and up to the porch.

"Go on inside," he said.

They entered the parlor.

Holding the rifle pointed in her direction, Paco took backward steps into his office. At the roll-top desk, he opened a drawer, fished around in it until he came up with a roll of silver-colored duct tape.

"Go into the bedroom, now," he said.

Walking close behind her, they entered the bedroom.

"Now, get your hands behind your back."

She heard the ratchet noise of the tape unrolling. He snipped a long piece of it, holding the roll in his hand and cutting it with his teeth. Slipping the rifle to the crook of his left arm, he took her wrists and began to wind the duct tape around them.

When her wrists were securely bound, he dropped the rifle on the bed, unrolled another long piece and wrapped it neatly over the other piece on her wrists. He turned Priscilla so she faced him. Touching her shoulders, he indicated that she should sit on the bed, and lie back.

Again, she heard the ratchet of the tape unrolling. This time, he wrapped the tape just above her knees, unrolling the tape as he wrapped it around. When he had finished, he took another piece of the duct tape and bound the piece on her wrists to the piece on her knees.

"What are you going to do with me?" asked Priscilla, lying flat on the bed, facing the ceiling.

"I've got to get going. Get my ass long gone out of here," he said. "Everything for me around here has turned to shit. It started with that redneck motherfucker Ralph Mason. It's not going to take long before they connect me with him, and once they do that, they'll know I killed him. I don't think I have as much time as I thought I did."

Priscilla kept quiet, trying to turn on her side. Paco Rangel lifted her legs up on the bed and then carefully lifted her shoulders to help her sit up.

"Comfortable?" he asked.

Priscilla nodded.

"So, I've got to get my ass out of here, get the fuck out of this country," he said, talking to himself more than to Priscilla.

"You still haven't told me what you're going to do with me," she said.

"That poses a problem for me, Priscilla," he said, crossing his arms in front of him. "I could leave you just as you are, on the bed here. It'll take you a while to get loose from that duct tape. If I could be sure that you'd stay tied up for a couple of days at least, this is where I would leave you. I really don't want to hurt you."

"I can stay here as long as you want me to," she said. "The police must be looking for me because they know I was with Ralph Mason when you shot him. That's why I asked to stay here with you. I don't want to get caught by the police."

"Yeah, I knew that's why you wanted to stay with me," he said. "All that other stuff was bullshit."

"No, it wasn't, Paco," said Priscilla, sincerely. "It wasn't all bullshit at all."

"I know you would give me time to get away, dear," he said, touching her cheek, drawing little circles on it with his finger tip. "In fact, I actually believe you. I think you were getting to really like me. We might have become a permanent thing, you know. You and me. That's the strongest reason there is for me to leave you here."

"You can leave me here," she said. "I don't care that you killed that redneck. I want to live, Paco. That's what I'm interested in."

"That's a good point in your favor," he said.

"When I get loose, I'll walk out of here and it'll be like I never met you at all."

"That's all well and good," said Paco Rangel. "But, there's more to it, Priscilla. A lot more to it than that."

47

I spent three years at the federal prison in Leaven-worth," said Paco Rangel. "This was back in the '70s. I'll tell you what happened. I was on a PT boat on the Mekong River. I found a nice plot of land, belonged to some old gook man. I made a deal with him to grow me some very precious grass. Stuff came up out of the ground as fine as anything anybody ever smoked. Never had an unsatisfied customer. I had it set up to make one good crop, sell it, and my tour of duty would be over. In fact, it turned out that business was so good, I extended my tour of duty for a year. That's where I learned one of the problems that come up when you're dealing with the best merchandise around. Word got around. Eventually, it got to Navy Intelligence and they caught me. I was brought back to the States, court-martialed, and I ended up serving three full years in Leavenworth."

"What's that got to do with me, Paco?" Priscilla asked. "That was a long time ago."

"I can't fault you for saying that, Priscilla," he said. "Those three years in Leavenworth did indeed make a very serious impression on me. I can't go to prison again. Thing is, you get good customers, you want to keep them supplied. You deal with the same customers, though, it will definitely increase your risk. Word gets out. There's more people want to buy your merchandise. There's always some risk involved, that's true of any business. I have all the risks of any business, plus I have the risk of going to prison, too.

"There's no way I could get rid of all the risk involved, but I could reduce it quite a bit. I came up with a plan. I told myself, how about setting up the operation, run it in one location for three years, no more, and then move on. Set up somewhere else. I can still supply my customers, but nobody knows where my operation is. That way, by the time the law begins to figure something's up, I'm already packed up and gone. The law is lazy in these small towns. They get wind of a problem, they have to do something about it. If the problem goes away by itself, then it doesn't concern them anymore.

"Where I fucked up is that I like this place. I extended my operation here by two years already. Two years ago, I was ready to make my move. I bought a place out in West Texas, near Stonewall. Out in the fucking desert. It was going to be more difficult to raise my plants, but it could be done. I've been all set to move, but I stayed because there's not been even a hint that the law is on to me. The signs that it was becoming dangerous were all there, but I guess I got lazy and didn't want to go. The last thing, I didn't figure on Ralph Mason."

Paco Rangel stopped talking and left the bedroom. A minute later, he returned, carrying two bottles of beer.

"I guess it's late enough in the afternoon to have a beer while we talk," he said. "Anyway, I have to wait until tomorrow morning before I can go."

He put the neck of the bottle to Priscilla's mouth.

"Here. Drink," he said.

Priscilla took a small sip of the beer. Paco upended the bottle and drank almost half of it.

"My mouth's a little dry," he said. "I really don't want to do this."

"Then, don't!" Priscilla said. "Give me a chance."

"We'll see," he said. "It took me two months to figure out what to do about Ralph Mason."

"What did he do to you?"

"Ralph Mason had a mouth that he let run too much. That was his problem, and eventually, it became my problem. He talked too damn much. Not only that, but pretty soon, he's flashing his roll around, trying to impress people with it like he never had more than twenty bucks in his pocket in his entire damned redneck life. He did his drinking and he brought his women to the Ligon Wells Saloon. I know for a fact that that ol' girl that owns the place is shacked up with a deputy sheriff. It's a very dangerous place to go shooting off your mouth. She's bound to know everybody's business in town, and how soon do you think it would be before she's telling her boyfriend? Then I'd have the law all over this place. All because some redneck fuck couldn't keep his damn mouth shut."

"You decided to kill him because he went around blabbing about you?"

"No, I'd'a killed him a lot sooner if it was only his damn mouth. You see, Ralph Mason was one of my drivers. When I first came into Larson, I stayed low-key, not going out too much, setting up my operation. The key to it was raising my vegetables. When I had a good crop, I took some samples to San Antonio, got me a list of clients, and with that part of the business going, I set about to where I make my real money. Once I got my marijuana field set up with good cover, I let my contacts know that I was ready to begin shipments, and I started to take in their orders."

"You sound like you're pretty smart about setting things up," said Priscilla.

"I made the runs myself for about six, eight months. Then, I was talking to this guy at the Ligon Wells Saloon one time, who works for a farm called Ranger Chicks, and they deliver fresh chickens to San Antonio, Houston, Austin, and

Corpus Christi. I do most of my business in those cities. The way the guy talked gave me some ideas. I got to know more of the people who worked on that farm. I made sure I got to know the drivers. Inside a year, I had it all set up."

"How did it work?"

"Not too difficult," said Paco. "I packed the shit in foot-square bundles. The Ranger Chicks people don't have the space at the packing house to park their trucks, so the drivers get to take the trucks home. I'd meet the drivers at different places, never the same place more than once or twice, and never, never near Larson or Lexington. It's where I'd transfer the bundles to them. Sometimes, I'd take off the camper shell on my pickup and load boxes of vegetables so that anybody passing by would think I'm a roadside vendor. Along with some vegetables I'd bag up for them, they'd take home my grass bundles and load them in the refrigerator trucks. A driver gets to Houston, let's say, makes his chicken deliveries, and nearby, there's a contact who takes delivery of the bundle I sent up. The driver picks up an envelope with my cash, brings it to me. I pay him what he's got coming and I give him another shipment."

"How long did you figure you could get away with it?"

"Oh, a year to set up, two years free and easy, and then another year, maybe two, with mounting risk. Except for Ralph Mason's mouth. There was a deputy sheriff not too long ago, his name is Hank Solís. He got on to Ralph Mason. He started to ask questions. In fact, I was in there at the Ligon Wells Saloon when he started asking questions of the Ranger Chicks workers. They didn't know anything. At least, Deputy Solís couldn't put Ralph Mason and the shit together, or he certainly couldn't connect me and Ralph. Nevertheless, that's when I knew it was time for me to move on."

48

"What did you do?" Priscilla asked.

"Before getting the hell out, I had to shut down everything here first. It was going to take me three or four months. Even though it was too damn risky, I couldn't afford to just leave my customers hanging. It's important to keep good relations with your customers, you know. But, I had the problem of Ralph Mason and the deputy sheriff snooping around, asking questions about him. I told Ralph Mason I was going to have to let him go as one of my drivers. I told him he was too hot to keep him going. He didn't like it at all. To pacify him, I let him make one last shipment. And, then another of my drivers couldn't make a run, so I got Ralph to do that one, too. I should've made the delivery myself. But, I let him do it. He made two deliveries that day, and he never came to our agreed meeting place to bring me my money. I had to track him down to the Ligon Wells Saloon, where he was buying drinks for everybody. I stayed away from him, so as people couldn't see us together, but I got to him in the bathroom and told him I wanted my money. He said he'd decided to pay himself a bonus with the cash he'd gotten in Houston. He said he deserved extra for making the run to Austin, so he'd keep that, too. He told me I shouldn't mind it, after all he'd done for me. In fact, he said he should've been taking a bonus all along, a bonus amounting to half of what he brought back."

"He got greedy then?"

"No, he got a case of the stupids. And, once he did the first stupid thing, it was only a matter of time before he did the next logical, but even more stupid, thing. Almost a month later, he caught up with me at the grocery store in White Leg. He was waiting for me out in the parking lot, where he told me he'd run out of the money that he'd taken from me as a bonus. He said I was making entirely too much money for a Mexican. Like it or not, he said, I had myself a partner. Only, he wasn't going to do any of the work. To keep things nice and easy, he said, he wanted me to meet him every week and deliver to him half of what I'd taken in. He said he'd trust me about adding everything up and delivering him his half."

"But, you were already going to move, weren't you?" asked Priscilla. "You could've left without killing him."

"What do you think? Before I could even ask, he said if I didn't go along with the way he wanted things done, he'd go to the sheriff. He would confess he'd been involved in the deliveries and tell them where they could find me. That's when he made my decision for me. I'd already bought the place in Stonewall. All I had left to do was meet my contacts and let them know I was going to shut down for a little while, but I'd be back in business in a year or so. In the meantime, I couldn't take the chance that Ralph Mason might make good on his threat."

"You took care of him, Paco," said Priscilla. "You can let me go. I'm not going to the sheriff."

Paco ignored her.

"On the day I decided to let him have it, I waited outside of the Ligon Wells Saloon. I was supposed to meet him the next day to deliver cash to him. It had to be that night, when he wouldn't suspect anything. My plan was to follow him out to where he lived with his brother, about five miles out of town. I'd stop him once he was off the road, before he got to the house. I'd come at him, pick him up, and drive him somewhere and shoot him. It would give me a few days before they found the body, and by then, I'd be long gone, and there'd be nothing to connect me with him."

"I'm the one who spoiled the plan," said Priscilla. "Is that it?"

"I had not planned on him picking you up at the Ligon Wells Saloon."

"He didn't pick me up," said Priscilla. "I picked him up."

"When the two of you left the saloon together, I couldn't afford to wait any longer. I thought for a minute I would have to shoot you in the motel room, but I decided against it. I didn't see any need to."

"There's still no need to, Paco," Priscilla said.

"Things have changed, Priscilla."

Paco Rangel finished his beer. He'd helped Priscilla to drink only half of the contents of the bottle he'd brought for her. He checked the duct tape to make sure she was securely tied up on the bed. At the bedroom door, he turned.

"I have a bunch of things to do before I can get on the road," he said. "I won't be too far away. I'm keeping the house in sight the whole time. If you get loose and make a run for it, I'll see you and I'll catch up to you. You won't get far. So, I suggest that you don't try anything. Stay calm, will you?"

She remained on the bed in a sitting position until she became uncomfortable and she felt the joints in her shoulders stiffening. She leaned backward to lie flat on her back, but this became too uncomfortable to bear and she rolled over to rest her body on its side. It felt better, and after a few minutes, she rolled over to rest on the other side. She tried several times to loosen the duct tape but was unable to.

She had no idea of how long Paco had been gone. The sun had already turned orange, casting eerie shadows inside the house at the onset of evening.

When Paco returned, he carried three black plastic trash bags, which he emptied, one after the other, on the bed beside Priscilla. The bags contained bundles of money, in two-inch stacks bound with rubber bands. From the floor next to the bed, below the window ledges, Paco pulled away a throw rug and lifted two boards which had been cut in short lengths. Beneath them was a combination safe. He dialed the combination, opened the safe, and took out more money. He lifted up one of the stacks bound with a rubber band and waved it at Priscilla.

"Did you ever get a look at a million dollars?" he asked.

"No, not in cash. I've seen more than that in bearer bonds, which are the same as cash," Priscilla said. "Is that how much you've made?"

"Yes, indeed! It's over a million. Took me twelve years," he said. "But, I did it. All of it is tax-free."

"That's better than municipal bonds," said Priscilla.

"You know, now that you mention it, I thought about investing it in the stock market, or something like that. A legitimate business, maybe," said Paco. "In the years of Ronald Reagan, I could've made a killing. Ronald Reagan, now, there was a president who did a lot of good in terms of people getting the chance to make some decent money."

Priscilla was tired and stiff from having her wrists and knees bound. She stared at Paco with wide-open eyes, trying to sound more alert than she felt.

"With some good investments, Paco," said Priscilla, "you don't have to set up another operation. You could live very comfortably on the earnings from that money. I know some people who could help you do that."

"Out of the question," he said. "No one will ever know I have this money. There is just no way anybody can know about it, if I'm going to keep it and stay out of the hands of the police."

"How do you plan on spending it?"

"Well, I'll tell you," he said. "This right here, all that you see, is enough for me to live on modestly. Except, when I retire, I want to live a bit more lavishly than that. I worked for it and I think I've earned it. I'm not aiming for extravagant luxury, you understand. My plan is to settle in some place for a couple of years, live well, and before people begin to ask questions about me and where I get my money, I will disappear. I'll find some other place and start over. Moving like that, and having to establish myself over and over again, takes money. More than what I have here. That means I've got to set up and go through one more operation. Maybe two."

Priscilla tried another tack.

"Why don't you take me with you?" she said. "I'd be next to you all the time. You could keep an eye on me, not that you'd have to. I know how to keep quiet. But, I'd be right there with you all the time."

"It's tempting, dear," said Paco Rangel. "In fact, I was thinking of doing just that. I thought about telling you everything and then asking you to go with me. I've never been with anyone as much into sex as you. That is a mighty fine blowjob you give. A man could get real attached to it."

"You don't have to give anything up," she said, trying to raise up to a sitting position.

"I'll tell you the truth, Priscilla. I'm the nervous type," he said. "No loose ends, that's me."

"So, you're going to kill me?"

"No, I'm not going to do it personally; but, yes, it amounts to the same thing. Come on, let's not talk about anything so unpleasant. I'm getting hungry. Why don't I throw something together for us to eat. All the excitement around here, we didn't have lunch, and now its getting on to evening already."

It took Paco nearly an hour before he returned bearing their dinner on a tray. It was ham and cheese sandwiches, with potato chips. There was one bottle of beer on the tray.

"I'm sorry, but you're going to have to pass on the beer," he said. "It'll cause problems if you have to go to the bathroom a lot, especially in the middle of the night. I want a good night's sleep since I intend to do a lot of traveling tomorrow. I may have to be on the road for a solid twenty-four hours or more. Day after tomorrow, I want to be in Oregon, or close to it."

They finished their sandwiches. Paco took the tray with the dishes to the kitchen. When he returned, he carried another bottle of beer.

Paco Rangel undressed, got into the bed, and snuggled up to Priscilla. He slipped his hand inside her T-shirt to fondle her breasts. She could feel his hard dick through the material of her blue jeans. He pressed hard against her.

"I promised myself I wouldn't do this," he said hoarsely. "It's just not my style, forcing myself on a woman. But, you do have a sweet ass on you."

"You don't have to force me, Paco," she said, assuming that Paco referred to oral sex. "I'll do it for you."

Without a word, he unsnapped her jeans and pulled them down over her buttocks and down her thighs as far as the duct tape would allow. He spread her cheeks and she felt the tip of his penis working its way into the puckered opening of her anus. Priscilla winced as it went in, silent tears beginning to flow from her eyes.

49

At two o'clock in the morning, Priscilla lay on the king-size bed with her eyes wide open, listening to the steady rumbling of Paco Rangel's snores. Less than a mile away, Orthal Mason slowed and then stopped his pickup on the sandy gravel road a hundred yards away from the entrance to Paco Rangel's place. The pickup truck groaned and clattered as if ready to cough for the last time and die. In the bedroom, Priscilla could hear the faraway sound of a sputtering engine.

Orthal Mason moved the truck forward, easing the tires over the rusted cattle guard, one pipe at a time to keep the clanging to a minimum. He knew the house was ahead somewhere. All he could see in the moonlight was a short piece of clear ground that edged into darkness in the mesquite brush.

He pulled the truck to the side of the entrance, where he left it, and went the rest of the way on foot. He carried the Winchester 30-30 close to his side, cleaving to the ruts of the road as he trotted onward. He was still well within the stand of oak trees. In what looked like an opening in a black wall, he could see the outline of the house in the moonlight. There was a dim yellow light inside the house. There had to be dogs and other animals, he told himself. They would make a commotion if he went any further. He walked off the road, weaving in his drunkenness among the thick trunks of the oaks until he couldn't see the house anymore. He sat on the ground to wait for morning. In a minute or so, he was fast asleep.

It had been late in the afternoon, although there was still plenty of daylight left, when Orthal Mason had driven into Lexington. It occurred to him that if he were to go into Paco Rangel's place in broad daylight, it would give the son of a bitch too much warning. The thing to do was wait for dark; in fact, the best time would be closer to daybreak. Let the son of a bitch get up and get ready to go about his chores. Go at him while he's half asleep and not yet alert. That would be the time to surprise the son of a bitch. Let him have what he had coming for killing his son.

The best place to pass the evening was in the Ligon Wells Saloon. He parked his pickup truck and went in. Orthal Mason took a table by himself, not wanting to be company for anybody. The bitch, Georgene Henderson, the one who lived with the deputy, brought him his beer, collecting the dollar each time, like she couldn't hold off charging him until he'd finished his drinking.

Orthal Mason began to think about his son, Ralph. He had been a good boy, wild like the others, but still a good boy. Where Ralph had been different was in him being a ladies' man. Women sure liked Ralph, and that was because he liked them back. In fact, he'd had a woman in the room, so the story went, and he'd been about to get him some when that cowardly Mexican shot him in the back.

It was a good thing that there were still some deputies in the sheriff's office who didn't like the way that the half-breed Mexican, Joe Blue, and that other full-blooded Mexican, Hank Solís, ran things between them, not giving anybody else a chance. He'd gotten around to talking to those boys, the good deputies. They'd told him about the woman Ralph had been getting ready to fuck that night.

It was too damn bad that his boy was gone. That Ralph was something, all right.

Orthal Mason remained at the Ligon Wells Saloon, drinking beer and getting drunker. His thoughts flashed to the 30-30 on the floorboard of his truck. He kept practicing how he was going to confront Paco Rangel. There was no doubt in his mind that Paco had killed Ralph. It was there all the time, except he'd been in too much grief to see it. If his boy was dead, then the Mexican sure must've had something to do with it.

Ralph sure must've had something going with that Mexican, Paco Rangel.

He'd taught his boys good. He wasn't much for working. Never was. He always managed to get what he needed for himself and his family. He could take pride in the fact that he provided. And, he'd taught his boys to do the same. None in his family ever begged for no government welfare. And, they never would. They would provide for what they needed, no doubt about that. And, not with no government welfare, neither. Not like the lazy damn niggers and Mexicans.

He'd always made sure that his boys were taken care of. Now that his boys were grown up, they returned the favor. He couldn't get around as much as he used to. He had his second wife, who'd stuck by him, and those two teen-age boys left in the house. Things cost more every year, it wasn't easy to make do anymore.

His boys did help out a lot. He'd taught them good. Everything that came their way, they set a little aside for him. He never asked where they got it or how they came by it. He'd never try to horn in on what deals they had going. His two youngest boys were pretty damned good with their hunting and providing meat for the table.

The other boys brought him money when they had it to spare, but they weren't like Ralph. That boy Ralph always had a way to make money, hard cash. Lately, Ralph was into something good, real good, because for a year and a half, he'd brought him twenty, thirty dollars every week. Sometimes more. He sure must've had something sweet and juicy going. And, it had to be that Mexican truck farmer who was in on it with Ralph.

After he started on his fourth beer, Orthal Mason looked at the clock on the far wall of the saloon. It said eight-o'clock. Still early. He thought about going home to sleep and getting up early to drive out to Larson to find the Mexican, but decided against it. It was better to get on the place and sleep for a bit in the truck.

Ralph was a good boy. His killing had to be avenged. There could be no doubt about that. He'd have to take care of that Mexican, else his boy, Ralph, wouldn't get any peace where he rested.

He raised his hand with the beer bottle in the air, signaling for another. The beers had flushed his face, and his thinking became sluggish. Repeatedly, he saw the image of Paco Rangel in the sights of his 30-30. He tried to get his mind clear on what he was going to do.

Now, killing the Mexican was one thing, he told himself. That part was right, he was going to kill the Mexican. His mind became even more thick and sluggish as he tried to think through to what it was that was trying to get to him. There was something on the other side of his mind that he couldn't figure out. He knew it was there, but he just couldn't get through to it. If only his head would clear for a second.

Orthal Mason raised himself out the chair where he sat. He stood up, having trouble staying on his feet. Sitting at the same damn chair for three hours without getting up had taken its toll. It had been more than an hour since he'd had the urge to go to the piss hole, but he'd held back on it. He wanted to save it until the end of his beer drinking, when he'd leave the place and head out for Larson.

He couldn't hold it any longer. If he sat any longer without going, he was going to piss in his pants. Goddamn! He wasn't through with his beer drinking yet. Since he'd come up with his plan to drive out and wait in the truck to get the son of a bitch at sunrise, Orthal Mason figured there was no harm in sitting where he was and drinking beer until the place closed.

Instead of going to the pisser at a rear corner of the bar, Orthal Mason went outside. He wanted to take in a breath of fresh air. Maybe the air would clear his head a little so he could make it through to what it was that he needed to think about. He walked out past the parking lot to an area in the dark. He got behind a tree to take his leak.

When he finished pissing, he zipped up his pants and was on his way back to the bar when it came to him. That Mexican had to have money in the house. How did it come that the Mexican had money? Ralph worked for Porter Labelle, made pretty good money driving his refrigerator trucks. The Mexican had to be involved in that business somehow. Could be they were stealing chickens.

For damn sure that the job with Porter Labelle didn't pay the kind of money Ralph flashed around. He'd bought himself a new truck, one that came with everything in it, air conditioning, radio, and lots more. Ralph had taken to wearing new boots, and not those $49.95 ropers, neither; and not just one pair, neither. And, he had a new hat to go with every one of the new pairs of boots he wore.

No doubt about it, Ralph was into a sweet and juicy deal. And that Mexican was in on it with him somehow.

Orthal Mason was ready to leave when that bitch that lived with the deputy, Georgene Henderson, came over to pick up his last beer. There was still a little bit in the bottle, and he didn't want to let it go.

"Take it with you then, Orthal," Georgene said. "It can't be on the table after midnight. Drink the rest of it on the way home."

"Let me have six more to go, Georgene," he said groggily.

"You should've let me know at last call, Orthal," said Georgene. "It's too late. It's past the time I can take money for it."

"Well, just let me have some beer. I'll make it up to you some other time."

"Not a chance, Orthal. You go on home now," said Georgene, tired, leaving him with his beer, going to the other tables to pick up beer bottles.

"Bitch!" said Orthal Mason under his breath.

"You say something, Orthal?" Georgene Henderson said as she turned to face him, hand on her hip.

"I'm just going home, Georgene," he said.

"That's what I thought you said, Orthal," said Georgene. "Good night to you."

Outside, he'd thought for a minute about tossing the beer bottle through the lone window of the saloon. That idiot, Johnny Watkins, the one she lived with, would probably come out and make him pay for the window. Besides, he had something important to do at daybreak. Maybe not drinking any more beer was a better idea. Of course, drinking had never interfered with anything he had to do.

He drove through Lexington and took the road past the twin bridges. A mile down, he veered to the right and headed in the direction of White Leg. Fourteen miles further, he came to a Y intersection, with the signs pointing to White Leg, four miles to the left, heading south.

He turned right, going north to Larson. In Larson, he turned right once more and continued up the paved county road until he saw the white church in his headlights. He turned off onto the sandy gravel road. In fifteen more minutes he was at the entrance to Paco Rangel's place. The noise of his pickup drifted in the air and into Paco's house where Priscilla could hear it.

He drove in and shut off the engine and headlights of his pickup. He got his Winchester 30-30 from the floorboard and continued on foot. He'd find a place near the house, maybe catch some shuteye before daybreak.

At daybreak, he'd kill the Mexican.

But, first there was something else to do.

The Mexican was going to have to tell him where he kept his money. It'd be a damn shame to have all that money on the place and not get his hands on it.

First, he'd get the money.

Then, he'd shoot the Mexican.

50

It was still dark when Joe Blue came out of his house in White Leg. There was a clinging wetness in the air. When he started the engine of his pickup truck and left it to idle while it warmed up, he looked down the street to see the low rolling fog under the street lamps. He backed the truck out of the driveway and headed for the center of White Leg.

At the crossroads, he turned into the gravel parking lot of the Dairy Queen, whose neon lights shone brightly in the hazy fog. There were a few figures inside, one of whom, Hank Solís, he recognized right away. His large, bulky shape was unmistakable.

"You're early, Hank," said Joe Blue, blowing steam from the Styrofoam cup of coffee that he'd picked up at the serve-yourself counter.

"I just got here, Joe," said Hank Solís, chewing the last of his first breakfast taco.

"How'd it go with the kids last night? They drive you out of the house at all?"

"Drove me out of my mind is more like it," said Hank Solís, rolling his head in disbelief. "Remember me telling you I was going to get fried chicken? What I had in mind is that we'd all sit at the table and have supper, like a family. Well, my kids had other ideas about that."

"I bet they did," said Joe Blue.

"They brought a grocery bag full of videos with them," Hank Solís said, beginning his second breakfast taco. "They rented six, eight of those things. There's not enough time in the evening to see all those movies, Joe! Each one of them came to the table, stuffed a biscuit in his mouth, grabbed a handful of french fries in one hand, and took a piece of chicken in the other. Off they went back to the television. The only word I got out of them came from my youngest, and she said she got cheated out of the last piece of chicken. I had to make her a bologna sandwich."

"They're just kids, Hank," said Joe Blue.

"The worst part is when I went to watch one of the movies with them. It was a movie called 'Reform School Girls.' Where do they get that shit? All through the movie, at least what I saw of it, there's these women with their tits hanging out all over the place, none of them gets dressed except in their underwear and you can see right through them. I didn't see any point to complaining about it, so I gave up and went to bed. This morning the television was on and all my kids were stretched over the living room floor, asleep."

Joe Blue smiled. "My kids'll probably be like that pretty soon."

"You're not eating, Joe?" asked Hank.

"I had breakfast at home," said Joe Blue.

"Anyway, she's raising them, not me," said Hank Solís, swallowing, taking a sip of his Diet Coke and then his coffee.

"At least you had them with you for the night," said Joe Blue.

"Yeah, I did at that. She and her new boyfriend wanted some privacy, chase each other naked around my ex-house," said Hank.

"Does that bother you, Hank?"

"Not anymore. It did at first, you know," said Hank. "I knew it was over when we got the divorce papers, all nice and legal, fair and square. But, then, I thought I could go on, you know, live a little like a single man, and then when I was done with it, she'd be there to take me back."

"Maybe she's got to go through her own phase of living single herself, Hank," said Joe Blue.

"Yeah, maybe so. Except from what the kids say, and don't get me wrong, I don't ask outright, this one's pretty serious," said Hank Solís. "Looks like they're asking the kids what they think of having a new dad in the house."

"Think she'll go through with it? Wasn't she close to marrying somebody last year?"

"She was, at that," said Hank, his joy betrayed by a thin smile. "Three ready-made kids is a lot of responsibility for a couple starting in a new marriage. But, I hope she stays lucky and goes through with it this time."

Hank Solís finished his breakfast. Joe Blue refilled the Styrofoam coffee cup and got into his pickup truck. They had agreed to drive out to Paco Rangel's place, leave one of the trucks at the entrance and then go on together in one truck. That way, they could drive on to Lexington after they spoke with Paco Rangel.

There was a hazy blue light of the sun coming up as they headed north out of White Leg. As he looked to the sides of the road, Joe Blue could see little patches of white fog that resembled discarded clouds on the gravel roads.

At the entrance to Paco Rangel' place, Hank Solís pulled his pickup to the side of the road and got out. Joe Blue stopped his pickup to let him come aboard and then maneuvered over the rusted cattle guard and stopped just beyond the entrance to the place.

They saw the battered pickup truck parked beneath the large oak tree that stood as a sentinel at the entrance gate.

"Is that his truck, Paco's, over there by that tree, Hank?" asked Joe Blue.

"Nope, I'd recognize that truck anywhere. Ain't another like it for fifty miles," said Hank. "That's Orthal Mason's pick-up."

"What the hell's he doing here?"

"I don't know, Joe. I say let's go and take a look in the truck before we go on. I got a feeling about this."

Joe Blue steered his pickup truck over to the oak tree. Hank Solís stepped out, looked into Orthal Mason's pickup, and then opened the driver's door. He leaned over to reach inside. He shut the door and came back to get in Joe Blue's truck.

"Take a look at this," said Hank Solís, holding the box in his hand, palm up.

"Thirty-thirties," said Joe Blue.

"You think Orthal's figured out that Paco Rangel killed his boy?"

"I don't know, Hank," said Joe Blue. "But, let's go find out."

Hank Solís checked his revolver to make sure it was loaded.

51

Priscilla awoke with her jeans still bunched around at her upper thighs. She lay in the darkness of the bedroom, her bound hands forming a tight knot at her knees. She stared with burning eyes straight up at the ceiling, listening to Paco Rangel murmur in sleep and occasionally snore. She'd been awake through the night, having drifted off to sleep for not quite an hour. She had been unable to quell the trembling that had overtaken her body throughout the night.

Several times in the night, as Paco slept, she had tried to slip her hands out of the duct tape that bound her wrists. The more she struggled with the tape without freeing her hands, the more she trembled afterward, overtaken with fright and frustration. As the light of dawn seeped in through the window, she despaired of ever getting an opening to get away from Paco.

The trembling shook her body to the point where the bed itself shook. Paco had left her with little doubt that he couldn't afford to leave her alive. For him it was more than the expedient of an extra few days to get away. She had seen his face, the marks on his body, and she could certainly give a very good description of him.

After he had forcibly taken her from behind, she had begged him again to let her go. She gave him every reason she could think of, assuring him and reassuring him that she would keep her mouth shut. All he had to do was take her with him, leave her some place, and continue on his way. No one would find her and ask any questions. But, let's say they did, she told him, he would be so far away and hidden in his new identity that he'd never be caught.

None of her entreaties had an effect on Paco's decision.

All of a sudden, next to her, she felt Paco stirring. She could feel the rustle of the bed as he slipped out to go into the bathroom. She heard the stream of his urine in the toilet bowl. She remained on her side, keeping her back to him. She stared out the window, seeing the gray dawn mottled with streaks of blue.

Paco returned to the bedroom, his soft steps coming around the bed to the side where Priscilla lay. He bent over and began to unwrap the duct tape. When he had it off completely, he pulled her jeans over her feet and tossed them aside. He spread her legs. She removed her T-shirt on her own.

"Let me go to the bathroom first," she said.

"Okay, but make it quick."

He followed her as she went into the bathroom. She knew to keep the door open. She was embarrassed to have him watch her sitting on the toilet. When she finished with the toilet, Priscilla rinsed her mouth, and returned to the bedroom. Paco moved aside to let her get back in the bed.

Priscilla lay on her back, her hands clasped over her stomach.

She spread her legs as Paco kneeled, got on the bed and dropped on top of her. He guided himself in and began to hump furiously. In a minute or so, he grunted and was finished.

"I want you to know that I've never done it like this before," he said, getting to his feet. He picked up his jeans from the floor, got into them, zipping them up.

"Why'd you do it, then?" she said.

"I couldn't tell you, right now," he said, "but I know I'll feel guilty about it some other time."

He left the room to go in the parlor for a minute and returned carrying her suitcase. He dropped the suitcase on the bed, opened it, and tossed away all of her clothes.

"You won't be needing so many clothes anymore," he said.

The money was in a pile on the floor beside the bed. He stuffed all of the money into Priscilla's suitcase. In a canvas duffle bag, he stuffed some clothes, jeans, T-shirts, and underwear. From the bathroom, he retrieved a bare collection of toilet articles.

Priscilla got out of the bed and onto her feet.

Paco looked at her intently.

"I'd like to put on my clothes," she said softly, as if resigned to her fate.

"Don't try anything," he said.

Priscilla dressed in her jeans and T-shirt. Paco waited, eager to get going.

"Come on," he said impatiently, "I need to get the fuck out of here!"

They stepped onto the porch and the black pit bull crept silently to stand beside them. Mariachi leaned his stiff furry pelt against Priscilla's ankle.

Paco Rangel jumped off the porch, walked rapidly along the pebbled pathway of the garden. At the white picket fence, he kicked the latch away and kicked again to send the gate flying to one side.

At the truck, he yanked the door handle of the passenger side and threw both bags on the floorboard. Priscilla stood close by the open door of the truck, Mariachi at her feet. Paco kicked the dog aside to roughly pull on Priscilla's arm. He shoved her into the truck, where she had to keep her feet on top of the bags. Paco slammed the door shut.

Mariachi wandered off into the short distance. He turned, sat on his haunches, and watched the truck.

When Paco opened the driver's door to get in the truck, Priscilla saw the nickel-plated pistol stuck into the waistband of his jeans. A chill ran through Priscilla's body and she began to shake uncontrollably. Tears welled up in her eyes.

52

Orthal Mason awoke with his dirty denim shirt soaked with the morning dew and the wet fog. He got to his feet, stretched, and made his way through the oak trees until he got a view of Paco's house. He watched Paco Rangel and Priscilla Arrabal get into the truck with the silver camper shell. He held the Winchester loosely at his side, thumb on the hammer.

He saw Paco shove the woman into the truck. She didn't look to be any too happy to be going with him. From the distance where he stood, he gritted his teeth. I can drop the son of a bitch right now, thought Orthal Mason. He gathered up the liquid in his mouth and spat. That boy's going somewhere. He could be going to get his money. He can stay alive until he gets to that money.

He continued to watch as Paco got into the truck, started the engine, threw it into gear and turned away to the right from the house. The truck went past the barn, rounded a clump of trees in the distance, and disappeared. He saw the black pit bull follow the truck, going at a quick trot after it. On the other side of the clump of trees, he spied the cab of the truck bobbing above the top of the young mesquite until it finally disappeared for good.

Orthal Mason decided to stay behind, out of sight, and follow the truck. The dog going after the truck was something else he had to contend with now. He'd have to stay far enough behind to keep the dog from getting wind of him.

A few minutes later, Joe Blue and Hank Solís parked in front of Paco Rangel's house. They waited for a moment for someone to come out. When no came, Joe Blue pulled the door handle on his side of the truck.

"Let's see what's shaking inside the house," he said.

"We don't have a warrant, Joe," said Hank Solís.

"If we see anything in there that we want to take with us, including Paco Rangel," said Joe Blue, "we'll get us a warrant after. Everything'll be nice and legal."

"That's the way I like to do things, Joe," said Hank Solís, grinning. "Everything nice and legal."

While Joe Blue went up on the porch and inside the house, Hank Solís decided to look around the place. After five minutes, they met beside Joe Blue's pickup truck.

"What did you find?" asked Hank Solís.

"There's women's clothes lying on the bed and on the floor," Joe Blue said. "Toilet articles, female variety, in a bag on the floor. From the look of things in the kitchen, it was dinner for two last night."

"I never heard that he had a woman living with him, Joe," said Hank Solís.

"Unless he wears those clothes himself," said Joe Blue, "he's got a woman with him. Question is, where'd they go off to?"

"There's the answer in that direction, headed out that way," said Hank Solís. "See these tire tracks here. The ground is damp, pretty good for leaving tracks. The truck backed up a bit, and then headed in that direction, going around those trees and then likely circling toward the back and away from the house. From the footprints on the ground here, there's a man and a woman."

"Let's go after them."

"There's also another set of prints," said Hank Solís. "They begin over there, like somebody came out of the trees, and then went after the truck."

"Orthal Mason?"

"Let's go and find out."

Paco Rangel parked his pickup truck on a high bank overlooking the dry creek. It was the same creek where Priscilla had left Ralph Mason's pickup truck three miles in the other direction.

"Come on, get out!" said Paco Rangel, his voice hard, urgent.

Priscilla opened the passenger door and stepped out, slipping on the soft dirt and falling over, struggling to regain her balance. She landed with her weight on her elbows.

Paco Rangel became short-tempered and rushed over to yank her to her feet by pulling on her shoulder. Priscilla was no sooner on her feet than Paco dragged her in the direction of woods thick with oak trees. They followed a cow path inside the forest that ran parallel with the dry creek.

Mariachi, who had already been kicked by his master, followed cautiously, staying behind, using the trees for cover.

Orthal Mason had lagged behind, nearly a quarter mile, continuing to follow their trail only after Paco's truck went out of sight. He came up to the truck after Paco and Priscilla were already deep in the woods. He could clearly see their footprints in the soft earth. He took his time following them. He wanted the Mexican to have plenty of time to dig out the money before he showed up to claim it and Paco's life.

Orthal Mason was a good five-hundred yards into the woods when Joe Blue and Hank Solís drove up behind Paco's truck and stopped. Joe Blue killed the ignition.

Hank Solís stepped down from Joe Blue's pickup truck, walked past Paco Rangel's truck, going ahead ten yards or so, before he stopped to get a good look at the ground. He came back to Joe Blue, who was looking inside Paco's truck.

"What did you find?" asked Joe Blue.

"Looks like the same two sets of footprints that got into the truck," said Hank Solís. "I make out another set of tracks following Paco, if it is Paco, and his girlfriend."

"There's a suitcases and another bag on the floorboard of the truck," said Joe Blue.

"So, the two of them are planning to go off somewhere," said Hank Solís.

"I'd say so, from the looks of things," said Joe Blue.

"And, Orthal Mason doesn't plan on either of them coming out of these woods alive."

"We'd better catch up to them before Orthal Mason does," said Joe Blue.

"How do you want to handle this, Joe?" asked Hank Solís.

Joe Blue said, "Let's follow their tracks for a bit. We don't know how far they plan on going. When we get a good idea which way they're headed, I want you to swing around, run as fast as you can and try to head them off. Come out in front of them."

"Looks like they might be following the course of the creek."

"That's what it looks like to me."

"Listen," said Hank Solís, hitching up his pants. "I'll just go this way here. Maybe I can get enough headway."

"Okay, you do that. And, I'll follow at a pretty good clip, and maybe I can get to Orthal Mason before he gets to them."

Hank Solís took off at a fast run, breathing tightly, swinging far from the creek, dodging the thick trunks of the oak trees and hanging vines dropping from the branches. The vegetation was sparse because of the tree shading, but he did catch the toe of his boots on some vines and nearly tripped. He kept going.

53

The creek made a sharp right-angle turn and the terrain sloped upward. At the bottom, in a ravine deeply gouged out of the earth, Paco spoke for the first time.

"Go that way," he said, pointing with his arm.

Priscilla turned to see in which direction his arm pointed.

After another hundred yards they left the shade of the woods. They were looking at a field of marijuana plants, higher than Paco's six feet. The plants were staggered, not planted in straight rows, but planted to resemble the random scatter of nature.

There was ten feet of clearing between the trees and the field of marijuana plants. When they had walked to the edge of the marijuana field, Priscilla was startled by the sudden appearance of three guard dogs, Doberman Pinschers.

They came out of the marijuana plants, their sleek black and tan coats glistening in the rising sun. They stopped at the end of the field and dropped back on their haunches, looking up, first at Priscilla and then at Paco Rangel. The dogs were lined up at the edge of the field, with six feet of space between them. Each dog had its mouth open, breathing in short, expectant breaths.

The dog nearest Priscilla made a leaping gesture, springing from its hind legs, its mouth wide open, its teeth bared, as if daring her to come forward. The dogs had been trained to not cross the edge of the field.

Priscilla turned to look at Paco Rangel, an imploring look on her face.

"Sorry," said Paco Rangel, his face a hardened mask. "This is how it's got to be."

Before Priscilla could fully assess the terror she faced, Paco Rangel lifted his foot and kicked her forcefully on her right buttock. Priscilla ran for a yard or two to keep on her feet, but fell forward, landing on her hands on the ground. She was still short of the edge of the marijuana field by a foot or two. Two of the dogs sprang in front of her face, baring their teeth, not more than a foot away from her.

She lifted her hands around her head and face to ward off the attack of the dogs, which she knew was coming.

The dogs growled menacingly, but nothing else happened. The attack she expected did not come.

She opened an eye, peering through her opened fingers. Inches away from her face she saw the stiff fur of the black pelt, and the white feet of the pit-bull terrier.

Priscilla lifted her head and saw Mariachi staring down the three Dobermans. Mariachi kept his head low to the ground, his jaws clamped shut. The Dobermans snarled, mouths opened, baring their teeth.

Priscilla sat up and then got to her feet. She heard the explosion of the shot behind her and saw the dirt spurt a foot away from Mariachi's head.

As if it were a signal for the fight to begin, the Dobermans leapt at once in Mariachi's direction. Mariachi opened his mouth wide as he saw the attack coming and grabbed the first Doberman's snout in his mouth. His powerful jaw clamped on the smooth line of the Doberman's jaw, crunched, and then he jerked his head, sending the Doberman flying off to one side.

It happened so quickly that the Doberman to Mariachi's right did not have time to pounce. The pit bull had finished with the first Doberman and was ready for the second. The Doberman, ready to pounce, checked itself and planted its feet firmly on the ground. It snarled, bared its teeth in a rolling, continuous growl as it stared at Mariachi.

Priscilla got quickly to her feet and took three steps backward. Out of a corner of her eye, she saw Paco Rangel moving his pistol to the right and to the left, trying to get a bead on Mariachi's head.

At the same time, the third Doberman came around Mariachi and attacked from the side, sinking its jaws into Mariachi's right leg. Mariachi ignored it, keeping his undeterred attention on the Doberman in front of him. The Doberman was cautious, making a leap, but checking itself, and then moving off to one side, sharpening its eye, looking for an opening before attacking Mariachi.

Mariachi still ignored the other Doberman whose teeth sank into his haunch. His eyes never wavered from the Doberman facing him, who desperately sought an opening for an attack. Mariachi was alert, his body tensed, but he didn't move an inch and he kept silent. He waited for the Doberman to attack. The Doberman twisted its head several times as if to shake something loose, and jumped forward, coming at Mariachi in a frontal assault.

The Doberman moved swiftly, lowering its head, going for Mariachi's throat, and failing that, his shoulder. Mariachi stood his ground, impassive, immobile. His teeth slowly bared as he prepared to intercept the attack. A low growl came out of his throat.

As the Doberman's head tilted, headed for his throat, Mariachi jerked his head down and then upward, as if he were going to nip something. As the Doberman's head jerked forward with its mouth open, Mariachi's massive jaws opened

and then quickly clamped shut, covering half of the Doberman's throat. Mariachi made a jerking, swallowing movement
with his upper body, and the Doberman was dead in a matter
of seconds.

Mariachi jerked his head to snap the Doberman's neck
and then swung his head to one side, as if tossing the dog
away. Only then did Mariachi take a look at the Doberman
whose jaws were sunk into his haunch. The Doberman let go
of Mariachi's haunch and scampered to a safe distance away.

Mariachi had not moved an inch from where he had first
planted his paws.

54

Priscilla turned to look at Paco Rangel, who had been watching the dogs fight. The unhurt Doberman stood a short distance away, cautiously watching Mariachi. It was not interested in continuing the fray with the pit bull. The first of the attacking Dobermans began to lick its wounds and limped away, shoving its snout into the soft earth to stanch the bleeding. Mariachi waddled over to stand with his head over the dead Doberman, as if claiming a conquest.

Paco Rangel lifted his pistol and took aim at the back of Mariachi's head.

"No!" yelled Priscilla, rushing forward, her arms outstretched.

Priscilla grabbed Paco at the waist, jerking him to one side. Paco lost his balance, his shot going into the air. Priscilla's weight and her arms around his waist brought Paco to the ground. As he tried to get to his knees, Priscilla balled her hand into a fist, and shot it into Paco's ribs. It knocked the wind out of him, and he fell once more to the ground.

Priscilla scampered away quickly, got up on her knees, and finally to her feet. Paco rose on his hands and knees. She took two steps toward him, coming within striking range, and prepared to kick Paco in the face.

Paco scurried a short distance away, lifting his torso, remaining on his knees. He shook his head and aimed the nickel-plated pistol at Priscilla. It was then that Priscilla heard the gunshot, this one farther away in the distance.

She saw Paco's body jack-knife, his arm jerking in the air. He took a short step forward as if walking on his knees, and dropped the pistol. He spun around, as if trying to see something behind him. Priscilla followed his gaze and saw Orthal Mason coming forward, holding his Winchester at waist level. Orthal jerked the lever to jack another round into the firing chamber.

"I want the money you got buried here, Mexican," said Orthal Mason, without preamble. He turned to Priscilla. "You! Get over next to him where I can see the both of you."

"He was going to kill me," said Priscilla, her facing filling with anger.

Mariachi sauntered over, his body swinging from side to side, until he stood between Paco and Priscilla, his eyes on Orthal Mason. He sat back on his haunches to watch Orthal Mason, his tongue hanging out the side of his mouth.

"Didn't you hear me? He was trying to kill me," said Priscilla again, unable to contain her fury.

"I don't much care what he was trying to do, lady," said Orthal Mason. "He killed my boy, Ralph, and he's got to die for it. First, I want that money he's got buried around here. Where is it, Mexican?"

"I was your son's friend," said Priscilla. "I was with him in the motel room when Paco shot him."

Orthal Mason ignored her.

"I'm waiting, Mexican," he said. "Where's my money?"

55

Hank Solís came out of the marijuana plants, holding his gun at waist level. He kept his eye on the two living Dobermans. The one unharmed sat moaning over his living comrade, who licked its wounds. The Dobermans no longer paid attention to the field they had been trained to protect.

"Orthal Mason!" said Hank Solís. "I've dreamed of this moment. I've wanted to shoot you so damn bad all of my life." Hank Solís grinned, lifting his arm, aiming his pistol directly into Orthal Mason's eyes. "And, here you are, with a loaded rifle aimed at me."

"It's him I want, Hank," said Orthal Mason, unsure of himself. "This ain't got nothing to do with you."

"Yeah, it does, Orthal," said Joe Blue, coming up behind the old man who held the Winchester rifle. "It's got everything to do with me, too."

Joe Blue had his gun in his hand, his arm stretched at shoulder level, walking sideways, keeping a bead on Orthal Mason.

"We're the law," said Joe Blue. "If Hank doesn't kill you with his first shot, you'll get a second one from me. Throw your rifle away, right now!"

Orthal Mason did not hesitate. He dropped the rifle.

Hank Solís ran to him and shoved him out of the way, still aiming the gun at him from waist level.

Paco Rangel got to his feet. There was a glassy, faraway look in his eyes. He had trouble holding his head erect. At last, with every ounce of strength that he had left, he took a step forward and collapsed. Hank Solís ran to him, dropping to one knee, and turned Paco over on his back. Hank Solís let out a soft whistle.

"This one's a goner, Joe," said Hank Solís.

Joe Blue came over, knelt beside Paco Rangel.

"The way the blood's pumping out, Orthal's bullet cut right through the artery."

"We can call a chopper from San Antonio," said Hank Solís.

"He'll be dead before the chopper gets airborne."

"You can't let him just lie there and die," said Priscilla, horrified at the casual manner of their discussion.

"What the hell you want to do? Shoot him? Put him out of his misery?" Joe Blue became angry at his helplessness in the face of the dying man.

Joe Blue and Hank Solís got to their feet. Hank walked behind Orthal Mason and put handcuffs on his wrists behind his back.

"You don't have to cuff me, boys," said Orthal Mason. "I got what I wanted. I killed the son of a bitch. That's good enough for me."

Joe Blue came over to Priscilla Arrabal. He took her by the arm.

Paco Rangel coughed several times before a profound stillness overtook his body. Hank Solís lowered Paco's head to the ground and got to his feet.

"Come on," he said to Priscilla. "Let's go back to the house, get you something to drink. This place'll be crawling with people before too long."

Priscilla squatted down, taking Mariachi's head in her hands.

"You saved my life, Mariachi," she said, rubbing his head briskly.

She turned her head to look up at Joe Blue.

"Can I ask you a favor?" she said. "Mariachi's been hurt. One of those dogs over there bit into him. I can't tell how bad it is, but I want to take him to a veterinarian, have him taken care of."

Joe Blue thought for a moment.

"We'll have to get Paco Rangel's truck into Lexington," said Joe Blue. "Impound it. There's keys in it. Suppose you drive it into Lexington. Veterinarian has a clinic on the bypass. You get him to take care of the dog. Then, you get a motel room, get you a good night's rest, and you come see me in the sheriff's office in the morning. Make it eight o'clock. Sharp. You understand?"

"Yes, I do," said Priscilla Arrabal.

The veterinarian in Lexington cleaned Mariachi's wounds and gave him some shots. Priscilla made arrangements with the veterinarian to board Mariachi until she came back for him in a few days.

From the clinic, Priscilla drove along the bypass, to the Settler's Motel. After she'd registered for a room, she parked Paco's pickup truck with the silver camper shell in front of her room. She walked back to the lobby, went into the motel restaurant to eat, and then returned to her room.

In the morning, with the suitcase of Paco's money lying on the floor at his feet, Joe Blue took her statement, which filled in all of the pieces of Paco Rangel's criminal activities. She told Joe Blue that she'd recognized Paco in the window, wearing wire-rimmed glasses, which they could find on top his roll-top desk. In one of the slots, she added, there was a green ledger with the names of the people who had worked with him.

Priscilla asked, "When's the bus to San Antonio come by?"

"It should pull into Tiny's in about ten minutes," Joe Blue said. "It'll be there twenty more minutes after that. You have plenty of time."

"I left my suitcase outside, in Paco's truck," said Priscilla.

"Don't forget," said Joe Blue, "you'll have to come back for Orthal Mason's murder trial."

"I won't forget," she said, thinking about the money in the suitcase.

"Come on, I'll drive you," said Joe Blue.